21·4·18

If You Should Ever Leave Me

LUCY ONIONS

Bekki.
Thank you fe
your support.

[signature]

TO MY FAMILY

Simon and Molly, Mom and Dad, Ella, Paul, Max and Harry. Thank you for being the best! I love you all very, very much.

PROLOGUE

"We'll take it!"

"Are you sure, Miss Jackson?" the Estate Agent asked, looking as shocked as I did, "Would you not prefer to go away and have a think about it? I don't have any more viewings on this property for weeks now."

"I'm positive."

What about asking me, Mum? I thought to myself, haven't I got to live here too? This was not a decision to be made lightly.

"Oh, sorry sweetheart," Mum said, turning to me as if she had heard my silent questioning, "Listen to me going on! I'm just excited, that's all. I think this place is exactly where we need to be. It's exactly right for us. What do you think?"

"It's lovely, Mum," I answered, trying to sound as convincing as possible. How can you be so sure of something? How can you be sure a house is perfect for you when you've only viewed it once? I suppose it's just instinct.

"So, it's settled then," she said, addressing the Estate Agent again, "we'll definitely take it."

DAY 1

I don't know if Mum was expecting to move in straight away, if she was expecting us to be in within a week of her making this monumental "life changing" decision but I thought she was going to go crazy with waiting. Not a week. Not a month. Almost two months later and we were finally there. Finally, in our new home. As Mum told the Estate Agent, our forever home. The moment she uttered those words, I very nearly vomited. I tried to be excited, as much for her than anything else. Maybe it's just going to take some time. I'm not great with change, don't handle it too well. But I need to start acting my age. I need to grow up. I need to show her I can be an adult. I'm not a child anymore and if I keep asking her not to treat me like one, I best sort myself out.

"Oh Henri, it looks beautiful," Mum gasped as she cast

her eyes around my room, "well done. You've done a lovely job with it."

Mum tends to overreact over most things, my new room being yet another one of them. All I had done was put up my posters, arranged things to suit and made my bed. That's it. I didn't even need to paint.

"Thanks Mum, glad you like it. How's yours coming along?"

She grabbed my hand excitedly and led me across the landing to her bedroom door.

"Tadah!"

I stood back in shock.

"You don't like it, do you?" she said. Her face dropped.

"I do, honestly. I really like it. It's just completely different to your usual style. It doesn't seem like your taste, but you know what? A change is as good as a rest."

The walls were a deep crimson. Too dark for my liking. The curtains were a deep green colour and looked as if they had been left there by the original owners who had built it in nineteen twenty-three.

"Good, that's exactly what I was going for. Henri, this isn't just a house move for us."

"I know that, Mum."

"We've been through the mire and back again. We've put up with way too much crap – oh, excuse my language."

"It's okay, Mum. I'm a big girl now," I smiled. I'd heard worse than that.

"Yes, I know – my beautiful big girl. Anyway, we've put up with enough you-know-what over the years. I don't want you to hate your Dad. I don't want that at all, but I hope you understand why I find it very difficult to see any good in him."

Ah, Dad. I knew it wouldn't be long before conversation turned to him. Yes, he had been a total pig to Mum. I mean, if you're going to have an affair with anyone, at least do it with someone with supermodel looks and legs up to her armpits, not your wife's closest friend.

"I don't hate him, Mum, I just hate what he did to you and I hate how he's treated you since."

"Oh sweetheart, so do I but just know that your father adores you, regardless of what's happened to us."

"Is that why he hasn't come to see me for the past eighteen months?"

"I imagine he's finding it pretty difficult right now. He really does love you, sweetheart. Just give him time."

Mum and Dad loved each other more than anyone else I've ever known. At times, it was embarrassing. They just seemed to fit together perfectly. Mum said the day they found out they were having me was the best day of their lives. That it bought them even closer together than they were before. I really don't know why they named me Henrietta because neither of them has used my full name since I was about two years old. No, scrap that. The full name always came out when I had been up to no good. Sometimes, I would be bad on purpose just so I could hear it.

"He's had more than enough time, Mum, and you know what? I don't give a damn. Who needs him anyway?"

An awkward, worried smile appeared on her face which quickly turned into a full on, unabashed beam.

"Anyway," she said, "this is nothing to do with

your father. This is all about us and our new life. I hope you're happy, my darling."

I threw my arms around her, closed my eyes and smiled.

I'm back at my old school, waiting outside the gates for my daily dose of abuse. They're close now, I can feel them. I'm shaking, and I can feel sweat on my forehead. My heart is beating so fast it feels like it will tear itself right out of my chest. I almost wish it would. I can disappear then – be gone from this world forever. I can't take any more of this.

Their hands rip my backpack off my wet, sweaty back. They zip it open and the contents spew on to the floor – my lunch, a book, a pencil case, my wallet and the jackpot, a small box of tampons.

Their howls and screeching laughter hurt my ears and I put my hands over them, trying to drown it all out.

The ringleader, Zoe, comes right up to me – gets right up in my face. She doesn't speak but I know exactly what she's thinking, and I know what's going to happen next.

She pulls my head right back by my hair. I'm wincing with pain, sure that she's ripped some of it out. Her cronies are laughing like this is the funniest thing they've ever seen. I feel tears brimming in my eyes, but I know now really isn't the best time to start crying. Suddenly, the pressure on my hair and scalp is relieved and Zoe is crying, saying, "No, please don't," again and again. I open my eyes to see something completely invisible throwing her round like a rag doll.

Blood explodes from her nose first, then her mouth as loose teeth shoot out of it. I can see where her invisible attacker's hands should be – they're leaving impressions on her fake-tanned skin. I don't know what's scaring me more, the fact that she's being attacked by something invisible or the fact that I'm quite enjoying it.

And now I don't want to see any more. I want to turn away, but I am rooted firmly to the spot and as quickly as it started, Zoe lies, beaten and bloodied, on the floor. The chaos stops, her cronies long gone. I feel strong arms wrap around my shoulders from behind and I am instantly calm.

"It's okay," the voice says, "I'll never let them hurt you again, I promise."

DAY 2

"Sweetheart," I hear, "Henri, darling – wake up now. Come on, open your eyes."

"Mum? Mum, is that you?"

"Yes, sweetie. I'm here. You're okay."

I had been having the same dream, pretty much every night, for the last three years. I really went through it at my last school. It started way before my father's little "indiscretion" and consequent retreat. I think it's fair to say that all the bullying I went through is what led to him doing what he did. I hate to say it, but I was the classic stereotype of a troubled, emotional teenager. I never used to be that way. Once I was happy all the time and then things started happening to me at school. Horrible, terrible things. I never asked to be bullied. I never asked to have the crap kicked out of me on almost a daily basis. I didn't do anything except be myself and *that* was the problem.

I excelled at that school. I worked damn hard. I

enjoyed learning, thrived on it. I could count my friends on one hand. I was happy the way I was and that did not go down well with Zoe and her flock.

My grades began to plummet because of this constant abuse. I became depressed. I was prescribed pills for it and I still take them from time to time, only if it's totally necessary. They help for a little while, but it never goes away – that sense of underlying dread. I don't think it will ever go away.

So, as I was saying, I think all this contributed to Dad having his way with Mum's *so-called* best friend. My depression triggered something in Mum. She was angry with everyone and everything, Dad being the focus of most of it.

Once upon a time, she was always beautifully turned out, either in casual, everyday wear or dressed up to the nines for parties or nights out with Dad but then she became slovenly, not even trying to be a wife or a mother. Fresh meals were a rarity so on the odd occasion where she had had a bit to drink and, if only for a few hours, felt happy, she served up some wonderful dishes.

They started to argue, pretty much every night, once I had gone up to my room. I mean, did they really think I wouldn't hear? On one particular night, I sat on the top step of the stairs and listened. I wasn't in full view but I'm sure they could have easily seen me had they actually paid me any attention. I heard him tell her that he had been sleeping with Christine, her best friend. I cannot explain the sound that came from her mouth. I'm sure it was the sound of her heart breaking. It was so incredibly sad, like a howl of pain. Then she started to cry, and yet it seemed that as soon as she had started, she stopped. She suddenly found her voice and, deadly serious, she told my Dad to get the hell out of our house.

He put up no defence. Gave no excuses. He wanted out, you could just tell, and I believe Mum did the hard bit for him. He left quietly that evening and never came back, not even to collect his belongings which, incidentally, all got taken to the charity shop.

All I've ever wanted, since that night, is to see Mum looking beautiful again. To see her being my Mum but also her own woman. I'm old enough to look after myself now – old enough to see she's finally coming back to me and to herself.

"Right, we need to get you back into school," Mum said as we sat opposite each other at the island in the kitchen.

"I know. Seriously, I know," I said after swallowing the food in my mouth, hoping that, in her elation of upping sticks and moving in, she had conveniently forgotten. I washed down the scrambled eggs and bacon she had prepared with a gulp of freshly brewed coffee. She looked at me disapprovingly.

"Seriously, you kids these days," she said, slightly shaking her head, "You shouldn't need coffee. It's not that good for you."

The words, pot, kettle and black sprang to mind. Mum had clearly passed her coffee addiction down to me. I can't help the fact that I love it so much.

I took another large gulp and forced a smile.

"What is it sweetheart?" she asked, "did you have a bad night? That dream again?"

I nodded but said nothing. I didn't need this, not at this time in the morning. I just wanted to settle down.

"Oh, honey, I thought we'd seen the last of those."

With all due respect, Mum, I thought, you haven't seen them. They were never yours to see.

"Me too," I said instead, "maybe it's just all the upheaval of moving. I'm sure I'll be fine once we're all settled in properly."

"Is this place bothering you at all, honey?"

"No. Why do you ask?"

"Oh, nothing really. It's just a feeling more than anything else. You just don't seem yourself."

"Like I said, it's just been a bit hectic lately."

"Yes, that's probably all it is. So, sixth form," she said, looking over the top of her reading glasses, "We've got a meeting with the Principal at Fallowfield at eleven. Once you've finished your food, you should really go and get ready."

"Okay, Mum," I replied before finishing the last dregs of coffee.

"So, all that's left for me to say, Henrietta, is welcome to Fallowfield Sixth Form College."

"Thank you," we replied in unison, my Mums voice sounding brighter and more eager than I had heard it in quite some time. She had really made an effort; her makeup was immaculate but not over the top, her hair tied back into a plait. Principal Stokes smiled.

"My pleasure entirely," he said, "So, Miss Roberts, we shall see you in the morning for your induction. It will be a relatively easy day, just a taster to ease you in. Please report to reception first thing and you'll be given a timetable and a welcome pack. I have a feeling you will fit in perfectly here. You seem to have exactly the right attitude."

I blushed. I don't know why because he hadn't said anything particularly cringe worthy. It just felt good to have someone other than my Mum being nice to me.

"Thank you," I said again, "I look forward to it."

"This calls for a celebration, don't you think?" Mum said as we pulled up outside a little Italian restaurant she'd read about in the local newspaper. I wasn't saying no to this.

We were shown to a table right by the window.

"Henri, I am so proud of you. You really do amaze me. I am honoured to be your Mum."

I couldn't help but smile at her.

"I wouldn't be me without you, Mum. Give yourself a pat on the back for raising such an awesome person."

We both laughed. It felt like all the worries of the world had been lifted off our shoulders. I couldn't remember the last time I felt so good.

Our food was delicious, the pasta fresh, light and cooked al dente. The sauce rich and moreish and the wine was a perfect accompaniment.

Mum paid for our food and as we headed to the car, I felt happy, happier that I had felt for quite some time.

"Mum, I've really got to head on up," I yawned loudly, "I'm exhausted."

"Okay, sweetheart. Night night."

We exchanged kisses and I made my way upstairs.

My bed molded to me as I sank into it. My pillows felt like clouds. For the first time in what felt like forever, I felt truly tired. It had been a good day. I could get used to this.

The pressure on my hair and scalp is relieved and Zoe's crying, saying, "No, please don't," again and again. I open my eyes to see something completely invisible throwing her around like a rag doll. Blood explodes from her nose first, then her mouth, as loose teeth shoot out of it. I can see where her invisible attackers' hands would be. They're leaving their impressions on her fake-tanned skin. I'm quite enjoying watching her being attacked and it isn't scaring me one bit.

I want to see so much more. I need to see her suffer for what she has done to me. And then he appears and although I have no idea who this boy is, I'm incredibly drawn to him.

I don't know how but I know he knows what I'm going through. He knows because he's been where I am standing. He knows how it feels to be bullied, beaten and broken by cowards.

Zoe lies in a beaten, bloodied heap on the floor. The chaos is over, her cronies long gone.

He turns to face me, and he is the most gorgeous, perfect boy I have ever seen. Sun bleached, dirty blonde, messy, neck length hair. His eyes are bluer than any ocean. He walks towards me and pulls me into his chest. "It's all okay now, Henri," he says, "I'll never let them hurt you again, I promise."

DAY 3

"Henri, come on! You're going to be late."

She was right, of course but I just couldn't get the dream out of my mind. It was more vivid, this time – more real than it had ever been before. I mean, the guy? I know I've never actually met him, but he feels so familiar to me. It's like I've known him forever.

"Henri, what are you doing in there?" she asks from outside the door, knocking it for good measure.

"Come in."

Her face is a picture when she sees that I am nowhere near ready.

"I'm sorry, I slept past my alarm. I had the dream again, Mum, and it was so real."

"We've just had so much on, like you said. Give it time sweetheart. I'm sure these night terrors will disappear in no time."

Here's the thing though, even though they unsettle me, I don't ever want the dreams to stop.

Mum took it far better than I expected when I declined her offer of a lift to school.

"I'm sure I can cope," I told her.

"I know you can," she said, "but no matter how old you are, you'll always be my baby girl. I don't care how silly that sounds."

I smiled widely and thought about what she had said as I crossed the school car park, towards the main entrance.

I half expected the funny looks and the giggles that followed me to the back of the classroom as I found a table as far away from the front as possible. It probably didn't help that I wasn't "trendy" or someone that could fit in with the "in crowd". It didn't help that my handmade school bag was covered with badges of my favourite rock bands, nor the fact that my long, wavy, auburn hair covered my face. I didn't want to fit in and it showed.

I shuffled right down into my seat and for a second, I felt like I could get through school if this was as bad as it was going to get but then...

"Hello students," the English Literature teacher said as she laid an armful of books on the table in front of her, "Are we all well today?"

The class groaned collectively.

"Good, good," she went on, "glad to hear you're all so excited for the new term. Now, with a new term comes a new face. Henrietta, would you please come to the front and introduce yourself to the class?"

The bubble I was living in burst instantly. The sniggers and whispers grew louder and stronger as I made my way towards the front.

"Class, this is Henrietta Roberts or Henri, as she prefers to be known. So, Henri, the floor is yours – tell us a little bit about yourself."

I'd rather not, I thought to myself but there was no way out of it now.

"Hi everyone," I addressed the class, "I'm Henri but you already know that, right? I live with my Mum. I have no pets. We're new here. I love to read, write, listen to music and take photos."

The words tumbled from my mouth without feeling. It was all I was willing to give away. I didn't want them to get to know me, not properly anyway. The less they knew about me, the better. They had no ammunition that way.

"Thank you, Henri," our teacher said, clapping her hands, urging the class to do the same but failing terribly, "that was lovely. Now, let's all knuckle down and open this terms text, The Catcher in the Rye. We'll read the first chapter together."

Something caught my attention at the window though and as I turned my head to look, I gasped. Standing there, right outside, was the boy from my dream.

The bell sounded and rather than join the stampede to get out, I waited back. My stomach churned, and I felt goose bumps break out over my skin. I wasn't dreaming, I was in class. What the hell was going on?

The boy was still outside, and I wondered if he had been looking at me the whole time. I couldn't take my eyes off him and was only broken from my trance when the teacher coughed loudly.

"Henrietta, class is over."

"Oh, sorry, yes. I was on another planet for a while there."

"Are you okay? Nothing's bothering you, is it?"

"Not yet," I smiled.

"Well, you know, being the new kid is hard but honestly, if anything gets to you, anything at all, you just come and see me, okay?"

"Thank you, I appreciate that."

I averted my gaze, looking back to the window, hoping to see the blonde-haired boy but all that was there was the breeze.

The best thing about taking your own lunch to school is that you aren't confined to the cafeteria, so I grabbed my lunch and notebook from my newly designated locker and headed outside. I spotted an empty space, right at the back of the playing field. I looked around and when I was happy that absolutely no one was paying me any attention, I sprinted to the little spot under the prettiest willow tree I have ever seen. I sat down. The grass was soft, almost spongy. I took my sandwich out of my lunch bag and felt my stomach churn with hunger.

My mouth started to water as I opened it wide, ready for the first bite. I felt a tap on my left shoulder and I dropped my sandwich.

"Anyone sitting here?"

I turned to see who the voice belonged to – it was the boy.

"Um, yes. I mean, no," I stammered. I was hoping that I'd imagined him standing outside the classroom window, that I'd somehow allowed my dream free entry into my reality.

"Do you mind?" he asked, sitting down right next to me before I even had chance to answer, "Henrietta, isn't it?"

I looked at him blankly and nodded.

"I prefer Henri though."

"Henri, it is then. You know that's a boy's name, right?"

"Really?" I rolled my eyes sarcastically.

"Oh, you're funny. I like you already."

"That's good then, thanks."

Usually, I wouldn't give strangers the time of day, but talking to him felt completely natural.

"So, if you were wondering, the name's Drew."

"Hi Drew," I blushed, hoping he couldn't see how red my cheeks were turning, "so, are you new here too?"

"Depends what you class as new, I suppose."

An awkward silence filled the space between us, but I knew I wouldn't be breaking it first.

"You're okay you know, Henri," he went on.

"Yeah?"

He nodded.

"Thank you."

I didn't feel entirely comfortable with the conversation but then again, it didn't feel wrong.

"I mean, at least you're listening, which is a damn sight more than anyone else has done since I've been here. It's like I'm invisible or something."

"Drew, if it helps, I feel the same. The only person who sees me, all that I am, is my Mum."

His face dropped; he looked so sad. I wanted to pull him into my arms but that would have been way too weird.

"Oh well, lunch time's over," he said, quickly snapping out of his trance and glancing at his watch.

"What? We haven't been out long."

The bell echoed out across the field. He let out a frustrated sigh and I followed suit. There came another awkward silence as I gathered up my things. I stood up, smoothing down my skirt, wiping the cut grass from my legs. Drew was making no effort to join me on the dreaded walk back to the school building.

"Come on, Drew, we have to go."

"Nope, not me."

"But."

"Free period," he shot in.

"Oh, okay, cool," I said, feeling instantly jealous.

"Could I meet you? After school?" he asked shyly.

A boy, this boy, wanted to see me again. It was so completely new to me and, a little scary. I'd never met anyone after school, let alone a member of the opposite sex.

"Um, yes – that would be nice."

His cheeks turned red. Mine did the same. Well, it felt like they did at least. I didn't know how to handle this kind of attention.

"Okay. So, I'll meet you at the gates? We could go for coffee or something."

"Sounds great."

It's hard to pay attention to anything when a boy asks you out on a date, if that's what we were going on. It's even harder when the boy is someone you've only ever seen in your dreams. That's another thing – should I mention that? Should I say, "hey, I've actually met you before! I was asleep at the time, though"?

"Okay class," the chemistry teacher said, his voice dragging me right back into the room, "that's it for today. Get out of here."

The home-time bell rang, and I couldn't get out of my chair quick enough.

Drew stood at the gates looking dark, brooding and unexplainably gorgeous. Something was happening to me. It was so unlike me to get worked up over anyone. Don't be too eager, I told myself, play it cool.

"Hey," he said coolly as I approached.

"Hi. Thanks for waiting."

"No worries," he said. He gently kissed my cheek, stopping me completely in my tracks.

"Oi. Oi, you - Henrietta!" I heard a girl shout from behind us. I turned to look. Drew did too.

"Yes, you," she went on, "hold on. We want a word with you." One girl turned into five and they all headed straight towards me.

"Me?"

"Yeah, that's right?"

I gulped hard, fear rising in my chest. I wondered if Drew would do exactly as he had done in my dreams. He was showing no signs of doing anything though as he stood, stock still, behind me.

"So, how's you first day been?" she asked.

"Fine, thank you."

"Well, that's great isn't it girls?"

The four girls forced fake laughter. If I didn't feel so scared, I would have laughed right back at them.

"Is everything okay?" I asked, "Do I know you? Should I know you?"

"Oh yes, everything's cool," she said, "we just wanted to catch up with you, you know? We wanted to find out a bit more about you – what makes you tick.

Zoe only told us a bit about you but that's not enough."

What the hell! They know Zoe. Zoe, the nasty piece of work from my last school. This was unreal. I thought I'd escaped all that. I thought the dreams were as bad as it would get from now on. Seems like moving a couple of towns away isn't a big enough escape.

"That's great. Thank you. It's good to know I've got people who I can talk to," I lied through my teeth.

Drew stayed still. Please, I pleaded silently, hoping he would pick up on how I was feeling, aren't you going to do something?

The girl got right up in my face. Her breath smelled of cigarettes and stale chewing gum.

"Just so you know…"

"Yeah, FYI," one of the others piped in. The ring-leader looked at her, clearly irritated.

"Just so you know, I'm watching you, Henrietta Roberts."

New start, same old shit.

I sighed with silent pleasure as the first, hot mouthful of coffee slid down my throat. I needed the caffeine. Needed it to settle my nerves, calm me down. Funny really because it should do the exact opposite. I couldn't quite bring myself to broach the subject of why Drew did nothing to protect me from the girls but, how could I, really? It's not like we were an item or anything.

"Are you okay?" he asked.

"Yes, I guess so. I'm used to it."

"You've been bullied before?"

"I've not really done anything to help my cause though," I said, blowing on my coffee.

"How do you mean?"

"Look at me, Drew – are you surprised?"

"Hey, you look pretty cool to me but then I suppose I'm drawn to weirdo's."

We laughed.

"Seriously though, Henri – you're great. Just because you're nothing like them doesn't mean you're less of a person. Those girls, they're awful. They're horrible. Get any one of them on their own and they'd run a mile if you stood up to them."

"I find the best thing is to just let it go. I don't care what they think of me. They mean nothing to me."

"I know that," he said, blowing at his drink, "and it's good to think that way but I know how it can grind you down."

A silence fell between us. We both had our own issues to deal with.

"I'm sorry I didn't do anything, Henri."

I looked up at him.

"Don't be. It's fine. Honestly."

"Well, anyway, I am."

It was close to six pm and although I didn't want to go home, I was starting to feel a little uncomfortable, sitting there, opposite him. The albatross around my neck was getting heavier by the second. At some point, I needed to tell him that I already knew him, even if it was only in my head.

"You okay?" he asked again, "you seem distracted."

He wasn't wrong.

"No, it's fine. I just best be getting back. I've left my phone at home and my Mum will probably be wondering where I am."

"Well, you're not going home on your own. I'll walk you back, okay?"

"I'd like that."

"This is it," I said.

"Well, I'll see you later then?" Drew said, leaning against the gate, looking down at his feet.

"Yes, see you at school," I said shyly.

"I've really enjoyed myself, Henri. I don't feel invisible with you."

I didn't know how to react to that. It was such an intense thing for him to say but it didn't feel creepy at all. Ordinarily, a guy coming on this quick would instantly turn you off.

"Thank you. I've enjoyed it too. See you tomorrow, Drew."

"Not if I see you before," he said, flashing a wink at me.

"For heaven's sake, Henri," Mum shouted, her arms crossed firmly across her chest, "where the hell have you been?"

"Mum, I'm sorry."

"Couldn't you have just phoned me? I've been having bloody kittens here!"

"It's not exactly late, Mum, is it?"

"That is not the point, Henri! You should have let me know if you were going to be late."

"I left my phone in my room. I'm sorry, I really am."

She softened a little, realising I was telling the truth. She knows I never leave my phone at home and she knows I always let her know my whereabouts if I'm not coming straight home from school.

"Who were you talking to outside?" she asked, a smile breaking on her lips, "I heard you chatting away about something or other."

"Oh, just a boy I've made friends with from school."

"Name?"

"Drew."

"Cute?"

"I suppose so."

"Cute enough to see again?"

"Well, I don't have a lot of choice on that one, Mum – he's at school."

"You know what I mean," she beamed.

"I think we're going to be really good friends. He's pretty cool."

"Well, it's nice you've made a friend, honey, and on your first day too? Wow, that's a record."

I laughed.

"Oh, Henri, I didn't mean it like that. I'm sorry."

"Mum, it's fine, seriously," I laughed again. She was right though – it's always taken me forever to form any kind of bond with anyone. I'm very much a loner. I don't need to be in the company of anyone else to enjoy myself. I don't answer to anyone, apart from her, of course.

"Do you have any homework?"

"No, not yet. I imagine I will do soon though."

"Well, now you're back, I'm going to jump in the bath. I need to destress."

I smiled and kissed her cheek.

"Don't turn into a prune."

My eyes don't want to close and even though I feel utterly exhausted, I know sleep is a way off yet. I can't shake off everything that's happened – my head is full. I want to sleep though. I need to sleep. What did Drew mean when he said, "Not if I see you before?" It may have just been a flippant remark, but it seemed quite the coincidence too. And the way he looked at me when he said it, it was just weird – like he knew that I knew I would see him.

Just sleep, I urged myself, you know you want to. If you sleep, you might see him again and you know you can't wait until morning!

Zoe lies in a beaten, bloodied heap on the floor. The chaos has ended, her cronies long gone.

He turns to face me, and he is the most gorgeous thing I have ever seen with his sun bleached, dirty blonde, messy, neck length hair.

"Drew, you came! You saved me."

His bluer-than-any-ocean eyes bore into mine and as he walks towards me, I feel excited and nervous. He pulls me into his chest.

"It's all okay now, Henri. I'm here. I'll never let them hurt you, I promise."

"I know you won't. I know. Please don't leave me."

"I'll never leave you. I'll always be here."

DAY 4

I could think of better ways to spend a morning than double math's. I thought they would take it easy on me for the first few days. Math's is not my forte. In fact, it's my worst subject. I haven't got an academic bone in my body.

"We'll start with a quick and easy trig test folks. Let's ease Miss Roberts in gently," Mr. Howell addressed the class. Great, that just made my morning even better.

"Right, turn your papers over boys and girls – you have fifteen minutes, starting now!"

Heads dropped in concentration all around me. I could only stare into space.

Math's filled me with utter dread and in all honesty, there was really no point in even trying to complete the trigonometry equation but apparently, showing your workings out is just as important as getting the answer right. Good job really. I stared at the numbers and triangles jumbled up on the page in front of me and wished I could just crawl into some dark, empty corner and hide.

Something caught my attention outside the window again and again, it was Drew. I looked straight at him and he smiled. I mimed at tying a noose around my neck and pulling it tight. His face lit up, his smile grew wider. He beckoned me outside and I silently responded, No!

Come on, he mouthed before flashing me an incredibly sexy smirk. I surveyed the room. Heads were still, very firmly, down. Pens were tapping tables in frustration. Mr. Howell had earphones in – bloody marvelous! Now that's how to set an example.

Pulling courage from somewhere, I got up from my desk and walked straight up to our so-called teacher. I stood directly in front of him. He hadn't got a clue I was there. I coughed and swayed from side to side, hoping he would notice me. Jackpot.

"Miss Roberts, is everything okay?"

"No, not really, Sir. I'm not feeling well. I shouldn't really be here to be honest, but my Mum didn't want me to miss my second day at my new school."

"I would have to agree with her on that one, but you do look very pale."

"Please, Sir, I think I'm going to spew," I said, putting my hands over my mouth for good measure, really laying it on thick.

"You're excused," he said, wafting me away, "Do you have anyone to pick you up?"

"I'll call my Mum," I assured, gagging, just to fire the point home.

"Okay, okay – just go. Get yourself home. If you're

not coming in tomorrow, you need to phone in first thing in the morning."

I nodded and ran out of the classroom like only a girl knows how.

"Are you ever in school?" I asked Drew as we lay side by side on a grassy bank in the local park.

"How can you make a judgment like that when it's only your second day?"

"Well, if you can count today, of course."

"Exactly!"

"Seriously though, how do you get away with it?"

"I don't have to. I told you, I have free periods."

"Every day?"

"Whatever," he huffed, clearly irritated, "anyway, what does it matter to you?"

"Hey, chill out – I'm just messing with you."

"I know," he said, "now you're getting a taste of your own medicine."

"Excuse me?"

"Nothing, it's cool."

"Um, no, what do you mean?"

"Nothing. Keep your knickers on."

If there was ever a perfect time to confront him, to ask him if he was all in my head, it was now.

"Drew, I need to talk to you, seriously."

"Fire away."

I took a long, deep breath. How could I ask him without coming across as a complete nut job?

It may have been easy to tell him that I knew him, albeit only in my dreams but just like me, he didn't get it.

"You haven't just made me up, Henri. You can't. It's impossible. You've obviously seen me somewhere around. Your subconscious has obviously kept me locked away in that awesome brain of yours."

"Maybe. I don't remember seeing you though. I would have remembered, wouldn't I?"

He shrugged.

"Look, shall we get out of here?" he asked, clearly eager to change the subject.

"Where do you suggest we go?"

"Come back to mine. I promise to get you home in time today too. I know how pissed off your Mum was last night."

I know I had mentioned that she would be worried, but he couldn't have known if she was upset or not.

"Well, I have my mobile on me today, so I can phone her if I need to."

"Cool. Come on, let's go!"

"Oh my God, this is incredible," I said, in awe as we made our way up the long driveway, "your parents must be rolling in it."

What a thing to say! How presumptuous of me.

Drew's face dropped. His demeanour changed in an instant.

"Come on," he said, "if you like the outside, you're going to love what's inside."

An ornate, mahogany staircase came into view as we entered. The décor looked traditional nineteen twenties with a modern twist. It was stunning and a feeling of warmth and welcome washed over me even though the house seemed imposing and far too silent.

I followed him through to his huge kitchen. There was an island in the middle which could have seated eight people easily, but there were only four high chairs.

I stood next to one of the chairs but didn't attempt to sit. I let out a small, fake cough.

"Oh man, sorry. Where are my manners?" he said, quickly pulling out the chair.

I smiled and sat down.

"Coffee or something stronger?"

"Just coffee please. I don't think my Mum would take it too well if she knew I was out drinking when I should be at school."

"Sure I can't tempt you to a beer? I have mints for after."

"Go on then, you've twisted my arm, a beer would be good."

I took another, quick look around whilst he was at the fridge.

"What do your parents do? They've got to have good jobs for you to be able to live like this." Not again. I needed to stop with the rude questions. Again, his mood changed. He stood stock still and stared at me.

"They're away. At conferences," he said. It was hard not to pick up the sharpness in his tone.

"Well, it must feel really good to be able to live on your own."

"So, what – don't you ever stay home alone?"

"Rarely. Since my Dad left, Mum's been finding it hard to trust anyone around us. I don't think she would settle if she had to leave me for any longer than a day. Seriously, it's ridiculous. I know she trusts me, completely. It's just everyone else she struggles with."

"Oh Henri, I'm sorry."

"Don't worry. It's a good job I love her company," I smiled.

"No. I'm… I'm sorry about your Dad. I know it's hard. I mean, I don't see either of my parents much but that's just because of their work."

"Don't be sorry, honestly. I don't have much sympathy for him. It took a long time for Mum to start clawing back her lost confidence. He really knocked it out of her."

"He beat her?"

"Oh no, nothing like that. Sorry, I didn't really make myself clear, did I? He had an affair with her best friend."

"Man, that's harsh."

"I know, right? And that's why she has trust issues."

"No wonder. Anyway, here you go. Enjoy," he said, handing me an ice-cold bottle. I put it to my mouth, took a large gulp and burped.

"Excuse me!"

"It's okay," he laughed, a smile lighting up his face.

"So, when are they home?" I asked, changing the subject.

"I'm not sure. Sometimes they're away for days, other times it weeks. It's different every time."

"Don't you get lonely? Is there no one else that could come and keep you company? Grandparents? Anyone?"

"My parents are the only family I have," he said, swallowing a mouthful of beer, "I really miss my grandparents. They were more like my parents than my actual parents. Don't laugh, okay, but I talk to them every day. It keeps them in my mind."

He looked at me with tears in his eyes, then looked at the floor.

"So now you understand why I feel invisible."

I nodded sadly.

"You're not invisible to me. You're here. You're real."

"Thank you, Henri," he said as he dragged his stool round to sit by me."

I blushed, averting my eyes from his.

"Sorry, I didn't mean to embarrass you," he said.

"You haven't, it's just that I'm a bit shy when it comes to talking to boys."

"That's cool. I understand. Hey, if it means anything, I really like you."

"That means a lot, actually. It really does."

"You know, you can come and stay any time you like?"

"As in overnight?"

"If you want."

"I'm not quite sure how my Mum would take it, what with only just moving here and meeting you, of course."

"Just tell her you've made friends with a girl at school. She'll love that."

He was right and staying with him was a tempting proposition.

"Do you think that maybe it's just a bit too soon to be having sleepovers?"

"You don't think I'm going to take advantage, do you?"

"Did I say that?"

"No, but I bet you were thinking it, right?"

"Maybe."

"Look Henri, if you do ever decide you want to come and keep me company in this stupidly large house, I promise I will be nothing but a gentleman. And anyway, have you seen how many bedrooms there are?"

I finished my beer and smiled.

"I don't doubt for a second you are a gentleman and I'm not saying I won't sleepover. I would love to spend more time here with you. Just let me sweeten my Mum up first. It might take some time, but I'll work my magic."

Drew's bedroom was tiny in comparison to the others. Just like my own, his room was covered with posters which told me he was a fan of pretty much every band and film I was into. So, we definitely had some things in common.

What little wall there was on show was painted a deep charcoal and with only one bay window on the far wall that was covered with a thin red drape, the room was dark and for want of a better word, gloomy. He had a couple of lamps; one on a small, bedside set of drawers and another on his computer table. There was a main light and two up-lights on the wall above his bed.

"So, why this room?" I asked, "Didn't you like any of the others?"

"I don't know. This is my room. It just is. I can't change. It won't let me."

"What?"

"I can't explain it," he shrugged, "I have tried. I mean, if I had the choice, this wouldn't be my first."

Not that it was a horrible room by any means. Even being the smallest, it was twice the size of mine.

"Do you want to see the room I think you'd like to stay in, if you can stay over?"

"Ooh, yes please."

Drew led me out of his room and across the landing to another and opened the door. The sight before me made me gasp. It was almost palatial. I've always wanted to sleep in a four-poster bed and this particular example was perfect.

The large, bay window housed a reading nook and was filled with an array of cushions of different colours and sizes. I just wanted to dive straight in. On the walls either side were shelves upon shelves of books. It was the bedroom of my dreams. The idea of staying over was growing more and more tempting by the second.

"Wow!"

"You like it then?"

"Like it? I love it!"

"So, you'll think about staying over sometime, then?" he asked hopefully.

"Sometime, yes. I promise."

We walked leisurely, all the way back to my house.

"Do you want to come in?" I asked. I hoped.

"Is your Mum in?"

"Yup," I sighed, knowing straight away what the answer was going to be.

"Do you mind if I don't? I'm not good with the old "meeting-the-parents" thing. That and the fact that I think, maybe, it's a bit too early for all of that. Is that okay?"

"Of course it's okay. It's not a big deal. Honest."

He smiled. Not a big smile. It was apologetic, almost pitiful.

"It's a beautiful night," he said, quickly changing the subject. I breathed an internal sigh of relief.

"It is."

He looked nervous as he took my hands. He couldn't bring himself to look at me for some reason.

"Henri, I know this sounds really stupid, but..." he stopped. Gulped.

"Are you okay, Drew?"

"Yes. I'm fine. Well, actually, no – I'm not. Shit, this feels so weird. Henri, I really like you. I'm sorry."

This was not the time at all to be speechless. If I didn't speak soon, he'd run a mile and I might never see him again. In dreams or at school. That's the last thing in the world I wanted. He shut his eyes tight and shook his head. I got the feeling he would rather be anywhere else but here, right now.

"Why are you apologising?" I spat out, as surprised at my outburst as much as Drew seemed to be, "Don't say sorry. I like you too."

His wide eyes relaxed and a smile started to break over his face.

"Erm," he said.

"Erm," I repeated.

"So, that's cool then. We good?"

"We are."

He leaned in slowly, tentatively. His mouth was a breath away from mine. I closed my eyes and waited. His lips brushed mine and, in that moment, everything changed.

"Hi sweetheart," Mum said as I dropped my bag on the floor, underneath the coat hooks, "what have you been up to?"

She wasn't angry but there was a certain tone to her voice that suggested she may have been a little annoyed. I don't know why. It's not like it was late or anything. Then again, I hadn't phoned her after school. Oops.

"Oh god, Mum. I'm sorry. I should have phoned."

"Oh, listen to me," she said, coming at me for a hug, "you're eighteen, not eight. It's just that I'm not used to…"

"Me going out after school? With a friend? No, neither am I."

"I'm sorry, sweetheart. That was a really insensitive thing for me to say."

"It's not. It's true. Like I say, it's a first for me, too. I know it's no excuse, but I got caught up in the moment and totally forgot to phone you."

She smiled.

"So, you've made another new friend then, huh?"

I nodded and hoped she couldn't see through my lie.

She did this funny little dance, grabbed hold of my cheeks and squeezed, making my mouth squish into a tight little pout.

"Ooh, that's just fantastic. Henri, I'm so happy!"

"It's no big deal, Mum."

"Oh yes, it is."

"Okay. Whatever."

"Henri, stop being such a misery. I don't care how embarrassing this is for you but it's just the best news. Oh, and how are things going with this boy you've met, Drew? I can't wait to meet him. You can invite him round for dinner one night after school, if you want?"

"Let's just slow down a bit, Mum. You'll meet him,

just not yet. Not for a while, anyway."

"Oh, so you want to keep your boyfriend a mystery, do you?"

"Mum, he's not my boyfriend! I've only just met him."

"Ooh, defensive are you, dear? That's a sure sign you like him."

"Yes. I do like him. He seems cool. That's as far as it goes."

"For now," she smiled knowingly.

I shook my head.

I ate my dinner far too quickly. Mum just stared at me in awe, obviously wondering why I was so hungry.

"Please tell me you're eating at school?" she said, still staring.

"Yes, Mum, I am eating my lunch. At school."

"I'm only saying, Henri. I've never seen you dig in like this before. Oh, I know, maybe it's because you're in love!"

I rolled my eyes.

"I am not in love. I'm just hungry. That's it."

She started giggling and as much as I didn't want to break, I did. We hadn't laughed together in such a long time. We were laughing like we were both crazy. Laughing for laughing's sake but it was worth it just to see Mum so happy.

"Oh, honey, I'm just being silly. It's just lovely to see you like this."

"What, covered in Bolognese sauce and belching?"

"Well, since you put it so eloquently, yes," she laughed again, "but seriously, I couldn't be happier right now."

"Neither could I, Mum," I smiled.

Before we knew it, it was almost eleven. We carried on chatting about Drew and what little I knew about him. She told me not to rush into anything even though she knew I had my head screwed on the right way. I agreed with her and nodded in all the right places and she was happy enough with that. I needed my bed. It had been an eventful day and I knew that as soon as my head hit the pillow, I'd be asleep. I hoped I'd be seeing Drew before sun up.

DAY 5

I caught a glimpse of dirty blonde hair outside the window again and waved at the boy smiling back at me. I laughed, and, in an instant, I knew I had been heard.

"Miss Roberts!" the history teacher said, drawing the attention of the whole class to me, "May I ask what it is that's so amusing?"

"Um, nothing, Sir. I…"

"Well, do you think you might be able to stop laughing at nothing and concentrate?"

The whole class sniggered in unison and I felt my cheeks start to burn.

I nodded.

"Good, good. Let's crack on then, shall we?"

I looked down at my hands and when I knew no one was looking, I peeked back to the window just as Drew flashed me a wink.

I couldn't get out the door quick enough when the lunch bell rang out it's shrill alarm, signaling one whole hour of freedom, albeit enclosed by all-round, eight-foot fencing. I could already see Drew in our spot and as I raced towards him, I could see his smile growing wider, beaming from ear to ear.

"Hey," he said, standing up to greet me.

"Hi," I responded, breathlessly.

"Happy to see me then, huh?"

"Might be."

He smiled and put his arm around my shoulder. I wanted school to disappear, leaving nothing but this field and the two of us.

"So, how's your morning been?" he asked.

"Not as good as yours, I'd say."

Drew loosened his tie, dropped his rucksack to the floor and looked down at his feet.

"Please, before you even think about it," he sighed, "don't bring up the fact that I'm not in school, again."

"Okay, I won't but…"

"See, I knew you couldn't resist!"

"It just baffles me, that's all. Yesterday was the first day I've ever skipped school and as much as I enjoyed every second of it, I feel so guilty."

"Yeah, but you were ill, right?" he smirked, "You can't help being poorly. I mean, in hindsight, what you should have done is have today off, you know, really make it look like you're not well."

He had a point and I wish I would have had the idea but I'm too much of a goody-two-shoes.

"Well, it's too late for that now, Drew but thanks for rubbing it in. Hey, listen to this. You know how you were stood outside the class, waving at me? Seriously, no one saw you. They all thought I was crazy."

"What do you mean? How does waving at your boyfriend make you crazy?"

In the very same second, we both realised what he had just said.

"So, is that what we are?" I asked, hopeful, "girlfriend and boyfriend?"

"I'd like it to be, wouldn't you?"

"Yes," I nodded, "yes I would."

He pulled me slowly to this chest and put his arms around me. I wanted to kiss him, like properly kiss him. Instead, I just sank into him and realised no one had ever held me this way.

"Does this feel weird to you?" he whispered.

"Does what feel weird?"

"That we barely know each other and yet it feels like this... this is meant to happen. That we are meant to happen. I know this is wrong for me to say. I feel wrong for saying it, but I think I more than like you."

Wait. Is he saying that he loves me? Surely not. You can't love someone when you hardly know them, can you? He's right though, it does feel weird because I feel the same too.

"I think I more than like you, too."

The end of lunchtime bell tolled and with deep disappointment, I broke my gaze.

"Got to go and let me guess, you're not coming?" I asked, knowing full well what the answer was going to be.

There he was again, waiting for me at the main gates. I sprinted towards them, eager to be near him.

"Hey," I said, "I almost toyed with the idea of skipping the rest of the afternoon off. Just leaving and not going back, but I was too much of a wimp."

"You don't seem a wimp to me, Henri. Quiet, maybe."

"No, I'm a wimp. I hate any type of confrontation, especially from the people I love. Can you imagine what my Mum would do if she found out I was skipping classes?"

"Well, no, actually," he sighed, "my parents may as well be on another planet. It would be nice to think they cared enough to punish me, I guess."

Why can't you just think before you speak, Henri? I scolded myself.

"Oh, Drew, I'm sorry. I didn't mean to sound so heartless."

"Don't be silly, Henri. To be honest, I'd probably hate their guts if they were around, anyway. I enjoy my own company. Good job, really."

"Don't they keep in touch?"

"I got an email from them not long after just to say that they love me, and to let me know they had transferred some more money to tide me over 'til they get back. Apparently, money can buy you love. Anyway, I'm not here to talk about my absent parents, I'm here to see you."

I blushed.

He looked down and the silence was deafening. He started to fiddle with his hands. He looked genuinely nervous.

"Henri, I know this is crazy and I honestly don't mind if you say no but would you like to stay at mine tonight?" he asked, his voice full of hope and fear.

I just stared at him. I couldn't the find words. Not straight away.

"Sorry, I should never have asked. It was a stupid

thing to say," he said, his voice now full of disappointment and embarrassment.

Come on, Henri, I thought to myself, say something. He's only asked you a question. Answer him. It's that simple.

"Drew, I would love to, but I obviously need to check with my Mum."

He smiled. A wide smile that stretched almost from ear to ear.

"Oh God, of course. Totally."

"Come with me."

"Where?"

"Home, so I can ask her."

"But I'm not ready to meet your Mum yet."

"I know. I know. You can wait outside if you must. Just be prepared though. She might not let me and I'm not going to argue with that. After all…"

"We've only just met," Drew continued, smiling at me.

"Mum? You there?"

"Upstairs. Just putting the last of my stuff away."

I dumped my bag and made my way upstairs. I could just about make my Mum out beneath open, upturned cardboard boxes. I knew she hadn't had time to completely unpack her stuff, but I didn't think she'd got all this left to do.

"You need a hand?"

"No, it's fine. Honestly, I'm almost done. It's just the odds and ends now."

"Looks like it," I looked around again and laughed.

There was hardly anything left to unpack, well,

not now anyway. She only had one more box left with not much at all in it. I cleared her bed and sat down, sinking into it.

"Mum?"

"Yes, honey?"

"Can I ask you something?"

"Of course you can," she said, spinning round and wiping her hair from her face. She sat next to me and I felt the mattress dip.

"Right, I completely understand if you don't want me to…"

"Oh, it's one of those kind of questions, is it?"

I smiled awkwardly.

"Like I say, I understand if you don't agree to it, but Drew has asked me if I would like to stay over at his?"

Her face went blank. I was not expecting a favourable answer.

"Did he, now."

I nodded.

"Henri, you've only just met the guy, I know you're old enough but even so, would you let you stay over if you were me?"

I shrugged. What would I do? I don't know.

"It's fine, Mum. It's okay. I understand."

She sighed, looked perplexed.

"You've got to see it from my perspective, sweetheart. I don't want to be an ogre."

"Mum, seriously. I know. You're not an ogre. I love you."

"Does he live in town?"

"Yes."

"And does he seem nice? Does he seem a gentleman?"

"I think so."

"You think?"

"Mum, yes. He seems like a gentleman."

It was clear she was thinking things through. Deeply.

"Can I trust you?"

Woah. That hurt.

"You know you can. You don't need to ask that."

She put her arm around my shoulder.

"I know. I'm sorry. It's just."

"Mum. It's okay."

"Last question. Do you trust him?"

"As much as I can do, yes."

"Well, then. You can stay over but I am telling you, Henri, do not let me down. I am putting all my trust in you. Please don't disappoint me."

I turned to face her and hugged her. Hard.

"Thank you so much. I promise I will not let you down."

She nodded and smiled.

"Right, just a little housekeeping. I want you to phone me when you get there, and I want you to phone me in the morning on your way to school. Go and get what you need."

"I love you, Mum. Thank you."

"I really didn't think your Mum would let you stay. I kind of thought that you might not have wanted to stay, yourself," Drew said as threw his house keys in a bowl on a small table in the hallway.

"I had serious doubts myself but here I am."

"She's one cool lady."

"She definitely is," I smiled, "and that reminds

me…"

I fished my phone out from my bag, tapped the screen and watched it come to life. I found Mum's number and hit call. I knew she'd be happy with a three-ring alert, but this occasion warranted a little chat.

It's surprising that I'd even contemplate staying over at a boy's house, especially one I had only just met but it felt right. It felt good.

"To be honest, Drew, it's that room you showed me. How can I resist that room? You never know, I might even want to stay over again, and again, and again," I trailed off.

"I'd like that," he smiled, "but let's just see how we get on with tonight first, huh? Anyway, what would you like to do to pass the time?"

"I don't know, whatever you want."

"Well, we can watch a movie or listen to music or just talk. It's up to you."

"What about we do all of that?"

We gave up on the movie about halfway through. It seemed pointless carrying on with it when we were talking and drinking and just generally enjoying each other's company.

"Why have I never seen you in school, Drew?"

"You have. You do."

"No, I haven't. I only you see you when you're lurking outside the windows of whichever class I'm in. You don't even know my timetable, do you?"

"Oh, lurking, am I? Well, thanks for making me sound like a nut job. And no, I don't know your timetable. I just take a guess and follow my instincts."

"It's not that I'm complaining or anything. Seeing you really lifts my mood. I just find it strange that I've yet to see you within the school itself."

"Why is it such a big deal? I told you, I have free periods," he said crossly.

"Here, now I'm letting you look at it," I said as I pulled out my timetable from my rucksack, "I have one free on Friday afternoon, that's it."

"Look, Henri, can we just change the subject? It's kind of bought the mood down. Let's move on, shall we?"

"I'm sorry, Drew. Of course we can. I hope I haven't upset you."

"Don't be silly, it's okay, honestly. Hey, do you want to go upstairs?" he asked hopefully, "I'd like to show you something."

"Oh, would you now," I said, trying to inject a little humour back into the atmosphere.

"That was not a euphemism."

"Christ, I'm just kidding! Now who's bringing the mood down?"

"Oh right, yeah. Anyway, come on please."

He took my hand and pulled me up from the sofa.

"Apart from my room, this has to be my favourite of the house," he said, taking an antique looking key out of his pocket. I thought it strange that it was the only internal door that was locked. Why didn't he show me this room on my first visit? Did he have some deep, dark secret hidden away inside? There was only one way to find out.

The key slid easily into the keyhole of the dark, wooden door we were stood in front of. With a turn of the key and a heavy click, the door creaked open.

It was hard not to gasp in awe as I stepped inside after him. I mean, the whole house was stunning, but it was easy to guess why this was Drew's favourite room.

There was yet another bay window straight ahead. An ornate, Victorian fireplace took pride of place on the wall to our right. To the left, the wall housed row upon row of LP records. I couldn't even guess how many were there, but it would easily be in the hundreds. My eyes were dragged away to an alcove next to the fireplace where there sat an old record player. It instantly brought back memories of Sunday afternoons when Dad would insist on switching off the television so that the three of us could sit and listen to whatever LP we were all hooked on at the time.

In the middle of this amazing room was a very comfy looking sofa, a couple of footrests and a nest of tables with a Macintosh lamp on top.

"Drew, this is just, well…"

"Wow?"

"Yes, wow."

He shut the door behind us and turned me round to face it. My mouth dropped open when I saw the bookcases that stood either side of it, full to the brim with books.

"Can I look around?"

"Of course," he smiled, "that's what I want you to do. That's why I brought you here."

I walked back to the 'record' wall and started to flick through a row. I smiled, noticing that his filing system was on point and the same as mine, alphabetical by artist and their albums in chronological order. Even though I had only just scratched the surface of this epic record collection, it was easy to see that Drew and I had so much in common.

I took out Rumours by Fleetwood Mac and smiled. A joint favourite for me and Mum.

"Would you mind?" I asked.

"Of course not. Go ahead."

I slid the record out of it's almost pristine sleeve and placed it on the turntable. There's something ritualistic about preparing to play a record. It felt like home. The turntable began to spin, and I carefully placed the needle on the record.

"Man, I love this album!"

"Me too," Drew agreed, "it's in my top ten, easily."

As the familiar sound filled the room, I sat down next to him. He was holding a book in his hands and as he began to flick through the pages, I realised it must have been some sort of journal. His handwriting, although readable, looked like frantic scribble.

"What's this?" I asked, gently pulling the book towards me, "a diary?"

"It's poetry I've written," he let go of the book completely, "I like writing. It's like therapy."

"Can I read some?"

"As long as you don't laugh."

"Of course I won't."

"Oh my God, Drew, this is amazing. It's beautiful."

"Really? Why are you crying then?

"Because it's so good. It's like it's been written for me. I can totally relate to it. It's like you know me."

"Hey, maybe I did in another life?" he said, and it didn't sound like too ridiculous a theory, "I'm glad you like it. You wouldn't believe how much that means to me."

I smiled through what was left of my tears and Drew smiled back.

He came closer, staring intensely into my eyes. I felt myself melt at the touch of his lips.

It was just no use, I could not sleep. I had been dozing on and off since getting in bed, but deep sleep was not forthcoming. The reason? No Drew. I had been finding such comfort in my dreams because of him. He made them good even though what was happening in them was bad. My brain just did not want me to let me see him, dream him on this occasion though. I tried my hardest to fill my head with him in the hope he would appear, but nothing.

"Henri," Drew called softly, as if on cue, from outside the door, "are you awake?"

My feet padded the soft carpet as I made my way over to the door. I opened it and let him brush his way past me.

"Clearly a yes, then. What's the matter, Henri? You homesick?"

"Dream-sick, actually."

"Come again?"

"I haven't seen you tonight, Drew. I haven't had an inkling of a dream, not one. I like it when you're in my head. It calms me. I feel safe."

"Wow, that's beautiful," he sighed, "I'm truly flattered. Here's what I think though – you don't need me in your head when I'm here in the flesh."

Why can't I have both? I thought.

"Henri, I know I said I would sleep in my own room and I still will, if you prefer, but would you like me to sleep in here with you?"

"I think it's a bit too soon for that, don't you?" My sensible side did my head in sometimes.

"I'm not trying to get in your pants, Henri, if that's what you think," he laughed, "I just think we both need each other's company tonight, don't you?"

"I do. I mean, yes, we do."

I got back into bed and felt my whole body, and mind, relax as Drew climbed in next to me. I lay facing him and everything felt right with the world.

"You're so beautiful, you know?" he said, stroking my cheek, "Sleep now, Henri. Let yourself go."

He turns to face me, and he is the most gorgeous thing I have ever seen. Am I asleep? I can't tell. All I know is that he's here, protecting me from all the cruelness in the world. I am safe. Nothing will hurt me with him here. I am his and he is mine.

"Henri, wake up," he says but this is too good to wake up from.

"Henri, wake up. You need to get ready."

"Really? Are you sure it's not the weekend? Can we not just stay in bed?"

"Sorry, no can do," he said, pulling me up from the bed and pushing me into the bathroom, "I'll make us a quick bite to eat and then once you're changed, we'll make a move."

"Why are you all ready? How long have you been awake?"

"Long enough to know we're going to be late for school if we don't get a wriggle on."

"Okay, okay – stop having a fit," I said before closing the bedroom door in his face.

"Shit," I mumbled through a mouthful of cold, limp, chocolate spread coated, toast, "we're going to be so late."

"I told you to hurry, didn't I?"

"Alright, Mr. Perfect!"

"That's my name, don't wear it out. Look, let's just try and get there as close to the first bell as possible, okay?"

I nodded.

We walked past a handful of kids from school. They were looking at us like we were a couple of crazies. I opened my mouth to shout at them, to tell them to shut up and leave us alone.

"Henri, don't give them the satisfaction," Drew said, stopping me from making matters any worse, "seriously, they're not worth it."

"I know, and I should know better but…"

"Look at me," he demanded, "do you honestly give a shit about what other people, especially those halfwits, think of you?"

"Well, no but I do have feelings, Drew. It's hard sometimes, you know? I'm just sick of being bullied. I've had enough."

"You have to believe me when I tell you I know all too well what it's like to be bullied. I went through two years of pretty much constant abuse, physical and mental. I know exactly how you feel."

My eyes found his and, in that instant, nothing else in the world mattered.

"Okay then, Mum. Love you," I said and ended the call. Thankfully, amidst all the rushing, I remembered my promise to my Mum.

"See you later then," Drew said, hanging back as I made my way to the school gates.

"Free period, again?" I asked. This was unreal.

"Just get to school, okay? What I do shouldn't be of any concern to you."

"How about I tell you the same?"

"Whatever," he shrugged.

"What's that supposed to mean?"

"Henri, look, I hate school if you really must know. I detest it. If I want to take days off here and there, that's up to me but you're new here and you're bright and clever and I don't want you getting into trouble by taking time off with me. You have so much potential, but me, I'm never going to change. I can't, no matter how much I would love to. I'm a loser."

"You are not a loser, Drew. Don't say things like that. If you were a loser, I wouldn't be hanging around with you. That's a fact."

He smiled, pulled me to his chest, kissed the top of my head and pushed me away.

"I'm sorry for being a dickhead earlier. I didn't mean to snap," Drew said as we made our way to the back of the field.

"Don't worry. It's all forgotten. And anyway, you weren't being a dickhead. I should learn to stop asking questions that don't need to be asked."

He smiled.

"Do you want to come back to mine?" he asked, hopeful.

"I'll leave it, if you don't mind."

"Well, as a matter of fact, I do," he smiled, "what could be more important than spending time with me?"

How could I tell him, nicely, that I just wanted to slob out at home, on my own?

"I've got loads to do," I lied, "and anyway, absence makes the heart grow fonder."

"I suppose you're right."

I nodded and decided, there and then, that I wasn't going to invite him round after school. It wouldn't hurt to have a little time apart and the last thing I wanted was to force the 'meeting my Mum' issue. The time would come. I just hoped it wouldn't be too long a wait.

Mum had clearly been cooking up a storm in the kitchen. She ladled the slow cooked, beef stew into two bowls. Her beef stew was incredible and if I had to live off one meal for the rest of my life, this would be it.

"That was delicious," I said as I soaked my last bit of crusty bread with broth, "just what I needed."

"Glad you enjoyed it," she said, waving a half full, bottle of red in the air, "would you like a glass?"

"Um, no thanks, Mum. I'm full. I don't think I could let anything else past my lips."

"Oh well, more for me, then," she giggled.

"So, how was your day?" I asked, leaning back on the chair and feeling bloated.

"Henri, it's been brilliant. I popped into town to have a proper look round the shops and I ended up in the pub."

"Oh, I see," I laughed, knowing what was coming next.

"I know. I shouldn't go out drinking in the day, but I only had one glass of wine," she justified. Not that she needed to.

"Mum, chill. You're a grown woman. You can do what you want... within reason."

She smiled.

"Henri, I can't remember the last time I had so much fun. Oh, sweetheart, I didn't mean it like that. We always have fun, I just meant…"

"Mum, stop! It's fine. I'm glad you had a great day. How was the pub?"

"It's lovely. So cozy and everyone was very friendly. I got chatting to the landlord. Nice chap."

"Oh, nice chap?"

"Yes, very," Mum said.

"Nice enough to go out with?"

"Blimey, Henri, I just had a chat with him that's all. Men and women can do that without having an ulterior motive, you know."

I giggled. It really didn't take much for my Mum to bite.

"Well, anyway, I'm glad you're getting out and about. It's good you're making friends."

"Yes, it is, isn't it? Which brings me to you. What's he like then, this Drew?"

Here we go, I thought.

"I like him, Mum. He's really cool. We have so much in common. Music. Books. Well, actually, I think that's all we have in common but, yeah, he's great."

She was staring at me, smiling widely and nodding. She seemed faraway.

"That's lovely, Henri. Actually, I needed to talk to you about something else."

"Fire away."

"I've got myself a job!" she spat out excitedly and smiled.

"Wow, Mum – that's fantastic news. You don't waste your time, do you? You didn't tell me you had an interview."

"I know, I'm sorry. I just didn't want to tempt fate and I didn't want to let you down if I didn't get it."

"Oh, Mum. Don't be daft!"

"I know. I know I'm being silly, but I just want to do my best for you."

"You always have, and I know you always will! I'm a big girl now and I want you to be happy. It's time you started doing things for you now. It makes me happy when you are. I love you, Mum, you're the best."

A tear began to trickle down her cheek but the smile on her face was wide.

"Oh, Henri – when did my little girl grow up? You're so clever and bright. So caring and loving."

"All your doing that is, Mum. I am the product of your work."

"I know that. I'm just saying though. I'm so proud of you. You've been through so much…"

"We both have! We have each other though and that's why we've come out the other end with smiles on our faces. We're stronger because of it all. So anyway, back to the new job?"

"Okay, so I'll be working Thursday nights, five until eleven thirty and then Friday and Saturday nights, six until midnight."

"Cool. So, as well as working, you'll be getting some socialising in too. It's brilliant, Mum. Really is."

"And you don't mind that it's night work?"

"Of course not."

"Maybe Drew can come over on the nights I am out – keep you company?"

"That would be great, Mum. I'll ask him. When do you start?"

"Tomorrow."

I got up, headed round the table to her and kissed the top of her head.

"Honestly, Mum, I am so pleased for you," I said, "I'm going to go to my room now. Just want to read for a while. That okay?"

She squeezed me tight and rubbed my back.

"Of course it is, sweetheart. I'm just going to relax with my wine and probably do the same if that's okay?"

I smiled at her and headed up the stairs.

Am I awake? I can't tell. All I know is that he is here with me, protecting me from all the cruelness in the world. His arms surround me. I feel safe. Nothing will ever hurt me again, he promises me that. I am his and he is mine.

He is standing at the end of the bed, looking at me. Looking at me like I'm the only thing in the world that matters to him. He climbs on to the bed and curls his body around mine, encircling me in him.

He kisses the back of my neck. His lips feel like electricity. I turn to face him.

"I need you," he says.

He doesn't have any idea of how much I need him too.

His mouth finds mine. I sigh into it. He does the same.

The sound is changing, becoming distant. The sound is not here, it's somewhere else.

"Drew!" I recoiled at the sight of him, "how did you get in?"

"Window."

"No, I would have heard."

"I doubt it. You've been fast asleep, snoring your head off."

I shook my head, dumbfounded. Maybe all of this was a dream. Maybe I was making this all up because I wanted it so badly.

"Now I'm here, can I stay the night?"

"I don't know, Drew. If you would have told me earlier, I could have asked her."

"She'll never know. I can be very quiet when I need to."

"Clearly."

He settled down next to me and I felt myself settle too, calming down as he pulled me to his side.

"Please, let me stay?"

I nodded. How could I not?

DAY 6

"Henri," I heard Mum call, "come on please."

I got up, ready to literally throw Drew out of bed and out the window. But he was gone and as I woke up properly, I noticed that there was no evidence at all that he had even been in my room. No scent, no sign of disruption, nothing.

"Henri, now! I don't want to have this every morning."

"Okay, Mum," I shouted, "I'm getting ready now."

"Drew," I whispered into my empty room, "you can come out now."

I didn't get an answer.

"I'm going then, Mum, okay?"

"Hang on a second," she ran after me, "just wait a bit."

"I'm going to be late. Can't it wait?"

"No. Don't worry, I'll be quick," she replied firmly, pulling on my arm. Her face turned serious.

"Was Drew in your room last night? I heard you talking to him."

"No, Mum. I must have been dreaming. I'm going to be late."

"Didn't seem to bother you when I was telling you the exact same thing a moment ago! Henri, I wasn't born yesterday. I really hope you're not lying to me. I definitely heard you talking to someone."

"Mum, I promise you, Drew wasn't in my room. No one was. He was on the phone, though."

Mum shook her head and looked at me in complete disbelief.

"Well, I'll just have to take your word for it," she said, "but if I find you're lying, Henri, I will come down on you like a ton of bricks. I don't mind you having friends round, boys or girls, but I won't have you sneaking them into my house. You want someone round, you run it by me first, understood?"

I nodded.

"Okay then," she went on, kissing my forehead, "I know you think I'm nagging but it's only because I love you and you're all I have now. Now go one, get yourself to school."

I approached the school gates out of breath but on time. My chest hurt like hell, but it didn't matter – no chance of detention for me. I pulled my laminated time table from my rucksack and felt more than pleased. English Literature was first up.

We were given homework, the first lot of the week and although I would never admit it to anyone, I couldn't wait to get started on it; a short story, didn't matter how many words, involving a very important person, or persons, in our life. Marks would be given for our work – *F* being the lowest, *A+* being the highest.

My story wouldn't just be about one person for now I had two very important people in my life. Thank heavens it was a fictional piece – no one would ever believe that I first met my boyfriend in a dream!

I had no mind to concentrate through chemistry. All I could think about was Drew and what kind of story I would be writing.

The bell rang for lunchtime and it's sound made me smile from ear to ear and put a spring in my step.

Once again, I ran like a crazy person, right into his waiting, open arms.

"Hey, you," he said, sighing.

"Hey."

As I sank into his embrace, the world, and everything in it, fell away around us. I couldn't tell where I ended, and Drew began. But then, something startled me – dragged me out of the paradise I had dived head first into.

A girl was laughing. I opened my eyes and looked deep into Drew's. He shrugged. I span around to face one of the girls that had thought it hilariously funny to laugh at me on the first day. The one that said she knew Zoe. I didn't know her name. I didn't want to.

"Henrietta, isn't it?"

"Yes. Why?"

"Oh, no reason. I'm Stacey. Maybe we can be friends?"

"Um, yeah, cool," I replied, noticing how quiet Drew had become, his silence practically deafening me.

"Everything okay?" she said.

"Yes. Fine, thank you."

"Oh, that's good then. You just seemed lost in conversation with yourself. You having a bad day?"

She sniggered. I could have slapped her face.

"My day's going pretty well, actually. And yours?"

"Yeah, great. Thanks. Anyway, I'll see you later."

She sauntered away, giggling snidely. I turned to Drew.

"What the hell was all that about, eh?" I asked light-heartedly even though my question was deadly serious, "She didn't even acknowledge you!"

He shook his head and shrugged his shoulders.

"I told you, I'm invisible round here."

"That's it, time to go," I said as the bell rang and I pulled away from him. I wasn't even going to ask the obvious.

He looked at me longingly. Didn't take his eyes away.

"Henri, I don't care what I am to anyone else. You're the only thing that matters to me now."

I threw my arms around him and hugged him more tightly than I have ever hugged anyone before. I wanted to kiss him, so badly, but the school playing field had eyes and I'd had enough drama for one day.

I like to think I'm a decent artist but how can drawing a bowl of fruit be so bloody difficult? It doesn't move. It doesn't fidget. It just sits there, doing nothing. Yet put a human, a dog, or any other domesticated mammal in front of me and, without being too big headed, I nail it every time.

I caught a familiar flash of movement ahead of me, just in my peripheral. Past my easel, past the art supply desks and out through the window. I smiled at him. He was exactly what I needed to see.

"Okay class, can you start packing up now, please?"

I didn't need to be asked twice. I gathered up my pencils and charcoals, headed to the desks in front of the windows and put them away. He watched as I washed my hands in the sink. I looked up at him and bobbed my tongue out. And then the laughing came, once again.

"Stacey was right! Look at her, she's crazy!" I heard one girl say to another.

"That's why no one wants to be her friend. No wonder she sits on her own. She's not all there," another said.

"Would you like to say that to my face?" I snapped as I span round to face the cronies that hung off Stacey's every word on the first day.

"Pardon me?" the one in the middle said.

"You heard me! Could you not get any closer before you started talking about me?"

"You shouldn't be listening in on private conversations," she shot back.

"What's private about it? If I can hear you, if it can be heard, it's not bloody private! So, come on, say it to my face."

My blood felt boiling hot in my veins. Adrenaline and anger coursed through me and I was amazed at this new, confident me.

The teacher came over, obviously realising something was amiss.

"What's going on here?" she asked, putting her hand on my back, looking straight at me, "Henrietta, is everything okay?"

Great, I thought, make a show of me, brilliant! That's exactly what I need. I nodded but said nothing.

"Girls," she directed to the Stacey's minions, "what seems to be the problem here?"

"Nothing," they said in perfect unison.

"Well, that means all of you are telling lies then, and that's not right. Now, whatever it is that's going on between you, just sort it out. If I have any of this kind of negativity in my class again, from any of you, you'll be going straight to the Principal's office. Understood?"

I nodded. They all nodded too.

"Right," the teacher carried on, still stroking my back, "get out of my class and go home. I hope the next time I see you, you'll all be good friends."

"What happened in there?" Drew asked, holding me to his chest. I nuzzled my face into it.

"Just some stupid idiots trying to wind me up, that's all."

"What were they saying?"

"Nothing. Can we please just forget it?"

"No. No, let's not."

"Look, Drew, it's all sorted, honestly. We dealt with it and well, that's it."

"I saw them, Henri, they were laughing at you. I could see that easily enough. You don't have to put up with it, you know? I can speak to them."

"And that would make everything so much better, wouldn't it?"

"Well, it would let them know that no one's going to be picking on my girl. I have a few tricks up my sleeve."

"No, seriously, please – let's just forget it."

"Okay, just this once but remember, I've always got my eyes on you. If I see any more shit going down, I'll have to teach them a lesson, one they would never learn at school. A lesson on how to be nice to people."

I smiled.

"Anyway, lecture over. Do you want to come back to mine?" he asked as we walked through the gates, leaving the school behind us for another day.

"Actually, that sounds good. Let me just call my Mum. Hold on one second."

I pulled my phone from my bag, found her number and hit call.

"Mum, is it okay if I go around Drew's?"

"I suppose it won't hurt. Will you be staying there tonight?"

Well, I wasn't going to ask, but…

"Is that okay?" I asked, hopefully.

"It's fine. You okay though? Do you have everything you need? Have you got any homework at all?"

"Yes, I'm okay. Yes, I have everything I need. No – no homework."

"Right, well, have a good time," she laughed, "make sure you get a good night's sleep."

"Okay, even though it is Saturday tomorrow and I haven't got to get up early. Actually, Mum, and only if you don't mind, could I spend the day with him tomorrow, too? Not sure what we're going to do yet. Would that be okay? If not, I totally understand."

I heard her sigh. It was a happy sigh though. She sounded pleased.

"Oh, go on then," she said, "why not!"

"Thanks, Mum, you're the best!"

"I know."

I woke up with Drew squashed in behind my back on the sofa. I prised myself from his grip and kneeled on the floor beside him. He looked even more beautiful when he was asleep.

I made my way, as quietly as humanly possible, to the kitchen. I felt ravenous and hoped his cupboards offered something in the way of sustenance. I found nothing. Well that's a lie. There were half used packets of dried pulses, some stock cubes that looked like they had been here as long as the house had and one particularly horrid looking, unlabelled jar of something. Something that had separated and had mould growing in it.

The fridge was stocked with beer and the wine rack was full. He clearly had his priorities well in order. He needed food, real food. Luckily, I had twenty pounds in my coat pocket. Mum always apologised for not being able to give me more and each time she did, I told her she shouldn't. I'm nothing if not thrifty when it comes to spending. Twenty pounds can go a long way if you want it to.

After writing a list of basics - teabags, coffee, milk, sugar, bread, butter, cheese, sliced meat, eggs and whatever fruit I could get with whatever money I had left over, and scribbling down a quick note for Drew, I left the house, shutting the front door behind me.

The town seemed like a ghost town. There was literally no one on the streets. No cars. No sound. Nothing. I was glad of the comforting glow of the lampposts lining each side of the road. Stop & Shop came into view, the light from its windows hitting the pavement like a beacon.

"Hi, Henri."

"Hi, John."

"You on your own tonight, Hun? Where's your Mum?"

In the very short time we had been here, me and Mum had visited Stop & Shop twice and, on both occasions, what should have been a quick grocery run turned into coffee and a chat. I could tell he liked Mum. I don't know whether that's possible in such a short amount of time, but I was in no way going to stand in the way of a blossoming friendship, especially since Mum seemed to be warming to John too.

"She's at home but I'm staying at a friend's house tonight and there's basically no food in the house."

"So, you're doing their shopping for them?"

"I know, I know," I laughed, "Someone decided to fall asleep though and I'm absolutely famished."

"A take-away normally helps with that, you know?"

"Yes, I know, and I do love Chinese food, but I just wanted to cook something from scratch. Something decent. That and the fact that his kitchen cupboards are bare."

"Where are his parents?" he asked.

"Out of town, apparently."

"What, don't you believe him?"

"Well, yes and no. Obviously, they're not there but it seems like they're never around, John. He just seems very alone."

"Oh dear, what a shame."

"Yeah. I mean, it's just this gut feeling I have. Maybe I'm reading too much into it."

"Gut feelings are usually right, Henri."

I nodded.

"Anyway, I'm going to get on with a bit of shopping."

"Okay. Just let me know if you need any help."

"I think that's everything," I said as I walked up to the counter John was lounging behind. I turned around in an instant, "Milk!"

I practically ran to the large, wall to wall fridges at the back of the shop and opened the door that housed all the dairy items.

"Shush," I heard behind me. I froze. Familiar hands covered my eyes and I relaxed instantly.

"For Christ's sake, Drew, you scared the crap out of me!"

"Sorry, I didn't mean to."

"Obviously. That's why you sneaked up behind me."

"Anyway," he laughed, "what are you doing here?"

"Didn't you get my note?"

"Duh, that's why I came."

"Does it not bother you that your kitchen is like Old Mother Hubbard's Cupboard? Seriously, Drew, how do you live? And don't say take-away. If you can afford that, you can afford to cook your own meals."

"What can I say?" he held his hands up as if ready to be handcuffed, "I can't cook for shit!"

"You can boil an egg, surely? Make a sandwich? You know, the basics?"

"Oh, I know the basics but that's boring. What I mean is I don't cook proper meals. I haven't ever needed to," he said, looking more than a little embarrassed, "I've always had everything done for me. I hate to admit, Henri, but you've fallen for a proper little Mummy's boy."

"Oh, so I've fallen for you, have I?"

"Erm, yeah! I'd say it's pretty obvious."

I couldn't disagree.

"Anyway, that's not the point! You need food in that house, even if it is just the basics. It's not healthy."

"You know, you'll make a great Mum one day," he laughed but there was a tone of truth in his voice. I slapped his arm.

"When did you get here? I never heard you come in. I never heard John say 'hello' and I'm pretty sure he says hello to everyone who walks through that door."

"Well, he obviously didn't see me. I've told you…"

"Yeah, yeah – no one ever does! Don't give me all that teenage angst crap again, Drew," I snapped, realising how sharp I must have sounded and regretted it instantly. I was just sick of him portraying himself as a victim. I knew where he was coming from. I knew how he felt but he needed to get his head together.

"Hey, are you angry with me or something?" he asked.

"Yes and no."

"Well that's helpful."

"I mean, yes, I am. I am because not only are you a complete mystery to me, you're making yourself a martyr. I know that sounds unfair, but it's not attractive. I'm also angry because you really aren't looking after yourself. At the same time, I'm not angry at you at all because you're all alone in that big house. I have my Mum. I don't envy you."

"Henri, my folks are away on business, a fact you already know. If you want to read anything else into that, whatever. I can't believe you're being like this. Oh, and by the way, I do look after myself, okay?"

"Yeah, with alcohol!" I snapped back.

"Henri, just shut up! Once again, you're making assumptions! For your information, I'm between grocery shopping at the moment. The reason why you see so much alcohol is because, believe it or not, I don't drink that much of it. I have a bottle of beer here and there and a glass of wine. And anyway, why am I actually justifying myself to you?"

I felt awful, so truly awful. He was right. I would have been the same had he talked to me like that.

"Hey, I'm sorry. I don't know what got into me. I shouldn't have spoken to you that way."

"It's okay, Henri. It's okay. Now, have we got everything?"

"Yes, definitely."

"Cool. Well I'll meet you outside. I need some air."

"You're just like me, Henri," John said as I made my way back towards the counter, "I'm forever arguing with myself over one thing or another. I hope you and your brain are friends again."

What? I thought to myself, What the hell is going on? He began to manually punch in the prices of all the items in my basket. Another reason why customers could never be in and out of this place.

"Oh, yeah, I do have this crazy tendency to talk to myself when I'm shopping," I said, thinking on my feet, "It's like I have to check with myself if I really need something or whether I'm just buying for the sake of it."

"Don't worry, love," John laughed, "Like I say, we all do it. Well, most of us, I think."

Had John heard anything of my conversation with Drew? I hoped not.

"That'll be twenty-one fifty, sweetheart."

"Damn it, I don't have enough John, can you take something out? I only have a twenty-pound note."

He looked at me tenderly.

"Don't be daft," he said, "I'm not going to go bankrupt by letting you off a few pence. Take it, Henri, please. I'd be offended if you didn't."

"Really, are you sure?"

"Yes, certain."

"Thanks, John, I really appreciate it."

"It's a pleasure, Hun. In fact, why don't you go and get yourself some popcorn and nibbles or something? I know these sleepovers require plenty of snacks. My daughter and her best friend clean us out when it comes to treats. Go on, help yourself."

"Wow. Thanks, John. Really."

"It's a pleasure. Enjoy."

Drew was nowhere to be seen. How could he have got home within moments of leaving the shop? This was getting way too weird. It's not like it's only been one occasion when he's gone completely unnoticed to everyone but me. I needed to get to the bottom of it, once and for all. Was he just a manifestation of my dream boy? Was I just going crazy? Was I making him all up to cope with the move, with my Dad, with everything? Maybe I needed to get back on my meds again or even go back and see the Doctor, which was the last thing I wanted to do. I hate the Doctor and I hate the surgery; horrible people, horrible place. They make you think you're crazy.

I opened Drew's front door, heaving the bags of shopping through, refusing his offer of help. I can do this, I thought, I am not weak. I practically threw the bags on to the kitchen table, my anger making itself physically apparent.

"Thanks for sticking around!" I said, barely able to look at him.

"Hey, look, I'm sorry. I had to get out of there."

"Why? Go on, tell me."

"I just had a bad feeling about staying, that's all I can say."

"Oh well, that's great. Thank you so much. It's a good job I'm not a wimp who won't go out in the dark, on her own, isn't it?"

"I am sorry, Henri. I really am."

It was pointless to keep going on at him. He clearly wasn't going to say anything more and as much as that utterly infuriated me, I didn't particularly want to keep nagging at him.

I let out a long, deep sigh, stopped trying to unpack, walked straight up to him and pulled him into a hug. He exhaled into my hair and I felt his body relax, giving up whatever he was keeping in.

"I don't know what's wrong with me," he said, his voice sounding like he was on the verge of tears, "am I that bad? Am I such a loser that no one will even acknowledge my existence?"

"Of course you're not," I assured him, "you're one of the loveliest people I've ever met, and you are not a loser! If it wasn't for you, I'd have no one, other than Mum. You're the only one apart from her who actually likes me. You're the only friend I have around here."

"Is that all I am to you, Henri?"

"No, what I mean is…"

"Because I need you, Henri," he interrupted, "I need you, so much. My life would be nothing without you in it. I mean that from the very bottom of my heart. Henri, what I'm trying to say is, I love you."

My jaw dropped to the floor, well at least that's how it felt anyway. Apart from my parents, no one had ever told me they loved me, and even then, it meant something completely different to what Drew was telling me.

"You do?"

"Yes."

"Is that even possible, yet? We've only just started to get to know each other."

"What more do we need to know about one another? If you told me, right now, that you pick your nose and eat it, I would still feel like this."

"Well, it's lucky for you that I don't," I smiled.

"What I mean is that nothing you could say to me would make me not love you. I don't think I can be me without you. I need you."

I couldn't deny him of his feelings. I couldn't stop him from loving me. I didn't want to.

"I love you too," I spat out quickly, as if the words were scrambling to leave my mouth. Drew's face changed from sad to stupidly happy.

"That means everything to me," he said.

"Same here."

Silence filled the air between and around us. It was heavy, weighted with anticipation and emotion. The look in his eyes was intense. He had me and he wasn't about to let go. My breathing became a little faster as he pulled me right into his chest. His hands slid around my waist and found their way to my backside. I let out a small gasp of surprise as he lifted me up. I wrapped my legs around his hips. They seemed to fit him perfectly. He carried me through to the living room and lay me down on the sofa, trailing kisses down my neck and across my collarbone. I closed my eyes and felt myself drift away.

We did pretty much everything apart from you-know-what and we had both gained quite an appetite.

"Now who's grateful I went to get provisions?"

Drew smiled between mouthfuls of popcorn.

"It's too late to cook now, right?"

"Um, I don't know, Henri. I could eat but if you're not that hungry…"

"I'm ravenous actually. I could eat a horse."

"Okay, so what will you be cooking, good-looking?"

"Nothing too fancy. How does Spaghetti Bolognese sound?"

"Sounds great," he nodded, "I can't remember the last time I ate anything home-cooked. I think I could get used to this."

"Well, unless I move in with you, that ain't going to happen."

"Now that is a great idea, Henri."

"What? You're joking, right?"

"Nope."

"It will never happen, you know that. My Mum would never allow it and I don't think your folks would be too pleased. I mean, they've never met me."

"You think they'd give a shit, Henri?"

"I'm sure they'll be back soon. They're obviously very busy with their jobs."

"With all due respect, Henri, you don't know them. I'm old enough to look after myself now, don't you know? They just keep putting more money into my account and they think that's all I need. Money is good, Henri, but it doesn't replace having them here."

I nodded. He was right, money is not a substitute for love.

"I admit, they've never been the greatest parents," he went on, "but there was a time when my Mum was a full time one. She loved it. I loved it. But then I guess she missed her job more. And then I became an inconvenience. I know I was a mistake, I overheard them arguing about it on more than one occasion. They hadn't planned on me. They never wanted a baby, their careers were their babies, but a baby is what they had, and they had to get on with it. As soon as I started high school, I became a man. I miss her, Henri, even though I'm pretty sure neither she or my Dad feel the same."

I couldn't speak. It made me think of my own life and realise just how lucky I was to have my Mum. I had someone to go home to, someone to talk to when I felt like talking, someone to cuddle, someone to scream at when I was angry. Drew didn't have anything even close to that. He had nothing other than brick walls and money. But now he had me, and I had to be his everything.

"Drew, you know I can't move in." I said, not wanting to say it was because I had everything he hadn't.

"I know but I can dream, can't I?" He smiled but he couldn't hide the disappointed look on his face, "I'm not going anywhere though, so you can stay here, with me, whenever you want."

I couldn't take my eyes off him. He walked to me, slowly, causing me to drop the packet of dried spaghetti that I forgot I was still holding. He wrapped his arms around my shoulders and kissed my forehead tenderly.

"And it's not just because I think you'll look after me," he laughed.

"That's okay, then," I giggled back.

"Come and get it!"

Drew raced to the dining table, almost falling over the chairs as he approached.

"Wow, it smells awesome and it looks amazing," he said, licking his lips.

"It's only spag-bol, don't have a fit!"

"You're talking to someone who lives off fast-food and take-outs. Please, Henri, let me just enjoy this moment."

"Okay," I laughed, piling strings of steaming spaghetti on his plate, quickly followed by two generous dollops of Bolognese sauce.

He could barely contain himself. No matter how trivial preparing a dinner was to me, I had to keep reminding myself that this was indeed a big deal to him. When was the last time he had been cooked for?

I can honestly say I've never seen anyone enjoy a plate of food as much. He wasn't rude, or greedy, but it looked like every mouthful he consumed was heavenly.

"Nice?" I asked between mouthfuls of my own food.

"Oh man, like you wouldn't believe."

"Would you like a glass of wine?"

"I won't say no," he said.

The cellar was pretty much fully stocked with beer, ales and wines from all over the world. It was clear Drew's parents were connoisseurs. I had picked out a nineteen ninety-seven Montepulciano earlier on, knowing it would perfectly complement the meal, no matter how amateurish a meal it may be.

I filled Drew's glass before pouring some for myself. The rich, dark claret liquid coated our glasses, leaving legs as it settled.

"Mm," Drew sighed, "delicious!"

"There's more where that came from," I said, heading over to the oven, where I had left a pot of sauce on a low simmer on the stove, "there's plenty left. I'd just need to put some more pasta on, that's all."

"I wasn't talking about the food," he gulped nervously, walked round to me and took my hand, "let's go upstairs."

DAY 7

Why is it that on the days you really don't need to be, you're awake before your alarm call? The weekends are meant for lie-ins and lazing about. No one should be awake at this time on a Saturday morning. It's ridiculous. What made it even more irritating was seeing Drew next to me, all snuggled up and cozy.

I quickly washed and changed whilst wondering where the hell I had left my phone. I knew it was in my coat pocket when I got back from the shop, but it wasn't in there now and that worried me. I didn't recall removing it and what with all the excitement the evening had bought, would I have even remembered?

Considering how well we ate last night, my stomach was groaning and gurgling like I hadn't eaten for days. I made my way downstairs to the kitchen, poured myself some juice and filled a bowl with cereal before splashing milk into it. I ate quickly and washed my food down with the juice. From the corner of my eye, I spotted my phone next to the bread bin. I don't know how it had got there and I didn't really care. I grabbed it and, hoping she'd be awake too, called my Mum.

"Hi, Mum."

"Oh, hi sweetheart," she yawned, "is everything okay?"

"I've woken you, haven't I?"

"No. I was just getting up. It's fine. Anyway, did you two have a good night last night?" she continued.

"It was great, Mum, really great. I cooked and everything!"

"Did you really? I thought you just ate junk at these sleepovers? Eat rubbish, stay up far too late and talk until you fall asleep?"

"You seem to forget, Mum – I don't do sleepovers. Have I ever had one? Have I ever been on one?"

"Well, erm…"

"So, yeah, I cooked and Mum, don't go crazy but we drank red wine. It was only with our meal. Drew's folks have an amazing collection."

Silence.

"Did you get drunk?" she asked, her tone low and accusatory.

"No, Mum – I promise. Do you think I'd be talking to you at this time in the morning if I had been?"

"Well, no, that's a point. All I need to know is that you're not being silly and you're keeping your wits about you. I let you have a drink at home because I can control it. Promise me you'll always be careful if you drink alcohol away from home?"

"You're talking like I've moved away to University, Mum and even if that was the case, you know I'd never let you down."

"Oh, I know, Henri. I know. Just humour me,

okay? I know I suffocate you sometimes, but I don't do it to make you unhappy. I do it because I love you so much."

"I know that, Mum and if you weren't keeping me in check, I'd start to worry. I love that you do it. I love that you are my Mum. Being with Drew has made me realise how important family is. His parents are never home. You let me have my independence, but I love being your little girl. I really feel sorry for Drew. I don't think he feels like anyone's child."

"Oh, Henri, that's so sad. Look, I've said it before and I'll say it again, any time he wants to come here, he's welcome any time at all. Please tell him that."

"Will do."

"Anyway, what are your plans for today?"

"Not sure just yet. He's still in bed. Actually, Mum, I know this sounds cheeky, but can I stay here again tonight?"

"What about your clothes and whatnot?"

"Um, well, I was going to pop back and make up an overnight bag and then come back but if you want me to stay at home for a while, I'll just go back later this evening."

Silence. Again. She was thinking, mulling things over.

"No, no, that's fine. To be honest, I was going to see if you would mind me meeting up with John. He's asked me out for an afternoon drink."

"Who's the daughter here, Mum? You haven't got to check with me," I assured her, "Go out and have a great time. I was in the shop last night, actually. I was getting a few bits and pieces. He's lovely, Mum. I like him."

"That makes me feel much better. I was worried

about telling you, what with your Dad."

"Mum, live your life. Dad lost any right to an opinion when it comes to this family when he walked out on us. You really don't need to worry about upsetting me because it's impossible. You can't."

Is it possible to hear someone smile? Because, I heard my Mum do exactly that.

"I'll be going out about twelve thirty," she sighed, "Will you be coming home before that or are you not sure yet?"

"Um, not sure. Probably before. If not, don't panic – I have my keys."

"Oh, okay then, great stuff. Well, I'll *maybe* you later then."

"Yes, Mum," I nodded even though she wouldn't see it, "Love you."

"And you, sweetheart."

"Hey. How long have you been up?" Drew asked sleepily, sliding his hands around my waist from behind.

"Almost two hours," I answered.

"What the hell?" he said, kissing the nape of my neck then behind my ear.

I headed upstairs and went to the bathroom. Drew followed me; stood behind me, looking at me through the mirror. I picked up his toothbrush, knowing full well that it's not great to use someone else's, but there was no way I was about to leave, feeling grubby. It was weird having him watch my every move, especially when I was trying desperately, yet failing miserably, to look sexy whilst white, minty foam was filling my mouth.

"How is it even possible for you to look more beautiful than you did last night?"

I shrugged my shoulders. If I tried to speak, I'd make a complete fool of myself. I spat into the sink as politely as possible and rinsed the toothbrush. I turned to face him and pulled his hips to mine. He gently pushed me up against the basin.

"Thank you," I replied, feeling my heart beat just that little bit faster.

"No, thank you. Last night was the best night of my life."

"Someone's been reading the book of romantic clichés, haven't they?"

He smiled.

I smiled.

"Seriously, Henri, I mean it."

"I know you do. If it means anything, I loved every second too."

"Anyway, why are you changed for?" he asked, peppering light, feather-like kisses on my face.

"I'm heading home to pick up a few things."

"No. No you can't," he said sharply, "I mean, no, you don't have to. I have everything you need, right here."

"Hey, chill out. I'm coming back. I've okayed everything with Mum. I just need fresh clothes, some fresh undies and some smells. Don't worry."

It was hard not to notice the panicked expression on his face. He looked as if he was losing control of something.

"Okay but please, please say you'll come back? Don't leave me."

"I promise I'll be back," I said, truly meaning every word but at the same time, feeling unnerved by his sudden change in demeanor.

"Hey, I could come with you?" he asked hopefully.

"Look, Drew, just let me go back, see my Mum and pick up my stuff. It will give us both a little break from each other and by the time I get back, I want you changed and ready to go out."

"But I don't want a break from you, Henri. I don't need one."

"You do, Drew. What about we go to the cinema and then for food? Or maybe even a gig? Anyway, we can sort something out later, when I get back, okay?"

"Okay," he said, head dropped low, eyes looking at the floor.

"Hey," I said, lifting his chin, "what are you so worried about?"

"That you won't come back? That this is all some sort of joke? That you're just stringing me along?"

I kissed him, long and hard.

"I'll be back. I promise."

"Mum, it's me!" I shouted as I pushed the front door open.

"Hey, up here," she shouted back.

I took the stairs two at a time, opened her bedroom door and nearly fell backwards as I took in the sight of her.

"Mum, you look amazing!"

"Oh thanks, sweetheart. I thought I better make an effort."

She looked stunning, but she wasn't over-dressed. She looked natural, but I could tell that she'd put a lot of thought into what she was wearing and her make up. I could feel my throat starting to tighten with emotion. I couldn't remember the last time she looked so beautiful.

"You're ready a bit early though, aren't you, Mum? I thought you were meeting John at lunch time?"

"Slight change of plan, Henri. Oh, sorry, I hope you don't mind. I should have phoned you back as soon as I knew. John's picking me up any minute now," she looked at her watch and gasped, "We're going for breakfast, then we're going bowling and out for lunch and finally, we're going back to his."

"Sounds like you're going to have a great time then, Mum."

"Yes, it does," she grinned excitedly, "Now, I know you're staying at Drew's tonight, but obviously if you did change your mind, just give me a call and I'll make my way home."

"Oh, so you're staying the night at his then, are you?" I grinned back.

"I don't know. Maybe. Is that okay?"

"Mum, you need to stop running your social life past me," I said, pulling her into a reassuring cuddle, "I'm old enough to look after myself and you know if I did really need you, I'd phone without a second thought."

A car horn sounded outside, and I ran to the bedroom window. John was sitting in his car, looking a little nervous. I pushed my Mum out the room and gently down the stairs.

"Do I look okay?" she whispered.

"Fabulous."

"You have your keys, don't you?"

I nodded and dangled my set in the air between

us.

"Okay," she went on, "right, I best be going then."

"Yes, you better. Have a great time, Mum."

"You too, honey."

I put my toothbrush, face wipes, deodorant, perfume and my "good" pants and matching bra into a bag, not forgetting an extra, dressier, change of clothes, just in case we decided to go out somewhere that required more formal attire. I booted up my laptop to check my email. While I was waiting for it to come to life, I ran downstairs to grab a quick bite to eat. I decided upon the last banana in the fruit bowl and made a mental note to either get some more or tell my Mum to.

Realising it was still early, and craving a bit of time to myself, I walked leisurely, taking in the sounds of the birds in the trees and the occasional car trundling past. I breathed in large lungful's of almost fresh air. It felt strange not to have my earbuds in; felt weird not to be looking at the floor. Usually, I was always on a mission when walking anywhere, never taking any time to appreciate the surroundings but now I welcomed the distraction. I just wanted to have my head to myself, if only for a little while. I love being with Drew, I really do, but I'm just not used to having anyone else other than my Mum in my life. And my new boyfriend is more than a little intense.

I walked past the handful of local shops and the post office and slowed down a little more, knowing that I was edging nearer to being holed up with Drew again. I stepped on to the field that led to the woods. I looked down at my feet and it was almost as if they were begging me to release them from their canvas covering so they could be free.

Glancing around, I noticed that I was the only person on the field. I crouched down and took off my converse and socks. I placed them to the side of me and stood up. I let my toes wriggle and caress the soft, green grass below and around them. I enjoyed the wetness of the morning drew, small drops of it visible on my skin. I let my eyes close.

"Hey, Henrietta?" I heard a girl's voice call from behind me.

I kept my eyes firmly shut. Maybe if I didn't see who was calling my name, they would just walk right on past.

"It's Henrietta, isn't it?" I heard again.

It was no use. I couldn't really ignore the girl now, could I? I turned around.

"Yes, that's me."

"Hi," she said, holding her hand out to shake mine, "I'm Nancy. I'm in Art with you."

That's exactly where I know you from, I thought.

"Oh yeah, right. Hi, Nancy."

An awkward silence filled the air between us.

"So, are you off anywhere nice?" she asked, clearly trying to break the metaphorical ice between us.

"Just to my boyfriends," I said, suddenly realizing I had just referred to Drew as my boyfriend, out loud to someone, for the very first time. I mentally scolded myself for giving away too much to this, Nancy, even though it really was only a little snippet of information.

"Right. Cool," she said, "so how are you getting on at school?"

"Oh, you know, fine."

"Cool," she said again, nodding, "I just thought I'd check you were okay. It wasn't so long ago that I was the new girl."

"Really? How long have you been there?"

"I've been here about a year now but I'm still struggling to forget those first, few weeks. Let's just say, I wasn't Miss. Popular."

"Tell me about it."

"I hope you don't mind," she said, looking down at her hands nervously, "but I saw those bitches having a go with you in class and I just want you to know that we're not all like them."

"I don't mind at all and thank you, I'm glad about that."

"So, what I'm trying to say is," she went on, "if you ever need to talk, I'm here to listen. Man, that sounds a bit creepy, doesn't it?"

"Nope. Not at all," I smiled, "thank you, Nancy. I'll definitely bear that in mind."

"Okay, cool," she said, and I wondered if that was her favourite word, "well, I guess I'll see you at school then. See you, Henrietta."

"Please, it's Henri."

She smiled, turned around and started to walk away.

"Hey, Nancy?" I shouted. She turned back round to face me.

"Yup."

"Are you doing anything right now?"

"Well, apart from walking home, no."

"Do you want to hang out for a while?"

"Um, okay, cool!"

"Mm," Nancy murmured as she looked over all the homemade cakes and biscuits on display, "it all looks so yummy. What are you having?"

"Just coffee for me."

"Really?" she asked as if I was out of my mind, "oh come on, how could you refuse any of these lovelies?"

I looked at all the cakes and sweet treats again and this time I felt my stomach rumble, even though I had eaten already.

"Stuff it, why not!" I said, choosing a moist looking piece of carrot cake and ordering a large cappuccino. Nancy ordered the same and pulled her wallet out of her bag.

"I'll get this," she said, and I was about to refuse and offer to pay when I realised I'd got no money left after spending it on shopping last night.

"Are you sure?"

She better be.

"Yeah, of course. I wouldn't have offered if I wasn't."

Relief washed over me.

We sat on a comfy sofa in the far corner of the coffee shop, aptly named, The Coffee Shop. It felt quite normal to sit right next to someone I didn't really know. It felt comfortable to be so close. Maybe I was just so happy to have found another friend.

"Oh my God," Nancy sighed with the kind of contentment and pleasure that only a sweet, indulgent treat can bring as she put a forkful of cake into her mouth, "this is amazing!"

I took a mouthful of my own.

"Oh man, yeah," I agreed, "it's heaven."

We both took tentative slurps of our coffees.

"Well, how cool is this?" Nancy smiled.

"Very cool. Nice place, good company. It's nice to have someone different to talk to."

"My thoughts exactly," she agreed before taking another sip of her drink, "So how are you finding school really, Henrietta?"

"Henri," I corrected.

"Sorry, Henri."

"Well, I haven't really been there long enough to judge just yet. Like I said though, it's going okay so far."

"Apart from the girls in art, right?"

"Oh yeah, but you know what? I try not to let it get to me."

"Well, you're a better person than me."

"So, I don't need to take it too personally, then?"

"No. They change their minds as often as they change their knickers. Give it a week and it'll be someone else's turn."

Nancy smiled.

I smiled back.

We both started giggling. I felt light and free. I felt amazing.

"So, is your boyfriend at school?" Nancy asked, plunging her fork into her cake, looking straight at me.

"He is but if I'm being honest, he never seems to be in any classes. Seriously, I don't know how he gets away with it!"

"Wow, that's crazy," she said, absentmindedly lifting another forkful of cake to her lips.

"I know, right? I mean, if it was me missing all these classes, I would be in a heap of trouble."

"Me too. One day he'll get found out though, surely?"

"You'd like to think so, wouldn't you? I mean, he's there but not there. He hangs around outside my classes and I meet him in our little spot at the back of the field at lunchtime. We sit and have our lunch together."

"Wow, you have a meeting spot? It must be serious."

"I know. I don't know whether it's all that healthy to be honest. I really like him, Nancy. I think I might like him a bit too much. I can't get over how fast it's all going."

"Aw, I know but it's so sweet though. I wish I was in a relationship."

I felt like saying, as much as it's nice, it's also a little stifling. I didn't.

"I'm sure you'll find someone, Nancy, when you least expect it. Oh my God, how clichéd is that? It's right though. When we moved here, the last thing on my mind was finding a boyfriend. Drew just turned up, totally out of the blue, almost out of nowhere. We just kind of happened."

"Drew?" Nancy asked, dropping her fork, her eyes wide, "your boyfriend's called Drew?"

"Sure is. Why?"

I couldn't put my finger on it, but something didn't sit quite right. Nancy looked shocked as she asked and there was more than a hint of disbelief in her tone.

"Oh, nothing. I just think it's a really nice name."

"I suppose it is?" I said before taking a large gulp of my now tepid coffee.

Nancy looked everywhere but at me.

"Is there something the matter, Nancy?"

"Nope," she mumbled through more cake.

"Really? You seem a bit off."

"Do I?"

I nodded.

"Honestly, everything's fine," she said, "You know what it is? I'm tired. I was up late last night and it's taking its toll on me today."

"Oh, that'll be it then, yes," I nodded again.

"Hey actually, Henri, do you have plans for tonight?"

"I'm staying at Drew's."

"Oh, cool."

"Why do you ask? Did you want to do something?"

"It'd be nice, wouldn't it?"

"It would. We'll have to arrange something for another night. That okay with you?"

Nancy beamed.

"Let's swap numbers, then," I said, "If we're going to arrange a girly night, I need to contact you and I don't think carrier pigeon is really the best option."

Nancy broke into fits of laughter.

"Of course. A number would help, wouldn't it?"

She took my phone from me, opened the keypad and punched her number in.

"Anyway, I've got to go now. See you at school."

"See you later, Henri."

"I thought you'd left the bloody country!" Drew almost shouted as I walked in.

"Nope. Still very much in this one. Did you miss me?"

He walked up to me, pulled me to his chest.

"Of course I did," he whispered into my ear,

causing goose bumps to break out all over my skin, "I always miss you when you're not here. What's the deal, anyway? I know you went home to get some stuff for tonight, but I didn't think it'd take that long."

For Christ's sake, I thought to myself, can't I just have a bit of time to myself?

"So, what if it did, Drew?" I asked, jumping on the defence. "I wanted to talk to my Mum."

"Even so, it wouldn't have taken that long, surely?"

"Might have done. Jesus, Drew, I didn't know it was such a big deal."

"It's not."

"Oh, really? Doesn't sound like it from where I'm standing."

"What? What's your problem, Henri?"

"I haven't got a problem," I barked, "but you obviously have."

"I only want to know what you've been up to. Where's the harm in that?"

"There's no harm in it. I just don't think I need to answer to you."

Drew shook his head and stormed off towards the kitchen.

"I'm just interested," he shouted, "that's all!"

So, our first, lover's tiff. Is that what this was? Is this what it feels like? Is this what it feels like to care? I don't want to argue with Drew. It's the last thing I want. But it just all seems a bit intense. Maybe it is all happening too fast. I couldn't leave it like this, though. I didn't want to spend the rest of the day, and night, with this awkward, stony silence between us.

"Look, if you must know, I bumped into a girl called Nancy today. She's in my art class. We got talking and we went for coffee."

"That's brilliant news," he said, smiling.

"I know, right?"

"It is. It's good that you're making friends."

"Well, she's only one girl. But yeah. It feels good."

"So, what's she like then, Nancy?" Drew asked.

"She seems great. I mean, I suppose you can't really make judgment after just one meeting which is why we're going to arrange a girly night. I'm not sure whether we'll be staying at mine or hers but it's going to be a great opportunity to get to know each other a bit better."

"Oh, I'm not so sure about that," he said, "don't you think it's a little too early to be staying over with her?"

Was this guy for real? I thought.

"You're kidding, aren't you?"

His face was deadly serious.

"Drew, how can you say that? How is what we're doing any different?"

His face was deadly serious. Still. Then a smile started to crack his composed face.

"You take things far too seriously, Henri."

He may have made out that he was just joking about me staying over with Nancy, but Drew's smile betrayed him. It wasn't natural, it was forced, contrived. He wasn't joking at all. At least that's how it felt.

I kept my feelings, like cards, close to my chest. Maybe it was just me. Maybe I was being oversensitive.

"Are you okay, Henri?" he asked, sidling up next to me, slipping his hands around my hips.

"I'm fine," I lied, because I wasn't fine. I'm not a fan of walking on eggshells around people. I like to know where I stand.

He pulled me in close, our noses touching, our eyes closed. He took a long, deep breath and sighed.

"Let's go upstairs," he whispered, and I pushed my feelings to one side. I could get them back some other time.

DAY 8

I should have woken Drew before I left but couldn't bring myself to. Once I'm awake, I'm awake. I'm not the kind of person who can stay in bed if I'm not tired. It makes me feel like crap. I made sure to leave a note for Drew. Left it on his bedside table.

If I was certain there was no one around to see it, I would have kissed our front door. I wanted to roll around on the welcome mat and if I would have had an arm span big enough, I would have hugged our new home like my life depended on it. Instead, I pushed my key into the lock and opened the door.

"Mum, I'm home," I shouted, throwing my keys into the bowl.

No answer met me, and I remembered she had stayed over at John's last night. I was sad she wasn't here but happy for her all the same.

I shrugged my bag off my shoulders and dropped it on the floor. I took my hoodie off and did the same. I looked at them both lying there haphazardly on the floor and scolded myself for making the place look a mess, so I picked them back up hung them in their rightful places, on the hooks by the door.

I checked the fridge, hoping to find leftovers of something. I don't know why I thought there would be anything. I'd been away for a couple of nights so why would Mum have cooked? But there, on the middle shelf, just peeping out from behind the milk and butter, was a plastic container. I pushed the dairy items out of the way and pulled out the tub. I opened the lid to be met with the smell of Chow Mein. Good one, Mum, I thought. I know it's wrong but leftover Chinese food, for breakfast, is so good.

I left the lid of the container loose and popped it in the microwave. I'd only have to wait a couple of minutes to taste heaven. The last twenty seconds before the ping felt like an eternity.

I grabbed at the container and passed it from hand to hand, almost juggling it until I placed it on the dining table. I ran the kitchen tap until it was icy cold and stuck a glass underneath. I filled it to the top, took a quick gulp and put it down next to my food.

I sat and ate in silence. I didn't want music and I didn't want noise, but I could just hear the birds chittering and chirruping outside. That was enough.

I put the empty container in the recycling bin and rinsed my chopsticks and glass. My room was calling to me and I wasn't going to ignore its plea.

"Henri, are you in there?"
    Knock. Knock. Knock.
    "Henri?"

My eyelids didn't want to open. I really had to force them.

"Yes, Mum."

The door slowly opened, my Mum creeping up behind it.

"Sorry, sweetheart. I didn't mean to wake you," she said as she sat beside me on the bed.

"It's okay," I lied.

"I really wasn't expecting you back yet but then I saw the stuff on the kitchen drainer and put two and two together."

"Yeah, thanks for leaving me that, Mum. It went down a treat." I didn't want to tell her that I'd eaten it for my breakfast.

"If you would have phoned me, I would have come back earlier."

"Don't be silly, Mum. I literally got back, heated up some food and came up. I didn't think I was that tired. I only came up to read."

"Well, I suppose you've had a busy weekend. Nothing quite as refreshing as a little afternoon nap."

Nothing little about this one, I thought.

"So, have you had a good time?" she yawned. She'd clearly had a good time herself.

"It's been great, Mum. I've loved it but I'm glad to be home."

She smiled and ruffled my hair. I'm eighteen, Mum, not eight, I thought.

"Good, good. I'm back a lot later than I expected. I'm sorry," she said.

"Mum, it's fine. And anyway, it's not late unless you've been up all night."

She didn't catch what I said straight away.

"What? Oh no, nothing like that," she blushed, "you know me, sweetheart – midnight, one 'o' clock. That's about my limit."

"Chill out, Mum," I laughed, "I'm just winding you up. Oh, forgot to say. I made another friend."

"Oh really. That's fantastic. Care to elaborate?"

"Her name's Nancy and she's in art class with me. She's really cool. We went for coffee yesterday. We clicked right away."

She pulled me into a tight hug.

"Oh Henri, honestly, I'm over the moon for you. Everything's coming together now, isn't it?"

"It is. For both of us it would seem. How did you get on with John?"

She blushed. Really blushed.

"Oh, it's like that, eh Mum?"

"Oh, stop it, you," she laughed, "we had a lovely time. He's a real gentleman. And before you ask, he slept on the sofa."

"I wasn't going to but, yeah, whatever you say."

"What? You don't believe me?"

"Of course I do," I said, raising my eyebrows.

"Henri, you can trust me when I tell you that nothing like that happened between me and John last night. I had a wonderful time and he treated me like a lady. I feel totally spoilt."

"I know, Mum. I'm just kidding. I believe you."

"Shall we get the records out?" she asked.

My heart filled with joy.

"Be rude not to."

"She really does sound like a lovely girl," Mum slurred slightly. It was easy to tell she'd had a great time and wanted to carry it on.

"Well, yes, as first meetings go, it was great, and I think the same. Actually, Mum, we wanted to arrange a sleepover. I don't know what night yet but is that okay?"

"Of course it is," she hiccupped, "why don't you invite her to come here?"

"I will do, yes but I have a feeling we'll be at her house for the first one."

"Oh, so there's going to be more then?"

"I think there will be, yes."

"Oh, that really is wonderful. I had this one, best friend. We did everything together. We used to stay at each other's houses all the time. At least once a week. It was always a Thursday night because there was this nightclub in town that played our kind of music and we loved it there. I never, ever told my Mum but her Mum, well, she was very open minded. She told us that as long as we were sensible, kept our wits about us and didn't get too drunk, we'd be fine."

She was talking so candidly, and it was brilliant. Of course, I knew what had gone on, I knew the story, but this seemed like the uncut, unedited, warts and all version.

"We had such good times," she went on, "we really were inseparable. Every Thursday, without fail. On the times she stayed at ours, we stayed in. Going out wasn't worth the hassle. If my Mum would have found out, well, I would have had to say goodbye to my best friend. It's where I, or should I say, we, met your Dad."

"The nightclub?"

"Yes. The nightclub."

Her face dropped, turned bitter. She downed what was left in her wine glass in one gulp. I knew what was coming next.

"You don't have to tell me anymore, Mum. Don't let this ruin your weekend."

"Oh, it won't," she said, pouring herself another glass, "Nothing could ruin it. I think I'm just happy that I've come through it all. She was having an affair with your Dad for far longer than I've ever let on. We met when I was seventeen. He was nineteen. We married five years later and the following year, we fell pregnant with you. Your Dad would have got married much earlier but I suggested we live together first, get used to each other properly. I knew getting married too early would have been a disaster."

"And that's when it all started?" I said, shaking my head, mouth open.

Mum nodded sadly. I hated seeing her so upset but I could sense that she was finding it cathartic.

"I believe, truly believe, that they were together within the first year of us all meeting. Of course, we were still only dating then, your Dad and me. But I had this feeling. The way they used to look at each other when we went out. I ended up feeling the gooseberry some nights. But your Dad was a real flirt. With anyone. We always went home together though. And because he was so good looking and, a lovely, warm, loving guy, I pushed all that to one side. He was a gentleman. Or at least, I thought he was."

I don't think I've ever listened to her so intently. The alcohol had loosened her and even though I didn't need to know all this, I was really honoured that she felt she could talk to me about it.

"Why didn't I do something, Henri?"

"Oh, Mum, don't. Hindsight is a wonderful thing. You did what you needed to do, what felt right."

"I'm sorry to be laying all this on you."

"No, don't you dare apologise. I'm glad you're talking to me. You clearly need to get it off your chest."

"I've been bottling this up for years, sweetheart. Maybe it's coming out now because I'm putting it behind me. Maybe I'm telling someone, and again, I'm sorry that that's you, because it's my way of putting it all to bed."

"And do you feel better for putting it to bed?"

"I do, sweetheart. I do."

DAY 9

I shot up out of bed. The light flooding my room suggested I should have been up earlier and I would have been if I had set my alarm like I told myself to do last night. I had it in my head that my Mum would be in no fit state to wake me up this morning. I had a feeling she'd be nursing a hangover and would need the extra time in bed to try and sleep it off. Did I set my alarm? No. What a start to the day.

I don't know exactly when my Mum had managed to wash, dry and iron my uniform but she had, and my shirt, tie, trousers and blazer were draped over my chair. I was quite capable of doing it myself, but the thought had never even crossed my mind. I quietly thanked her and dressed quickly. I brushed my hair and fashioned it into a loose plait. That would hide the fact that I hadn't washed it for a few days. I washed and brushed my teeth in record time and ran down the stairs. I pulled my bag and coat off the hooks and grabbed my keys.

"You know how to cut things fine, don't you?" Nancy giggled as she grabbed my hand and pulled through the school gates.

"Tell me about it. I seriously don't know how I've got here for this time. Oh, actually, I do. No breakfast."

"Tut tut, Henri! You know that breakfast is the most important meal of the day, don't you?"

"Yeah, yeah. Whatever," I snapped. I didn't mean to.

"See, it turns you into a right cranky bitch."

I couldn't help but laugh. She was right.

"What you got first?" she asked.

I stuck my hand in my bag and rifled around for my timetable.

"Oh shit. Physics."

"Ooh! I couldn't think of a worse way to start the day. And Monday, as well!" She broke into laughter.

"Yeah, thanks for your heartfelt concern, Nancy."

"Remember, we need to arrange for you to stay over, okay? Catch you later."

"Okay. Cool."

We hugged briefly and went our separate ways.

There was still a crowd of kids hanging around outside class. I looked up to the ceiling and whispered thank you. I don't know who exactly I was thanking but it seemed appropriate.

I hated physics at my last school. I think it was mainly to do with the teacher. He smelled. A mixture of body odour and bad cologne. He looked more like a down-and-out than a teacher. His hair was wild, and his beard looked like he was storing leftovers in it. His lab coat was always filthy. He wasn't married, and it was easy to see why. As he was teaching, he would rub his beard, clearly deep in thought. It made me gag sometimes, seeing all the little bits and pieces falling from it. I hoped, beyond all hope, that this teacher wouldn't make me feel like I wanted to vomit.

I looked up at the ceiling again and said thank you. The man who walked up towards us and opened the class door to let us in looked pretty normal. He looked a lot younger than my previous Physics teacher and, most importantly, looked smart. He looked like a teacher should.

The class filed in, the looks on their faces matching mine.

"You're the new girl, right?" the Physics teacher asked me just as I got to the door.

"Yes. Henrietta."

"Hi, Henrietta. I'm Mr. Jackson and as you've probably guessed, I'm the Physics Teacher."

"I did gather that, yes."

"Well, now that we know each other, let's get this class started."

I raced out of class and out through the doors, heading towards the usual place. Something caught my ankles and I went flying through the air before hitting the asphalt with a crunch. Pain shot through my hands and up my arms as a result of using them to try and break my fall. Luckily, my head bounced off them so hard that I tasted blood. I instinctively put my scraped, shaking right hand to my mouth and felt for loose teeth. No, nothing loose but on running my index finger inside my bottom lip, I felt a cut.

I got up slowly, brushed myself down and looked back towards where I tripped over. There was nothing on the floor, no object that could have caused me to go flying. And then I saw Stacey, stood there with her cronies. They were all laughing, sniggering. I could feel my blood pumping in my veins and my heart felt like it would burst out of my chest. I wasn't standing for this any longer. I needed to start standing up for myself.

"What the hell was that?" I shouted as I walked up to them.

"What?" Stacey said, "What was what?"

"Have you got nothing better to do than trip people up?"

"Well, actually, yes, far better things but it was funny. Come on girls, it was funny, right?"

Her sheep laughed on cue. Clearly, they couldn't do anything unless prompted by the shepherd.

"You're pathetic, you know? All of you. I'd like to see what you'd be dishing out if you were on your own. If you want a fight, let's fight. Let's have a proper, all out, fight. None of this namby-pamby crap. Tripping people up? Yeah, that's going to give you a right reputation, isn't it?"

Now, bullies can't fight a war with words. They don't have the brain cells to do it. I hadn't heard Stacey string a decent sentence together since I'd been here and as for her minions, Christ, they had fallen out the stupid tree and hit every branch on the way down.

I grabbed Stacey by her shirt collar and she cowered backwards, trying to pull out of my grasp. I saw someone running towards me out the corner of my eye. It was Nancy. I didn't let her distract me.

"You touch me again, you even so much as

breathe in my direction and I will show you that I'm not one to be messed with. Do you understand?"

I don't know where this confidence had come from, but I was liking it. Stacey's eyes were wide and glassy. Her little friends had creeped off whilst the fracas was going on and her face was a picture when she looked round to see that they had indeed disappeared. Nancy was standing next to me, arms crossed and brooding. She let me carry on.

"Aww, where have your friends gone now, Stacey? Not very nice, is it?" I let go of her collar and smoothed down her shirt, "Oh well, never mind. I'm sure you'll cope. Anyway, see you around."

She walked away, her pride wounded.

"I don't think she'll be bothering you again," Nancy said, stroking my arm, "You told her what's what, that's for sure."

I let out a long, shaky sigh. I felt like crying but managed to hold it back. I wiped my mouth with the back of my hand and bought it away to see a line of blood smeared across it.

"Are you okay, Henri?" she asked, full of concern.

"Yeah, I'm fine."

"Maybe you need to go to sick bay? They might be able to do something about your lip."

I didn't want to argue with her. It was painful, and my head was throbbing. I hadn't got the strength to say no to her. I let her lead me back through the doors I had tumbled out from to be met with Principal Stokes doing his rounds.

"Henri," he said, walking straight at me, "what on earth has happened?"

"Tell him the truth," I heard Nancy whisper under her breath.

"Oh, I tripped and fell."

"The truth," she whispered again.

I shook my head and let out a long breath.

"Someone tripped me up and I fell."

"Someone tripped you up on purpose?" he asked.

I nodded.

"Who, Henri? Who did this?"

I needed to think about this. Would it create even more of an issue if I did?

"Henri, I do not tolerate bullying in this school. I do not tolerate it at all. I want you to tell me who did this to you and I will deal with them accordingly."

Nancy nudged me in my side.

"It was Stacey, Sir."

"Stacey Kemp?"

"I don't know what her surname is, Sir."

"Well, there's only one Stacey I know of and this doesn't surprise me in the slightest. I've already suspended her once for this kind of thing. I'll be doing more than that this time."

"Sir, it's okay. Honestly. I've dealt with it. She won't be bothering me again."

"That's beside the point, Henri. This kind of thing needs to be stamped out. She's already been warned, and I won't have it. Even if she doesn't bother you again, I've no doubt she'll find someone else to terrorise."

I nodded. He was right.

"Now, would you like me to contact your mother?"

"No, Sir. Please don't. I'm fine now. Honest. I'll tell her when I get home."

"Okay, Henri. We'll see you tomorrow then?"

I nodded again.

"Thanks, Sir."

"Do you want me to walk you home?" Nancy asked, her arm hooked through mine.

"Not, it's fine and anyway, I don't want to get you into trouble."

"Don't you worry about me. I can handle myself."

"I know you can but honestly, it's fine."

"Well will you at least text me when you get in?"

"Of course I will. Oh, and we need to sort a night out."

"Well, we can do that now, can't we? How about you stay over on Wednesday? I know it's a school night, but I can't do the weekend."

"That sounds great. I'll speak to my Mum, but I can't see it being a problem at all."

"Okay, honey," Nancy said, pulling me into a hug, "you just take care and I'll see you in the morning."

"Hey, Mum," I said quietly as I walked up behind her in the kitchen.

She turned around, clearly shocked to hear my voice. She was even more shocked when she saw my face.

"Oh my God, Henri! What's happened?" she said, stroking my face gently.

"I got tripped up," I knew the truth was the only way to go.

"Tripped up? You mean someone tripped you up?"

I nodded.

"And what did you do back?"

"Don't worry, Mum. I put her in her place."

"I hope you did. I hope she knows exactly

who she's messing with. Did you find a teacher?"

"Didn't have to find one. Principal Stokes found me. He saw me and Nancy in the foyer and that's why I'm here. He sent me home. He wanted to phone you to let you know what had happened, but I told him not to. Said I would tell you myself."

"Who did it?"

"A girl called Stacey, she knows Zoe. I think that's why she's been bullying me. I think Zoe had told her all about me."

"Well, if I ever catch hold of her, she won't know what's hit her."

"Principal Stokes has got it all in hand, Mum. She's been in trouble before about it and he's got it covered."

"I certainly hope he has."

"He has. I know it."

"Oh, sweetheart, I wish I could stop it all for you," Mum said as she cleared our plates from the dinner table. It seemed neither of us had much of an appetite.

"I wish I could wave a magic wand," she went on, "Do you want me to come to the school? I can talk to Principal Stokes myself and see what he's going to do about this."

"Mum, honestly, it's fine. I have every faith in him. He really did sound adamant that he was going to sort it out."

"As long as you're sure?"

"Totally."

She nodded but looked completely unconvinced.

"Actually, Mum, I needed to ask you something?"

"That sounds ominous," she said, clearing our

plates and cutlery away.

"Don't worry, it's nothing bad."

"And that makes me feel so much better."

"Can I stay at Nancy's on Wednesday night?"

She turned, a look of relief on her face.

"Of course you can," she beamed widely, "Will you be going straight after school?"

"I think so. Is that okay?"

"Yes, it is. It's absolutely fine."

I walked up to her and gave her a big hug.

"Thanks, Mum."

"Don't mention it," she smiled.

I don't know who was more excited about all of this but by the look on her face, I would have put money on it being her.

"I'm going to go to my room, Mum. I'm so tired. Today's really took it out of me. Think I'm just going to go up and read or something."

"You do look pale, sweetheart. Are you sure you want to be on your own?"

"I'm sure, Mum, honest. I do have a little bit of homework," I lied, "so I'll get that done first before I start reading."

"Okay, sweetheart. If you need anything just shout me."

"Will do."

I slumped, like a rag doll, onto my bed. I felt physically and emotionally drained and I just needed to relax. My peace was disturbed by a knock on my bedroom door.

"Come in."

"I know you haven't asked me, but I thought you might want these?" Mum said.

She was holding a lap tray with a steaming mug of hot tea and a side plate with a selection of biscuits on it. I thanked her sleepily, knowing full well my tea would go cold and the biscuits would just have to wait.

She stroked my face and ruffled my hair.

"I'll leave you to it then, sweetheart," she said as she headed for my bedroom door, "Try to relax."

The door creaked shut and I allowed my eyes to shut out the world.

I am face down and flat on the asphalt. I stand up and brush myself off and turn to see Stacey and her cronies laughing. I walk right up to her. Our faces are inches apart. I give her what for. Tell her she's messing with the wrong girl. Her friends have long gone. They know what's good for them, obviously.

I turn back round, and smile. About time I started standing up for myself.

I'm walking home, and I feel free. Freer than I've been in a long time.

I'm in my bedroom. I'm tired. I settle down on to the bed and something catches my eye in the shadow cast by my wardrobe.

"Hi, Drew"

"Hey, you" he says, "don't you worry about Stacey. Don't worry at all."

"I'm not. Not now."

"I know. You did good today. I'm so proud of you."

"Thank you. I'm proud of me, too."

"Don't worry about Stacey. I have plans for her."

"Oh really? Drew, what are you up to?"

"Let's just say she won't set a foot near you ever again. I'm going to make sure of that."

"*Drew, what the hell are you talking about? What are you doing to do?*"

"*That's for me to know and you to find out.*"

DAY 10

"Henri, wait up!" Drew called as I approached the school gates. I slowed my pace to allow him to catch up. I liked being early for school. I hated being in a rush. If I start a day off on the wrong foot, it impacts on everything else.

"Come here," he said, pulling me so close to the perimeter hedging that we became practically part of it. The surprise of it made my breath catch and it seemed he was a little breathless too. He looked around quickly to see if anyone had noticed us and when he was happy that no one was really looking, he kissed me deeply. Our clinch was brief yet thrilling.

"Wow, what was that for?" I giggled as we composed ourselves and headed through the gates.

"Just felt like it," he whispered into my ear.

"Well, thank you. It felt good."

He smiled cheekily.

I didn't mention that I'd seen him in my dream. I hadn't really got time for the conversation that may have ensued.

We walked in happy silence to the school entrance and as I expected, he left me to carry on.

"Right, see you later," he said.

I nodded. I wasn't going to question him on it again, I was in too much of a good mood.

The good mood stayed all morning and as a result, my lessons went by in a bit of a blur.

"Henri!" Nancy shouted, running right at me as I walked out onto the playing field, "Henri, you are not going to believe this."

She was jumping round like she had itching powder in her pants.

"Calm down. What's the matter with you?"

"I can't calm down. You will not believe this!"

"So you keep saying. Go on."

"Stacey. She's not in school today."

"And?" If this was classed as gossip, she needed to get a life.

"Take a wild guess why, go on."

"Erm, I don't know. Chipped her nail?"

"Nope. Shall I tell you?"

"Yes. Please."

The look on Nancy's face was a fusion of joy and shock. Mostly joy.

"She was attacked!"

"What?"

"She was attacked on the way home from school."

I didn't know what to feel. I couldn't stand the girl, that's true but I wouldn't wish that on anyone, even her. I know what I said to her would suggest otherwise but when it boils down to it, my words were just an idle threat.

"Oh my God. What happened? Is she okay?"

"You're asking if your arch enemy is okay? Are you okay?"

"Nancy, I may hate her guts but still."

"So, yeah, she got attacked on the way home yesterday."

"How did you find this out?"

"Don't say anything but I heard her friends talking. They were pretty cut up, actually."

"Well, I'm not surprised. They might be gutless wonders but they're still her friends, I suppose."

"Apparently, Stacey's Mum phoned one of their Mum's."

"Oh God, can you imagine if our Mum's had to make a call like that?"

"I know. I don't want to imagine. But anyway, I hung around. I was pretending to listen to my music. I was nodding my head to nothing. Think I did pretty well."

"Oh, Nancy, you sneak!" I couldn't help but smile at her audacity.

"I know, right?" she giggled, "So, yeah, back to the gossip. It was in an alleyway…"

"What? Please don't tell me she was…"

"No. God no. Even I wouldn't wish that on her!"

"Me neither. So, what happened?"

"Just got roughed up, apparently."

"Badly?"

"Depends what you class as bad."

"For Christ's sake, Nancy. How is she?"

"Let's just put it this way, she's at home, not in

hospital. From what I could make out, she's got some minor bruising to her neck and arms. No other injuries."

"And that's it? Honestly?"

"That's what I heard, yes."

I breathed a sigh of relief. Nancy was right, I suppose. I don't know why I was feeling any pity for Stacey. I'm pretty sure she wouldn't feel the same about me if roles were reversed.

"I've called you all here to deliver some bad news," Principal Stokes announced in assembly hall, "one of your fellow students was attacked on the way home from school yesterday afternoon."

I didn't expect to hear gasps of shock, it was clear to see that the news had already been doing the rounds, but I did expect to at least hear some form of sympathetic chattering. Nothing. No emotion from anyone. She may not have been everyone's best friend, she certainly wasn't mine, but my fellow pupils seemed so indifferent, so callous.

"I am aware that some of you didn't get on with her and I know she isn't the easiest person to get on with," he went on, "but regardless of that, she is still a pupil at this school and to think that someone has done this to one of our pupils makes me very sad and very angry. I spoke to her Mother this morning and she tells me she's not badly hurt but she is shaken up, which is understandable given the circumstances. I don't know when she will be back at school but when she does come back, may I kindly ask that you treat her as you would wish to be treated even though I know that may be difficult for some of you."

I looked down at my feet, feeling like he was talking directly to me. I felt guilty, so guilty, even though I had absolutely no reason to be.

"Hi, Mum," I mumbled as I dropped my bag on the floor.

"Hey, sweetheart," she said, not even looking up from whatever crappy, gossip magazine she was reading.

Seriously, how can people read that rubbish? My Mum, she's bright, clever. I can't understand why someone like her would ever even pick one of those things up. She never used to read them but since Dad scarpered, there's always one or two in the house, rehashing the same, shitty, sensationalist stories. I suppose it's just escapism. I suppose it's just like me reading a book. Oh well, each to their own.

"Are you okay?" she looked at me, dropping the magazine to the floor, "you look terrible."

Wow, thanks for that, Mum!

"Yeah, I'm fine."

"No. No, you're not. I know my own daughter. Your face is telling me you're anything but fine. What's going on? Is it Drew?"

"No. Nothing to do with Drew."

"Well, something's the matter. Spit it out."

Her arms were crossed. She meant business.

"You know the girl that tripped me up?"

"Yup."

"She was attacked on her way back from school yesterday," I said quickly, the words tumbling out of my mouth.

"Oh well. Serves her right."

"Mum! That's so not like you."

She shook her head. She knew I was right.

"I know. I know."

"Can you imagine what you'd be like if it was me who'd been attacked?"

"Don't, Henri. Please don't."

"Well, there you go then."

"Is she okay?"

"Just minor bruising. More shaken up than anything else. Apparently."

"I'm assuming the police are involved?" she asked, sternly.

"I would have thought so. Principal Stokes announced what had happened in a special assembly this afternoon."

"Well, let's hope they catch the scum that did it. I can't bear to think of someone being out there, doing this."

"I know."

All the emotion of the day had finally caught up with me. I felt my bottom lip tremble, water filling my eyes.

"Oh, come here, sweetheart!" she demanded, dragging me into her arms, "let it all out. Go on, let it all go. This hasn't been the easiest time for you, has it?"

I sniffled and sobbed into her jumper. Felt my shoulders shaking, my chest heaving.

I didn't want to leave her arms, her embrace. I relaxed almost instantly, felt her body calm mine. You're never too old for a hug off your Mum. My eyelids became heavy and I didn't nothing to keep them open when they finally shut the world out.

"Henri. Wake up!"

What was that? Who was that?

"Henri. Wake up. It's me."

My eyes opened. Slowly. My room was a blur. I couldn't focus. I rubbed my eyes with fisted hands and took them away. Now I could see everything.

"Drew!" I croaked.

"Hey. You okay? Just thought I'd come and see how you are."

"How did you get in?"

"Window. Open again. You need to be more careful. Any Tom, Dick or Harry could have sneaked in to have their wicked way with you."

I shuddered at the thought.

"And you need to stop creeping into my room when I'm asleep. My Mum's a force to be reckoned with. I think it's you that needs to be careful."

"I've already told you - I can be super quiet when I need to be."

He shimmied up next to me. I turned to face him. I felt my cheeks burning. I needed to get my head out of what I was feeling.

"I can't remember coming to bed. I must have been tired."

"Busy day?"

"Not particularly. Just been thinking about Stacey."

"Oh yeah? Why have you been wasting your thoughts on her?"

"You haven't heard?"

He shook his head.

"She was attacked on the way back home from school yesterday. Surely you know that?"

"I didn't, no."

It clicked. Why would he know? He wasn't at the assembly Principal Stokes had called and come to think of it, I hadn't seen him since our little rendezvous that morning.

"So, what happened?"

"I know she was attacked, and that it's shook her up. That's all anyone knows."

"Nothing life threatening then?"

"Nope, not as far as I believe. The injuries are mainly superficial I think."

"That's a shame."

"Drew!"

"It's called karma, Henri. It's about time she got her comeuppance."

"Maybe so, Drew but I wouldn't wish that on anyone, not even her."

"Well, let's hope this little scuffle she got herself into will knock her down a peg or two."

I couldn't argue with him. Maybe it would change her. Maybe it would make her realise what she did to me wasn't that far removed from what happened to her. Even so.

"Maybe."

"So, you're awake now?"

"No thanks to you."

"What shall we do to pass the time, then?"

"Anything, as long as we're quiet!"

DAY 11

My alarm buzzed to life on my bedside table. I fumbled for it and hit it with as much might as I could muster. As I sleepily suspected, there was no sign of Drew.

"Henri, are you awake?" my Mum asked, outside my door.

"Yes," I called back. You know I am, that's why I set an alarm, I thought.

"Okay, sweetheart."

I couldn't take the smile off my face. I usually rush getting ready. It's tedious at best but this morning felt different. I felt great. Happy. Refreshed.

I packed my rucksack with the necessities to stay over at Nancy's. I couldn't wait.

"How did you sleep?" Mum asked as I hit the bottom stair.

"Great thanks, Mum. Must have been good because I don't remember going up to my room."

"You dozed off in my arms, you haven't done that for a very long time," she smiled, clearly reminiscing, "I don't know how you managed it, you didn't look comfortable at all. I woke you up as gently as I could, and you stood up, said goodnight and went straight up. Just like that."

"Wow. I have no recollection of that at all."

"It was like you were sleepwalking again."

The idea of sleepwalking has always freaked me out. I used to do it a lot when I was in the last school and I was having problems with Zoe. My Mum often heard me wandering round the house in the middle of the night. A few times, I woke up, abruptly, in strange places like inside my wardrobe, in the bath and the little nook under the stairs. Thankfully, the sleepwalking stopped when I knew I was moving school and moving home. Hopefully, last night's little blip was exactly that and nothing more.

I grabbed the carton of orange juice from the fridge and poured a glass.

"What do you want for breakfast, sweetheart?" Mum asked.

"Whatever's easiest, Mum. Whatever you're having."

"I was just going to have toast and jam. That okay?"

I nodded

"Sounds great."

"Nancy!" I called out just as she approached the school gates. She stopped dead in her tracks, spun round and jogged up to me.

"You got your stuff for later?"

"Of course."

"God, I can't wait. It's going to be so much fun!" she said, clearly excited.

"I know."

She hooked her arm in mine and we walked up the school drive.

"Oh my God!" Nancy spat out and pointed towards the main entrance, "Now, I was not expecting that."

I followed where her finger was leading me to and felt my mouth drop open. Stacey was standing in the middle of a group of pupils. Where usually, she would be animated and putting on a show for her followers, there she stood looking tiny and frightened. I felt a pang of sympathy.

"What the hell is she doing here?"

"She's obviously come in to show off her war wounds. Look at her, she loves it. She's got her audience."

"Nancy, you can't think like that! Look, you can tell she's not her usual self."

"It's all an act, Henri. One big act. She knows exactly what she's doing."

Maybe Nancy had a point. Maybe it was just another excuse to show off. To add to her group of cronies. If it was all an act though, she deserves an award.

We walked past, and I couldn't take my eyes off her. She turned and looked straight at me. She was as white as a ghost and her sunglasses looked gigantic on her gaunt, pale face. Her attacker had obviously blacked her eyes too. She certainly wasn't the Stacey we were all used to seeing, that's for sure.

I waited for Nancy in the foyer. I wanted to go straight out to see if Drew was in our spot, but I needed to catch up with her.

"Aw, you've been waiting for me?" she said.

"Yup, of course I have. Heard any more about Stacey?"

"Oh, so you're just using me, then?"

We both laughed.

"Well, you are a great source of information," I said.

"Someone's got to be, right?"

"Exactly."

"Actually, Henri. I can't come out with you. I haven't done my history homework so I'm going to use lunch and then my free to at least try and rustle something decent up."

"Oh, okay. Well, do you want me to come with you. I might be able to help."

"Henri, as much as the offer is lovely, I know I won't get anything done because I'll just want to talk about Stacey. Hope you don't mind."

"Of course I don't. Don't be daft. I'll catch up with you later."

She threw her arms round my shoulders and hugged me far too tightly.

"See ya later, alligator!"

I walked out the doors, on to the asphalt. I looked into the distance, towards our spot. I was glad he hadn't shown up outside one of my classes because now I saw him, standing there, under our tree, I felt even happier to see him.

I heard sniffing and snuffling and looked to my right to see Stacey, sitting on her bag, against the wall. She didn't look at me. It seemed the floor between her feet was far more interesting. Just carry on, I thought, leave her and go to Drew. As much as she didn't deserve even an ounce of my sympathy, I couldn't help but feel it.

"Stacey?"

"Yeah?" she sniffed, not even looking up at me.

"Are you okay?"

Stupid question.

"I've been better," she said.

"Yeah, I bet. Anyway, I'm sorry for what happened to you. Hope you feel better soon."

I walked away and didn't expect another word from her.

"Henri. Wait."

I turned back.

"What?"

"I'm sorry," she sighed, her breath shaky.

"Okay. Thank you. Apology accepted."

"No, I'm really sorry. I've been such a bitch to you. I know you won't believe me and I wouldn't expect you to but what happened to me has made me realise how awful it is to be on the receiving end of abuse. I am truly, truly sorry."

I sat down next to her, apprehensive but more confident than before.

"Are you sure you're okay?"

"No. No, I'm not. Not okay at all. I'm terrified."

"That's understandable, Stacey. What happened to you is awful. I hope the police catch whoever did this to you."

"I'm not so sure they will, Henri."

"You've got to have faith in them, Stacey. They'll find your attacker. That's their job."

"They won't. Seriously."

"Look, did you see the person that did this to you?" I pointed at her bruised neck. The bruises bore a distinct resemblance to hands. Oh my god, she was strangled? I thought.

"No. I couldn't give a description."

"Was it a man? Was the person wearing a mask?"

"I don't know, Henri. That's what I'm trying to tell you. I didn't see anything!" she broke down into tears. I put my arm across her shoulders.

"I don't understand. Could you not make out the colour of the clothing? What was the person wearing?"

"I've got nothing, Henri. Nothing at all."

I shook my head. She might be right. Maybe the police won't catch anyone. How can they if they have no information?

"I don't know what to say, Stacey. Maybe you'll remember something soon. You're probably in shock. That's what it is."

"I won't remember a thing. There's nothing to remember, Henri. It wasn't a man. It wasn't a woman. Something attacked me."

Please don't say she's going to tell me a vampire attacked her? I thought. Maybe all this is all part of her big story? Maybe she'd taken some strong painkillers that were affecting her brain?

"Something attacked you?"

"I felt hands grab my neck and arms. I felt a fist punch me," she took her sunglasses off to reveal one hell of a black eye, "I felt it all, Henri but whatever was doing this to me was invisible!"

Nancy laughed so hard I thought she was going to pass out.

132

"Invisible?" She howled, putting her hand on my shoulder to steady herself.

"Invisible."

"The girl's gone crazy. I think she needs psychiatric help. Maybe the attack has sent her funny."

"I think that's highly likely but honestly, Nancy, she was adamant. Deadly serious."

"She's on cloud-cuckoo land. You can't go around saying stuff like that. People will rip the piss out of her so bad."

"She apologised to me."

"She said sorry, too? She's definitely lost it! She's never apologised to any one of her victims. Including me."

"She said that what happened to her made her realise how awful and abusive she was being to others."

"And you believe that?"

"Yes. I think I do."

"Well, you'll make perfect roommates in the funny farm."

I jabbed her playfully in the arm.

"Seriously, Nancy, if you would have sat where I was, I think even you would feel the same."

"Not on your life! That girl deserves everything she gets. Karma has well and truly bitten her on the backside. Anyway, let's get out of here before Mr. Invisible comes for us!"

"Mum," Nancy called out as she opened the front door, "I'm back."

No answer came, just the sound of feet padding down the stairs.

"Hi girls," her Mum greeted us, "it's Henri, isn't it?"

I nodded. I felt so nervous. Weird.

"Hi there, Henri. Nice to meet you, finally. Nancy's told me all about you."

"Nice to meet you, too. Thank you for letting me stay over."

"It's a pleasure, Henri. It's nice to have you here."

"Thank you, Mrs…" I didn't even know Nancy's surname!

"Walker," Nancy's Mum smiled as she finished my sentence, "but please call me, Sarah."

"Sorry… Sarah. I hadn't even got around to asking Nancy what her surname is."

"Don't apologise, Henri. It's not something that comes straight up in conversation."

I smiled. I liked Nancy's Mum.

"Now, you girls go and head upstairs. Hope you have a great girly night."

"Thank you, Sarah, Mrs. Walker."

She nodded silently, smiled and headed into the kitchen.

Nancy's room pretty much mirrored mine; from the furnishings, to the books and music collection, and even the posters. Her computer desk was littered with gig tickets and post-it notes. Her bed was unmade with numerous items of clothing scattered all over it. Yes, we were alike, very alike, and it felt good.

"Well, do you want to listen to some music or something?" she asked.

"Yeah, I'm easy. I'm happy with whatever."

"Music then," she decided.

I nodded and the opening notes of 'Porch' by Pearl Jam filled the room. I wanted to have a good look around, wanted to be nosey, because I really am very nosey, but I didn't want to appear impolite. I sat on the bed and watched her potter around, pulling out cd's, looking at them and then putting them back; obviously trying to pick just the right album.

"You have a great collection," I said, walking up behind her, hoping she wouldn't mind me looking over her shoulder, "it's pretty much the same as mine."

"Really? That's so cool."

My eyes skimmed over the shelves and out of the corner of my eye, I spotted a record player.

"Do you use this?" I asked.

"Hell yeah, every day. To be honest, there's nothing better," she said excitedly, "I love the sound quality, even if there are a few scratches. I think it adds something."

"Exactly," I wholeheartedly agreed with her.

"Mind you, I haven't bought any new records since the shop shut down. It breaks my heart that I can't go and get lost in there. I suppose my Mum's records will get even more rotation now but it's not the same. I spent pretty much every weekend in that place. And now there's nowhere I can get my nerd on!"

"It's so sad, isn't it?" I smiled, but I knew exactly what she meant."

"It is. I know I can go online and buy, and I'll have to soon because I need more. I'm getting withdrawal symptoms."

"I know that feeling," I agreed enthusiastically, "I've got tons of cd's but even they're seen as old fashioned now. I mean, don't get me wrong, I am guilty of succumbing to convenience occasionally and download an album here or there, but I still like to have physical copies."

"I know, same here" she smiled widely, "You want to see the vinyl?"

"Of course," I said as she opened the double doors beneath the turntable. I flicked through her collection cautiously. Some of the records were likes of which my parents would listen to, "So all of these are yours?"

"Well, no. Some of them my Dad gave me. He said he trusted me enough to look after them, which if you knew my Dad, you would know how much of a big deal that is. We used to spend hours listening to his records. It was our time. Dad educated me, music wise."

I picked up straight away on the way Nancy talked about her Dad in past tense, the same as me, and so I deduced that he had, just like my Dad, left or even worse, he was dead.

"My Dad wasn't cool enough to leave me his records," I said, "which hurts because we used to do the same, just sit for hours, listening to them."

Nancy looked straight at me. She was shocked. That was easy enough to see but I also saw empathy. She understood, which is exactly what I wanted from her. I needed someone other than Mum and Drew to get me.

"What happened, Henri?"

"I'll tell if you do too."

She nodded.

I told her all about my Dad and what he had done and that no matter what he said about always being there for me, only ever being a phone call away, it felt like he was on some far away planet, completely out of reach. I explained that, even with all the will in the world, it would never be the same. I told her that he tried his best and maybe it's just me. Maybe it's because I hate what he had done to my Mum. I will never forgive him for that.

My Mum desperately wanted, no needed, me and Dad to stay on good terms because like she always said that no matter what happened between the two of them, he loves me more than life. I know that may be the case, but I've never been able to trust a liar, especially when it's a family member doing the lying.

"Henri, are you okay?" Nancy asked, hugging me tightly. I didn't even try to stop the tears that began to fill my eyes.

"Oh, sorry, I…"

"It's okay. Don't be silly. You know what though, I think maybe your Mum's right. I appreciate what he did was totally wrong, and I can't imagine how you must have felt but at least you still have a Dad. I think I'd prefer to be shouting and screaming at mine over not having him at all."

"Oh God, Nancy. I am so, so sorry," I said. I half expected her to tell me that, but it was still a shock to hear, "you must think I'm so selfish."

"Of course not," she said, pushing me gently away, "we both lost them, lost our heroes. It's not a competition to see whose story is best. Sometimes I hate him. I hate that he left me. I hate to see what it's done to my Mum, but like I say, I would give anything to shout that to his face."

"I bet," I said, finding a brand-new perspective on my situation because of hearing about someone else's, much worse one.

"You'll never forget what your Dad did, Henri," she went on, "but one day, you will forgive him."

"I know. I do. Thank you."

"For what?"

"For telling it exactly how it is."

"That's kind of what I do and the reason I have no friends."

"You have now," I smiled.

"Nice doze?" Nancy giggled.

"Oh man, I'm so sorry," I yawned, stretching out my arms and legs.

"No sweat. I didn't want to wake you up. You looked so cute."

"Oh well, thanks. How long have I been out?"

"About an hour."

"Did I snore?"

"No, not really. Well, not what I would class as snoring, anyway. You were dreaming though – going on about Drew and saying you were sorry."

I usually remember my dreams.

"Oh, well, sorry about that."

"You say sorry a lot."

"I do, oh, s…"

We both laughed.

"Anyway, do you fancy going out tonight?" Nancy asked once we had both composed ourselves.

"So, we're not having a girly night in now?"

"Well, you see, I've just found out there's live music on at The Loft."

"Oh okay, cool. Anyone we know?"

"I couldn't tell you. I didn't really pay much attention to who was on the bill. I just love the place, that's all. The atmosphere is always electric and there's always a load of guys to drool over."

I smiled awkwardly.

"I know, I know. You're already taken. Why don't you ask Drew to come too?"

"Nah, it's okay. We said tonight was going to be just us, so let's keep it that way," I said.

"Agreed."

Luckily, I'd packed clothes suitable enough for a gig. I brushed my teeth and washed quickly then I pulled my hair back into a messy bun, which my new best friend went crazy about. She said it looked awesome and asked me to do her hair.

The queue went down quickly, considering it looked like it went on forever. I half expected security to turn us away at the door, but Nancy casually led me in. I didn't feel too casual, I felt nervous.

"I didn't think we'd get in for a moment there," I shouted over loud, pumping music as Nancy dragged me to the bar.

"Don't worry about it! You need to relax, and I know just the thing," she shouted back.

"Right, so you think we're going to get served?" I said into her ear, scared someone might hear.

"Why not?"

"Look around you, Nancy," I urged, "we look like we're the youngest people here."

"You're correct, we do, but if security have let us in, we'll be fine. Anyway, I've got ID on me."

Of course she has, and I must remember to have mine with me next time. If there is a next time.

"I'm assuming you haven't got yours with you?" she asked.

I shook my head, feeling foolish.

"No worries. I'll make the trips to the bar even though I really don't think there'll be a problem."

Nancy called in our drinks and we made our way to a table. I sank down into the faux leather sofa while she perched on the edge and took a gulp of her JD and coke.

"Come on," she said, "get it down ya!"

I put the bottle of beer to my lips and sipped tentatively.

"What's the matter?" she asked.

"I don't know. It's just weird. I have a glass of wine, occasionally a beer, at home and I have a drink with Drew, but I've never been served alcohol at a club. It just feels strange. How do you afford it anyway?"

"I get twenty pound a week off Mum but then I work every other Saturday night at the pub."

"Which one?"

"The Dog and Duck," she said, "I love it. It just gives me a bit of freedom and, I appreciate the money more. I earn it rather than just get it given to me. Don't get me wrong, I really am very grateful to Mum but working for the money makes me feel good about myself. And it gets me out of the house and talking to people."

"That's great, Nancy. If there's ever another job going, let me know."

"I was just going to say exactly the same. Can you imagine us working together? It would be so cool."

"It would," I smiled.

A guitar was strummed, a snare drum hit. Mics were being tested. Nancy grabbed my hand, desperate to get me up and out onto the floor.

"Come on, let's go to the front," she said more than a little enthusiastically.

"Oh, I'm not sure. I'd rather stay here; the sound will be much better."

"You sound like my Mum," she said, "but I'm not going to force you. See you in a bit."

With that, she sprang away, bouncing and darting in and around the bodies of the ever-growing crowd. I took a sip of my beer and tried my best to relax.

I took out my phone. Drew hadn't been far from my thoughts all day and now I was here with Nancy, I wished he was too.

"Hey," a voice shouted from behind. I felt a hand on my shoulder, "enjoying yourself?"

I span round.

"Hey, Drew," I said, not even attempting to hide my grin.

He came around to the side of the table and pointed at the sofa.

"Mind if I sit?" he asked.

"Of course not," I replied.

"So, what brings you here? I thought you were staying at Nancy's?" he asked, looking around, scanning the area.

"I am but she sprung this on me. How cool it this place? This was totally unplanned but I'm loving it."

"Glad you're enjoying yourself," he said, but his tone betrayed his words. He didn't seem all that happy about me being here, for some reason.

"So, where's Nancy?"

"Getting squashed up the front."

Drew looked toward the stage.

"I can't even remember the last gig I went to," he

said.

"So, that means you're staying then?" I asked hopefully.

"No. Far be it for me to cramp your style."

"Oh, come on, at least you can keep me company whilst Nancy's off going crazy."

"No, honestly, it's fine. I just wanted to see if you were okay, not spoil your evening."

"Okay then," I smiled, "see you tomorrow?"

"Yeah, see you at school. Love you."

"You're alright, too, I suppose."

He flashed me a wink and smiled before heading out of the club.

Nancy bounded over, looking bedraggled but still beautiful.

"Oh my God," she shouted, "these guys are bloody amazing!"

"I know," I shouted back as she slumped down next to me, "they sound really good. Who are they anyway? I don't think I heard them say."

"Shout the Call. I'm sure that's what the lead singer said."

"Oh right, okay. Never heard of them before."

"We have now," she said, taking her glass, gulping down the last of her drink and slamming it on the table, "want another?"

"I'd thought you'd never ask. Yes please."

"Same again?"

I nodded.

"There you go," Nancy said, putting our drinks on the table. I took a sip of my bottle almost immediately. I didn't realise how thirsty I was.

"Hey, are you okay, Henri?"

"Of course, yeah. Why?" I asked, puzzled.

"Oh okay, cool. Just checking."

"Well, thanks for checking," I giggled.

Nancy's face and body language suggested that she didn't believe me.

"What?" I asked.

"Hm?"

"Is there a problem?"

"No. Should there be?"

"No, but you looked at me funny, that's all."

"Did I?"

I nodded.

Nancy looked down and past me, doing everything she could to avert her eyes from mine.

"Look, I saw you, Henri."

"Okay, you saw me," I said, shaking my head, totally confused, "and?"

"Henri, are you sure you're okay?" she asked, emphasising 'sure'.

"For Christ's sake, Nancy, what the hell are you going on about? Maybe it should be me asking you the same question!"

Nancy shook her head his time.

"Look, forget about it," she said, "let's just enjoy the rest of the night."

"Well, I was enjoying myself until you started acting up! Spit it out or I'm going home now."

"You were talking to yourself, Henri. No, actually, you were talking to something."

"What do you mean, I was talking to something?"

"Well, it was like you were talking to someone but there was no one there."

"I was talking to Drew, actually. Maybe you just didn't see him. Maybe your view was obstructed by something."

"Yeah, that must be it. You're right."

Why did I not believe her?

The cold, crisp, night air was a welcome distraction from the steely silence between us. Nancy had already acted strangely when I mentioned Drew before and now she was being even more weird.

"Hun, what's Drew's surname?" she said, scuffing her feet as she walked, just like a child would do.

Shit, what was his surname?

"What kind of a question is that?"

"I don't know, a valid one? You do know it, right?"

"You know what? I don't," I answered, feeling ashamed and embarrassed.

"Are you shitting me?! Would that not be an important thing to know about your boyfriend?"

I shrugged my shoulders but of course, she was totally right.

"And you're sure he goes to our school, yeah?"

"Yeah, why?" I agreed slowly. Now I felt shaky and nervous. I didn't like it.

"Well, the only Drew at our school that I know of isn't here anymore."

"What do you mean, isn't here?"

"Henri, there was a guy called Drew at school, but we held a memorial for him just over a week ago."

Did I just hear her right? I laughed at the mere thought of it.

"Okay, whatever!"

"Henri, this is no joke. Drew's dead. He died a couple of weeks back," she said sincerely.

I couldn't get a word out of my mouth. All I could do was look at her.

"Henri, are you okay?"

I wasn't.

"Henri, is everything okay? Damn it, answer me!"

Um, no it isn't, actually! Are you honestly trying to tell me that my boyfriend's dead? I thought. No words came out though. I just couldn't get my head round any of it. She rubbed my back, as if that would take all my troubles away.

"I'm just… I can't…" I stuttered.

"I know," she sighed, squeezing me even tighter."

"So, are you telling me that Drew is a ghost?"

"Well, surely that's the only explanation, right?"

"I guess," I said, pulling myself out of her arms and shaking my head, "but… oh, I don't know."

"Look, let's head back, huh?" she said, linking her arm through mine.

Nancy cussed at her computer as it slowly booted up.

"What are you doing?"

"I thought you might want the proof," she said, typing the name of the local newspaper into the search bar.

"I believe you, Nancy," I said, "you don't need to do this."

"I know. I just think you should see it in black and white."

"What, because that makes if official?" I spat.

"I'm sorry. I really am."

"It's not your fault," I sighed, immediately

regretting the way I'd snapped at her.

"Here goes," she said as the screen filled with text and a photo.

NO MOTIVE BEHIND THE DEATH OF LOCAL FAMILY

By *Heath Jenkins*

Two weeks ago, this small, friendly town was rocked by the news that a local family man, Geoff Hardy, shot and killed his wife, Sandra Hardy, and son, Drew, before turning the gun on himself.

The crime was committed at the family's home, here in Invention. The Hardy's had no remaining family and as such, no funeral was held. However, a collection set up by the Principal of Fallowfield Sixth Form College, along with money donated by the local community, raised over £4'000 to help towards the cost of burial for Mrs Hardy and her son.

No, it wasn't.

It couldn't be, could it?

Yes. It was. This made it all so real. I had wondered if Nancy was being completely truthful at first but how could anyone lie about something as awful as this? There was still this tiny little part of me that refused to believe her. Well, now it was right in front of me, just like she said, in black and white.

My phone buzzed to life. It was Drew. Funny how he can phone me, but I can never get hold of him! I gulped and took a long, deep breath, hoping it would allow me some kind of composure.

"Hey," he said, "just checking up. You okay?"

"Fine," I said simply.

"Any idea when you're coming around, next? Only, I have a little surprise for you?"

I bet you do! It wouldn't happen to be something to do with fact you're dead by any chance?

No. I had to keep my head. I didn't know anything for sure. There must have been another Drew in town. There had to be.

We changed and washed in silence. Silence seemed the only way to deal with this situation.

"Come on, get in," Nancy said, holding the duvet up for me.

I thought I would be sleeping on the floor, or at the least, top-and-tailing. I was a little taken back by her request, but I was in no mood to argue. I shuffled in next to her and lay, looking blankly up at the ceiling.

"Try to get some sleep," she said softly.

I knew for a fact that that wasn't going to happen.

LUCY ONIONS

DAY 12

I wanted to go home. I wanted my Mum. I wanted one of her cuddles, you know, the only kind Mum's can give? But, of course, going to school meant that I would have to wait, and wait, and wait until I got what I wanted. I looked at Nancy. She was blissfully asleep.

I gathered up my clothes and went into the bathroom to wash and change. I looked into the mirror to see a girl who looked exactly like me, but her eyes were rimmed with dark circles. She had birds-nest hair and dull, almost lifeless eyes. I turned on the cold tap and splashed handfuls of water at my face, hoping it would perk me up a bit but no such luck. As if a bit of cold water would sort this whole mess out.

I finally pulled myself away from the mirror and headed out onto the landing. Nancy's Mum was in the kitchen, cooking up a storm. The smell of sizzling bacon and freshly brewed coffee would usually drag me along, trailing after the vapour's like a sniffer dog.

149

Not today though. Breakfast was the furthest thing from my mind.

"Oh, hi Henri," Nancy's Mum smiled at me, "just in time. I take it Nancy's still away with the fairies?"

I nodded.

"Are you okay, Henri?" she looked concerned. I wonder if she'd guessed that I'd had a troubled night.

"Just didn't sleep that well, that's all."

"Oh dear. I'm sorry about that. I bet the last thing you want to do now is go to school?"

I nodded again.

"Here," she said, handing me a glass of orange juice, "get that in you. The vitamin C will do you good."

I took it from her and drank.

"Now, sit down," she went on, "have some breakfast. Hang on a bit, Henri."

Nancy's Mum walked to the bottom of the stairs and, far louder than was necessary, shouted her daughter. Her shrill, bellowing call hurt my head but I didn't want to let on. I picked up the knife and fork and scooped up a dollop of fresh, hot scrambled eggs. Maybe eating would help me forget.

"You make sure you eat it all if you can. Nothing like a good breakfast. Finally, she has risen!" Nancy's Mum sighed.

Nancy sat down across from me and looked at me pitifully. I could tell she felt awful about having to tell me about Drew. I mean, if it was true, well, I don't know but if she was telling me one hell of a lie, that'd be it – I would never speak to her again. I don't think she would lie, not about something so monumental.

We both finished our food in silence and got up to leave.

"Hope you manage to have a good day, Henri," Nancy's Mum said, stroking my hair.

"Thanks, Mrs. Walker."

"Goodbye, girls."

"Are we okay, Henri?" Nancy asked, tugging lightly at my arm outside the school gates.

We'd walked in complete silence. Partly due to the fact I was exhausted and partly because we were both feeling more than a little awkward with each other.

"Of course we are, Nancy. I'm so sorry. My head's somewhere else right now."

"I know it is and I'm sorry that it's me who's caused that."

I put my arm around her shoulders and kissed the top of her head.

"Don't worry about it. You only told me what I needed to hear. Anyway," I let her go, "Catch you later, yeah?"

She nodded, and we went our separate ways.

His face was the last thing I wanted to see but there he was, by the tree, waiting. I couldn't do this. I didn't want to. My brain was struggling to come to terms with the bombshell Nancy had dropped on me yesterday.

"Hey, you," he practically chirruped, his arms wide open, inviting, completely oblivious to what I was feeling.

"Hey," I shot back, looking at his feet. Looking anywhere but his eyes.

"What's up?"

I shrugged.

"Henri, what's wrong?"

"Nothing."

"Look at me."

I shook my head. Didn't he understand? I couldn't. I couldn't look at him.

"Henri?"

"I'm sorry, Drew, I've got to go," I mumbled, hoping he wouldn't ask me to explain.

"But you've only just got here!"

"I know, I'm sorry. I have to go."

Thankfully, Drew didn't try to follow me back to school. Why would he? He's not the biggest fan of the school as it is and now, I've probably made it one hundred times worse. I'm the only person who gets him, the one person who wants to be with him and I'd just left him hanging with not even a word why. I wonder if he'll ever want to speak to me again? I wouldn't want to speak to me again if I'd just behaved like that.

I couldn't bring myself to wait for Nancy. I just needed to get home. It's all I'd been thinking about all day. I couldn't concentrate on anything. I felt utter relief the second I rounded the corner to our street and saw the house. My home. Our home.

"Hi, Mum," I sighed as I walked in to see her rush upstairs.

"Hi sweetheart," she shouted back, "I won't be long. Just getting ready for work. Have you seen my mascara?"

I shook my head.

"No. If you can't find it, just use mine."

"Okay, sweetie. Thank you. What would I do without you?"

I sat down at the kitchen table, rested my elbows on it and held my head in my hands. My mind was a whir and I wanted it to slow the hell down.

"Right, there's a jacket potato in the oven, you've just got to decide on the filling. It should still be warm because I've left the temp on low," Mum said, looking flustered but fantastic, "I've got to go now though. You going to be okay?"

I nodded. I lied.

"Sweetheart, are you okay? Look at me!"

I looked into her eyes. I wanted to tell her everything. I wanted to tell her my boyfriend was a ghost, but I don't think I could have handled all the fuss and commotion.

"I'm fine, Mum. Just tired. Stayed up too late on a school night, that's all."

"Well, I have no sympathy then, if that's the case," she smiled and pinched my cheeks.

"Mum, actually, could I go around Drew's?"

"Can't he come here?"

I shrugged.

"Mum, please," I whined and realised I sounded like a little kid.

She looked at her watch and shook her head.

"Okay, but you make sure you eat that dinner first and you make sure you let me know when you get to his and you make sure he walks you back home. Oh, and I want you back home by eleven pm. Do you understand? I trust you Henri. Please don't let me down!"

I hugged her hard and she kissed my forehead.

"Sorry, honey," she said, rushing out the door,

"just be careful."

"Wow, it's beautiful. You've done a great job!"

The living room and the kitchen were spotless, and paintings and ornaments had been carefully placed on walls and tables. It looked lived in. It looked like a home. I felt my throat go tight again and I struggled to keep from crying, but I did, somehow.

"I just want you to feel at home," he said, reading my mind.

"Well, you've nailed it. That's exactly how I feel. Where did you get all this stuff?"

"Attic. Must be all the stuff from the old house. They want this place to be kept minimal but I'm sick of it. It's boring and lifeless. They're never here, right? So, I thought it was time for a change."

"Exactly, Drew," I agreed, "you've got to stay here and live in it. Let's hope they have a change of heart when they come home and see what you've done to the place."

"Yeah, whenever that'll be."

Do I tell him now? Should I tell him that his parents are never coming home?

Drew went into the kitchen, leaving me to carry on looking around.

"Beer?" he asked, already clutching two bottles in his hand.

"Well, I suppose so. Go on then," I heard the crack and pop of tops coming off bottles, "No family photos?"

"Somewhere," he said, walking over to me, handing me a bottle. I got the distinct feeling he wasn't in the mood to talk family.

"Oh, okay."

"Look, Henri, you've obviously guessed by now that family means nothing to me. I've been left to my own devices since I hit my teens. Apparently, I was deemed old enough to hold my own, in pretty much everything. I've had to grow up quick even though all I've ever wanted is a Mum and Dad. I want to be told off when I'm bad and I want so, so much to be held, by one or both of them, when I need to be. I just want them to love me like they used to do when I was a kid. Up until a few years ago, before they started these new jobs and we moved here, I was the love of their lives. I've tried everything to make them proud of me but I'm just an inconvenience. I don't know why they even had a child. So, what's the point in school and doing well when they clearly couldn't give a shit?"

"Oh, Drew, I'm sorry."

"Don't be. I don't want to force the issue anymore. I'm not going to beg for their love. Anyway, what they lack in parenting skills, they make up for financially."

He threw his arms around my shoulders. I could feel his chin on the top of my head and he squeezed me tightly.

"Henri, you are an angel and you've been sent to me just when I needed someone the most. Can I tell you something, honestly?"

"Of course you can," I mumbled into his neck.

"Don't be angry with me, okay?"

"Okay?" I said, dreading what he was going to say next.

"I tried to kill myself. About a year ago."

I hugged him tighter but didn't say a word. I wanted him to get it all out.

"My father drinks. A lot. Too much. My Mum's a

coward really. She likes to think she's this strong, confident, independent woman but she's not. She's a doormat. I used to hear him knocking her about pretty much every Friday when he got back from the pub. I often heard her crying. I'd had enough, so one Friday, almost three years ago now, I went downstairs and caught him in the act. Mum's face was bloodied and bruised, and I saw red. I punched him, Henri. I punched him so hard I felt his nose crack. It felt amazing. I felt incredible. Finally, I'd grown a pair and stood up to him. He deserved so much more than what I did to him but at least I did something."

Never judge a book by its cover. Those photos that I saw, they were just images of what a family should look like. I've got to admit, they looked happy in the images but obviously, it was just a façade.

"Jesus, Drew. That was such a brave thing to do and it was exactly the right thing you did."

"Yeah, maybe," he nodded softly, "for Mum it was, anyway. Suddenly, they were like the best of friends. They giggled like school kids, they went on dates. They had friends round and they even started having sex again. It was all very disturbing. It was like the abuse had never even happened but then, after about six or so months of relative peace and quiet, it all started up again. This time round though, I was his victim. It was as if he needed to have someone to abuse now that Mum was out of the equation."

Drew paused, letting out a quivering sigh. Without realizing, I did the same.

"I told her, Henri. I told her I was Dad's new punch bag. I told her because I thought she would sympathise. I thought she'd get on the phone to the police and I thought we'd get him put away for good.

He needed to pay for everything he had done to us. But no. Shall I tell you what she did?"

I gulped. No, I didn't want to know but at the same time, I didn't want him to feel like he had to keep this huge secret to himself any longer.

"She did sweet fuck all!" he shouted, letting his resolve completely slip, "She turned a blind eye to all of it. Even after he had done the one thing no father should ever do to his son…" he stopped, wondering if he had gone too far, said too much. Tears filled his eyes. My eyes copied.

"You don't need to say any more," I assured him, "if you want to, I will listen, but I totally understand if it's too much."

He pulled out of our embrace.

"Even after he did that to me," he carried on bravely, "and even after I told her – nothing! She did nothing. He got away with everything, Henri. No one could help me. I couldn't tell anyone what had been going on. I didn't have the balls to. But Principal Stokes called me into his office one afternoon as I was about to leave school. I thought I was in trouble because I'd started to act up a bit. My grades weren't the best. I wasn't myself."

Drew stopped and sighed sadly.

"Anyway, I told him what had happened and without going into too much detail, how Dad had turned on me. He took me home with him that afternoon and we talked more openly. He told me that he wouldn't betray my trust and would only speak to the police if I wanted him to, but he urged that it was the best thing to do. I told him I would deal with it myself, that I would speak to the police when it was safe for me to do so. We both lied to each other that day. I never phoned the police. I had no intention of doing so."

"Oh, Drew, why? Why didn't you?"

"I don't know. I was ashamed? It felt good to speak to Principal Stokes. He made me feel at ease, but I didn't want to tell my secrets to a complete stranger."

I nodded sadly.

"A few nights later, the Police knocked on our front door, said they'd had a phone call that suggested domestic violence was taking place here. I knew who had made that phone call. My Mum and Dad denied all knowledge and because I knew I'd just get yet another beating, I did the same. I denied that my Mum and I were being used as punchbags. I didn't hate Stokes for phoning the police. I know he only did it because he was concerned and because of that, I lied, again. I was getting good at lying. When I saw him at school the following morning, I made out that the police now knew everything, and I thanked him for his intervention.

My Dad thanked me for protecting him and it made me feel physically sick. It was easy to see the guilt etched on his face and remember, my Mum wasn't exactly innocent in all this either. She may not have raised a hand to me, but she didn't exactly do anything to stop my Dad. She had the same reasons as me, I guess. And then they started to work away a lot more. I think it was all the guilt.

Three years has gone by so quickly and I'm so happy I'm alone. I'm pleased that their way of parenting is purely financial now. I don't care if I never see them again."

Drew's body eased and relaxed beneath my touch and I could almost see the huge weight lifting off his shoulders. Maybe that's why he's still around? Was he stuck in some kind of limbo? Maybe he needed to confess all of this to someone in order for him to move on. I didn't want him to move on. I didn't want him to go. I had only just discovered him, this truly wonderful boy. Ghost or not, he couldn't leave me. Not now.

"I'm really going to have to go now," I said, pulling myself out from Drew's side, "I told my Mum I'd be back for eleven."

"Why don't you stay, Henri? Phone her and ask."

Man, I knew there something I was meant to do. I grabbed my phone and saw Drew's face turn hopeful. His hopes would be dashed as soon as he realised I wasn't going to ask my Mum anything.

"Hi, Mum. Yes, I'm leaving now. See you later."

As predicted, he didn't look all that happy. He looked deflated.

"I can come around at the weekend, yeah?" I said, doing my best to cheer him up.

"Of course you can," he smiled and followed me to his front door, "I'm sorry if I seem pushy, Henri. I just love having you here."

"I love being here too."

"Come on, I'll walk you back."

I hugged him hard and we walked out.

"Goodnight, Henri," Drew said, placing a soft, gentle kiss on my lips.

I sighed.

"Goodnight, Drew."

We both hesitated. There was a definite air of

anticipation between us. Drew leaned into me, his face pulling up just short of mine. I closed my eyes and he kissed me again. Not so soft and gentle this time.

"Sorry," he said, pulling away and leaving me with my mouth wide open and my eyes still closed, "I just needed to do that."

"I know what you mean."

"Love you, Henri."

"Love you, too."

I watched him go. Watched him walk, all alone. I thought ghosts, well, you know, disappeared into thin air? Isn't that what they do?

I washed and changed and climbed into bed. I was too restless to sleep. I looked at my phone. Mum had only asked me to be in by eleven but here I was, lying in bed, my brain refusing to let me drift off.

DAY 13

"Hi, Mum," I mumbled as I ambled into the kitchen.

"Hey," she said, spinning round and pulling me into a hug, "I'm proud of you, you know?"

"Yeah, I know," I smiled tiredly.

"No, I mean it. I'm so proud of you. I know you've heard me say it before, but I don't care. I half expected you to not come back last night, and yes, I would have been so bloody angry but it's what teenagers do. We've all been there you know, Henri. We've all been teenagers and we've all, at some point, done things that disappoint our parents. That's just the way things go. You've never done anything to disappoint me, Henri. Not one thing."

I squeezed her tighter. I don't ever want to let her down.

"You're not letting Drew cloud your judgment," she went on, "and that's so important. Keep your independence, Henri. Keep your own mind. I know it's difficult. You get a boyfriend, you fall in love and it's so easy to allow yourself to go blind with it. You're a bright, clever girl and you still amaze me."

I pulled away from her and kissed her cheek tenderly.

"I obviously get it all from you, Mum."

She beamed.

"If you want to stay at Drew's tonight, you can," she said, "it's the weekend and I'm working so you're not going to have much company. Unless Drew wants to come here, of course."

"Are you sure?"

"Yes, of course."

"Well, I imagine we'll be staying at his. As usual. Does it bother you, Mum? That we only stay at his?"

"If I think back, I always stayed at your Dad's when we first started seeing each other. He lived in the basement of his parents. He had it done out lovely. He had everything he needed. Why would I have wanted him to come around our house, a two bedroom, semi-detached with just about enough room for the three of us? No. The only way we got our own space was to be at his. So, no, you staying at Drew's does not bother me, unless you start staying every night, of course?"

"Nope. Never going to happen. I love my room too much."

"Oh, so it's just the room then?" Mum punched me playfully in the arm.

"Yeah, pretty much."

She smiled widely and skipped off back to the breakfast bar to carry on reading the newspaper.

I opened the cupboard above the bread bin and pulled out a box of cereal. Mum slid a bowl across the worktop without even looking at me. I filled it half full of cornflakes and poured cold milk all over.

"I read a terrible story in here the other day," my Mum said, tearing me from my reverie.

"Oh yeah, what was it about?" I spoke through a mouthful of wet cereal.

"A local man killed his wife and his son. Then he killed himself. How awful. How horrible."

"Oh god, really? That's so sad," I said, feeling a cold sweat wash over me, hoping that she hadn't read it in too much detail, "How local? From here?"

"I'm not sure exactly where they lived, but they were definitely local."

"Did it give any names, the article?"

"I think so. Yes, it did."

"Who were they?"

"Oh, sweetheart – you know what I'm like! I can barely remember what I had for lunch yesterday, let alone anything like that. I'm sure it said they were, oh hang on," she looked up and rubbed her chin in concentration, "Hardy. The family name was Hardy."

I looked into my bowl, staring at what was left of my cereal, doing everything I could to avoid my Mum's eyes. I would give too much away, leave myself open, and then there would be questions, questions that I didn't want to, and couldn't, answer. I quickly finished what was left of my cereal and drank the leftover, sugary milk straight from the bowl.

"Shouldn't you be getting ready?" she said.

I looked down at myself and realised I was still in my pyjamas. I ran up the stairs and into my room. I threw on my uniform, taking no time to smooth down. I quickly washed and brushed my teeth and then pulled my hair back into a loose ponytail. I grabbed my rucksack and shoved in a change of clothes, underwear and toiletries. I hadn't even asked Drew if I could stay over but I don't think he'd say no. In fact, I knew he wouldn't.

"See ya, Mum!" I shouted on my way out.

"Hey, Henri!" Nancy shouted, running after me.

I turned around to face her.

"Hey."

"Are you okay? I was worried. You know, about the Drew thing?"

How could I forget?

"I don't know how to feel, Nancy. I don't know what to think."

She nodded sympathetically.

"I can't imagine what you're going through," she said, "I don't think anyone could."

"Tell me about it."

"Have you seen him today?"

"No. Not a thing. I'm going around to his tonight though."

"Are you?"

I nodded.

"Shit, Henri. Are you going to say anything? What the hell would you say anyway?"

"No offence, Nancy but you're seriously not helping the situation."

"I'm sorry, Henri. Just tell me to shut my mouth."

I pulled her into a hug.

"No, I'm sorry. I shouldn't have spoken to you like that. You're my best friend."

"Hey, don't apologise. I just don't know what else to say."

"At least we're in the same boat, then."

She pulled out of my arms and smiled at me.

"Well, I know you'll handle it perfectly. Are you going to his place straight after school?"

I took my rucksack off my back and gave it to Nancy to hold.

"I guess that's a yes, then," she said, her arm sagging with the weight, "have you packed your entire bedroom in here?"

I laughed. It sounded strange. Forced.

"We'll talk more at lunch, okay?"

I nodded but food wasn't high on my list of priorities.

"You'll let me know how you get on, won't you?" Nancy said as she chomped away on her chips.

"Of course I will."

"I mean it, Henri. Whatever happens. You need to talk about this. Please don't keep it bottled up."

"Yes, Mum."

"I'm being serious," she scowled.

"I know you are. I can't take you seriously when you're being serious though. You're funny."

We both laughed and this time it didn't feel forced at all.

"I don't know if I'll definitely say anything to him yet. I don't know whether it's the right time."

"I'm not saying you've got to, Henri. You'll know when it's the right time. Just let me know how you are. That's all I'm asking. Promise?"

"Promise."

I knocked at the door. No answer. Knocked again, a

rhythmic seven times and the door opened.

"Hey," Drew said, pulling me inside, "come in."

"I know we hadn't said I'd come over tonight, but Mum said I could stay without me even asking. That and I really needed to see you."

He pulled me into a deep hug.

"Well, I'm not going to argue with that. I'm really glad you're here."

"Me too."

"So, what shall we do?" He asked hopefully and somewhat suggestively.

"I hadn't thought that far ahead. Do you have any ideas?" I smirked.

There wasn't even an inch separating us, but he slid his hands around my waist anyway, letting them rest on my behind. He pulled me even closer. I sighed with expectation. Our noses touched, and he grabbed my bottom lip between his teeth, pulling it into his mouth. My legs felt like they had turned to jelly so I put my arms around his shoulders to steady myself. If this was his idea, I was happy to go along with it.

"Well, we're still no closer to a decision are we, Henri," Drew whispered into my ear.

"Hm. What?" My mind wasn't really focused on anything other than what had just happened.

"What are we going to do? Go out? Stay in? Your choice."

I didn't really want to go anywhere. I just wanted to be alone with him. That would do me just fine.

"Can we just stay here?"

"Of course we can."

Yes, can we stay here so I can tell you you're a ghost?

I smiled at him.

"So, you fancy watching a film?" he asked.

"Sounds good."

"Come on then," he pulled at my hand and I got up off the bed.

I sat down on the sofa and made myself comfy.

"What do you want to drink?"

"Beer if you have any."

"Silly question."

He headed back off again and came back with two bottles of ice, cold beer.

"I think we should go for horror. Think you can handle it?" he asked, adding an 'ooh' for good measure.

"As long as you don't mind if I watch from behind a cushion and squashed up against you?"

"Doesn't sound too bad to me," he said, leaning in for a kiss.

If I never kiss anyone else in my whole, entire life, I'd be happy. Each kiss with Drew felt like the first. Exciting. Breathtaking.

He unfurled himself from the sofa and made his way over to the television and entertainment unit that took up most of the wall in front of us. I could feel myself tensing up already. I'm not brilliant with scary movies. He looked at me and smiled sexily.

"You're going to love this," he said.

"You realise I won't sleep a wink tonight now!"

"That's kind of the plan."

"Honestly, Drew, how do you watch that stuff on your own. I'd be a nervous wreck?"

"Don't know. Never seemed to bother me, I suppose."

"I wouldn't be able to look out my windows at night. It's actually freaking me out that you've not closed the curtains."

"What can I say? I'm a hard guy."

I blushed as I took his statement totally out of context.

"You have a dirty mind," he said.

I blushed again.

"You want to watch another?"

"Do we have to?"

"No. But it'll be fun."

I shrugged. I had a feeling he was going to put another scary movie on, regardless of what I wanted, and I suppose it was just another excuse to get up close and personal with him.

DAY 14

A dull but loud buzzing woke me with a start from a deep, dreamless sleep. I turned over as quickly and quietly as I could and picked up my phone from the bedside table.

I know it's early, I know it's the weekend and I know you said you'd let me know how you got on, but I've hardly slept a wink all night with worry and because I'm awake, you should be too. I'll just keep pestering you until you answer me. Nancy xxx

I shook my head. Yes, it was too early. Yes, it was the weekend and yes, I told her, promised her even, that I would let her know how things went but as much as her text irritated me, I couldn't be angry with her.

I swung my legs out of bed and slowly got up, being as careful as I could not to wake Drew. I pulled on the dressing gown that had been hanging from a hook on the door and, with phone in hand, headed downstairs.

I spooned eight level tablespoons of ground coffee into the filter of the coffee machine, filled up the water reservoir and shoved the carafe into place. There's nothing like the sound and smell of coffee brewing in the morning. Nothing in this world.

I filled a mug and dropped a teaspoon of brown sugar in. I stirred and became mesmerised by the little whirlpool I had created. All this procrastinating was pointless. If I didn't text Nancy back soon, she'd be messaging me left, right and centre. Just do it, I ordered myself.

Hey. Thanks for the wake-up-call. Much appreciated. Nothing to report, I'm afraid. I couldn't tell him. Like you said, I'll know when the time is right. Stop worrying. Henri xx

I hit send and turned my phone, face down, on the table. I took a gulp of coffee, savouring it's bitter warmth as it slid down my throat.

It buzzed again.

I picked it back up.

I am sorry, Henri. Honest. I'd bloody kill someone if they woke me up at this time on a Saturday. Yes, you'll know. Hope you're okay. Nancy xxx

It felt weird to have this, this relationship, with Nancy. I had never, ever had a friend like her. A best friend. I had to keep that in mind. The girl was just worried about me. I know I'd be the same if the roles were reversed.

I'm fine. I really am. We had a great night even though I was petrified for most of it.

Petrified? What of? I hope Mr. Ghostie hasn't done anything to scare you?

We just watched some pretty shocking horror films last night.

Aww, it's only so you'd snuggle up to him, I bet. That's exactly what it was.

Nancy text back with smiley-face emoticons. Two were laughing, tears coming out of their eyes. Two were blowing kisses. I responded with a *Mwah.*

So, what are you two love birds up to today?

Haven't got the foggiest.

Well, whatever you get up to, enjoy! Love ya oodles, ya nutter!

Love ya more!

I put my phone back on the table, secretly hoping that that would be the last of the texts.

I lifted my bag up from the floor, put my hand in blind. I pulled out my book, tipped my now tepid coffee down the sink and poured another. I retreated to the living room, curled up on the armchair and began to read.

"Hey," Drew said, kissed the top of my head.

"Morning. Sleep well?"

"Must have done. How long have you been up?"

"Half past eight, thanks to Nancy."

"What? Has she been here?"

"No. It would have been far easier though, the amount of texts she sent me."

"Everything okay?"

"Yeah. Just Nancy being Nancy."

"You really like her, don't you?"

I nodded enthusiastically.

"I do. She's brilliant."

"It's good, you know. Really good."

"I know."

"So, what are we doing today?" he yawned.

"Nothing if that reaction's anything to go by."

"Sorry," he yawned again.

I laughed.

"I'll check with my Mum first but how about we just do the same as last night? Stay in and watch films? Maybe even listen to some more of those records of yours?"

"Well, that sounds like bliss to me but are you sure you don't want to do something different?"

I didn't want to tell him that I was afraid people would catch me talking to thin air because, that's what he was. I didn't want to tell him that he really was invisible.

"I couldn't think of anything better."

"Are you sure you don't mind, Mum?"

"Not at all. I'm working tonight, anyway. Actually, John's meeting me at work and then he might stay over. Is that a problem?"

"You know it's not. I don't mind at all. Not that it should matter."

"I know, I know. I'd just hate for you to walk in on us. Oh hell, I don't mean it that way. I mean..."

"I know what you mean," I laughed, "So, I'll see you tomorrow then, okay?"

"See you tomorrow, sweetheart."

"Hi John," I called as I entered the shop, "how's things?"

"Good, Henri. Very good."

Hang on, was he blushing?

"Great."

I smiled knowingly at him.

"And you?" he asked.

"Good, John. Very good."

"That's good, Henri."

I smiled again and picked up a basket, ready to fill it up with movie-time snacks. This time, I hadn't got to use my own money. Not that that would have bothered me. Drew had given me his bank card and pin number. Told me to use whatever I needed. I took the heavily laden basket to the counter and heaved it up on to the surface.

"You at Drew's tonight, then?"

The question took me back a little. I wasn't angry, just surprised. Mum had only been with John for what felt like a few minutes and already, she'd told him about me and Drew. It's not like it was a secret, I hadn't specifically told her it was, but the timing could have been better. Then again, would there ever be a good time for her to realise, for me to tell her, that my boyfriend is a bit different?

"I am. I hear you're staying at ours too?"

If he was red before, he was crimson now.

"Erm. Yes. I am. I hope that's okay with you?"

"Of course it is, John. You're great for her. It's about time she felt good about herself again."

"Thanks, Henri. The feeling's mutual. She's good for me too."

John stopped, looking at anything but me.

"You really like her, don't you?"

"I do. Yes."

"Well, I'll let you in on a little secret. She really likes you too."

He smiled. A huge, wide smile.

"Anyway, let's get this totted up for you so you can go and enjoy your Saturday."

"Yup."

John took out each item in my basket, tapped in their prices and packed them neatly into a bag

"That'll be fifteen pounds, Henri."

"I'm paying by card, that okay?"

"Sure is," he nodded.

The price appeared on the card reader screen and I followed the instructions that appeared, punching Drew's pin number in from memory. I'm good like that. I'm terrible at remembering directions, names and stuff like that but numbers, they just get stuck in there, somehow.

The words, "card declined", popped up on screen. I must have put the number in wrong. Or maybe Drew had messed up. I tried again. And again.

"Everything okay, Henri?"

"Forgot the pin number. Sorry, John, I'll put it all back."

I held out my hand to take the bag from him.

"No, it's okay," he shook his head, "take it. Please."

"I can't, John, you're running a business, not a charity."

"You can, and you will. Don't worry, this is my treat."

He smiled widely.

"Thanks, John."

Drew rushed towards me, searching the bag I was carrying like a child rooting around for treats.

"Mm, yes," he said, pulling out a couple of bags of sour, chewy sweets, "how did you know I like these?"

"I didn't. I do now though. Who doesn't like them?"

He shrugged.

My shopping bag was full of junk food. Crisps, sweets, chocolate – that's all I wanted right now. That and Drew.

He took the bag from me and emptied it out onto the dining table.

"Is this a hint that we'll be watching some girly shit later?"

"Girly? Do I seem, in any way, girly?"

"Well, when you put it that way."

I slapped his arm playfully.

"Look, I don't mind what we watch but please, nothing as scary as last night's offerings?"

"Oh," he said, pulling an over the top, sad face, "but you're so cute when you're scared."

"Oh really?"

He nodded. I couldn't take my eyes off him.

"Really," he breathed into my ear.

I shuddered and felt goose bumps prick my skin.

He peppered kisses from my ear, down my jaw and then softly landed his lips on mine. He kissed me deeply and I followed suit.

He pulled away, leaving me pouting at nothing and started pouring crisps into a bowl. He broke up the block of chocolate and did the same with that. I hoped we'd start watching films sooner rather than later, so at least daylight was on my side. I could manage scary movies while it was still light outside because monsters only come to get you at night, don't they?

"Anyway, let's leave all this until later," he said, taking my hand and leading me up the stairs.

"No way," I said, looking at my watch, "I can't believe we've been up here so long."

"I know, time flies when you're having fun."

"You realise how cliché that sounds, right?"

"I do. Nothing wrong with a good cliché, Henri."

He grinned, a big, cheesy grin.

I laughed.

"Anyway, film time. Come on," he said, pulling me up off the sofa, out the room and down the stairs.

"I thought I'd mix it up a bit," he shouted as he headed down the basement stairs.

"What do you mean?" I shouted back.

He reappeared, a bottle of red wine in hand.

"We'll do one horror and then a young adult, rom-com thing. Does that suit you better?"

I nodded.

"It does."

I watched as he pulled a couple of wine glasses from a cupboard and poured wine into both.

"Here you go," he said, sitting down next to me.

I took the glass he offered me and sipped from it. It was delicious, rich and moreish.

"Amazing, isn't it?" Drew asked.

I nodded.

"This is one of my Mum's particular favourites. I'm sure it's the only reason she goes to Italy."

"Do you know where they are now? Do you have any idea at all?"

"Nope. Like I say, I haven't heard a single thing from them for a few weeks now. Oh well, out of sight, out of mind."

I rubbed his leg, hoping this small gesture would comfort him.

"Anyway, enough about parents. Let's get this show on the road."

He is sitting at the end of the sofa, smiling sweetly, staring.

I sit up and reach out to him.

"What's wrong with me, Henri?" he asks.

I ask him what he means but I know exactly what's wrong with him.

"Why aren't they coming back? They've never been away this long before."

"I don't know, Drew. I just don't know," I lie.

"Why does everyone ignore me?" he pleads.

"I don't ignore you," I say.

"I know, but it's weird, right? You've got to admit that."

I woke up, my head resting in Drew's lap. The television screen was totally black. It had entered standby due to its viewers doing the very same thing. I looked up to see he was fast asleep, his head hanging over the back of the sofa at an awkward angle. The dream was a surprise. I hadn't had a Drew dream in a while. I don't have them when I'm with him. I must admit, I missed them. Missed the secrecy and fantasy of having him in my head. Of course, I wouldn't want to be without him. Not now. Not ever. Why had I dreamt of him? Was it my head's way of telling me that I needed to tell him the truth? To tell him what he really is? Could I tell him? Could I shatter this bliss? Because if I told him, told him everything would we still be a we?

I wriggled from his leaden arms and picked my phone up off the table. It was eleven thirty-five. Not that late. Not for a weekend. And even though I'd slept for, well I don't know how long, I still felt exhausted. I nudged him gently in the ribs. He caught his breath, mumbled something completely incoherent but did not wake up.

I didn't want to leave him down here. Didn't want to leave him all alone. I began to tidy the things away, taking the empty bottle and wine glasses into the kitchen, along with the empty bowls. I closed curtains and checked that doors and windows were locked and then I checked them again. And then again.

Drew started to stir. He yawned, well more like roared, and stretched his body right out flat. His eyelids flickered open slowly and for a moment, it looked like he didn't know where he was. He turned his head towards me and he was most definitely back in the room.

"Hey," he yawned again, "what's up?"

"Nothing. Just clearing stuff away and then, I'm sorry, but I need to go to bed."

"What time is it?"

"Gone eleven thirty."

"What the hell?!"

"Yeah, I know."

"Did we even watch anything?"

"Possibly? Maybe. I don't remember to be honest. We must have started to watch something because the wine bottle was empty when I woke up and the television was in standby mode."

He shook his head and rubbed his hands over his face as if he was washing it with invisible water.

"I dreamt about you," he spat out, like the words had literally just come to him.

"You did?"

"Yeah. It was weird."

"Did we talk?" I remembered the conversation we had in my dream vividly. I wondered if he'd had the same dream. I wondered if he remembered too.

"Yeah. Well, I think so."

"Do you know what about?"

"It's really fuzzy, Henri."

"Look, no worries. Shall we just head up to bed?" Maybe a change in subject would take his mind off his dream.

"What's wrong with me, Henri?"

"Nothing. Nothing's wrong with you. What do you mean?"

"Why aren't they coming back? They've never been away this long before."

"Your parents? I don't know, Drew. I just don't know," I lied.

"Why does everyone ignore me? It's like I don't exist," he pleaded.

"I don't ignore you."

"I know, but it's weird, right? You've got to admit that."

"What is there to admit, Drew?"

"I don't know. I just feel like if I dropped off the face of the planet, no one would notice let alone give a shit."

"Don't you dare say that."

He looked down at his hands, his index fingers picking at the skin around his thumbs.

"I know I have you, Henri and you will never understand what that means to me. What you mean to me. I love you so, so much. But, be honest, I'm nothing. If I didn't have you, I'd have no one. I'd be nothing."

"We've had this conversation before, Drew."

"Yes, I'm aware of that, Henri," he said condescendingly, "but you have to admit I'm totally right."

I shook my head.

"Drew, you're just going through what lots of teenagers do," I lied, feeling absolutely awful for spinning him a yarn, "I went through exactly the same. Anyway, let's just forget about it now. Let's go to bed."

I took his hand and led him up the stairs.

DAY 15

Drew didn't take his eyes off me as I finished off my toast and orange juice. It was more than a little awkward, he was staring so intently. I was aware of how my mouth was moving, taking care not to show exactly how ravenous I was. I'm not a pig but when I'm hungry, manners and etiquette go out the window.

"So, I'm guessing you're going back home today?" he said glumly.

I nodded.

"I am. I'm sorry."

"Why are you apologising?"

"Well, we've had such a good weekend."

"We have, and you don't need to apologise. No doubt I'll see you tomorrow, anyway."

"What, in between your many classes?"

We both laughed.

"You got it."

"So, I'm going to finish up with this feast and then

get ready, okay?"

He nodded.

"You want me to walk you back home, Henri?"

"If you want to."

"I sure do."

"Come here," Drew said, pulling me behind the huge rhododendron bush at the end of our driveway.

He put his lips on mine and kissed me longingly. I sighed blissfully.

"What was that for?"

"Nothing. Just wanted to do it."

"You can do it again, if you want."

He kissed me a little harder and pulled away.

"I love you, Henri. I know I've told you already, probably too many times, but I mean it. I really, really do."

"I love you too."

A wide smile broke on his face. I could look at that face forever. I've never seen a smile quite like it.

"Anyway, you better go," he said, pushing me away from him.

"I'm sorry," I said.

He shook his head and smiled.

"Just go."

"And the wanderer returns," Mum called from the kitchen.

"Hi, Mum."

"Good night?" We both asked at the same time.

"You first," I said.

"Well, actually, it was. Perfect, in fact. I haven't

had so much fun in ages. John's an absolute gentleman. Your turn."

"Same. It was brilliant. The whole weekend was."

What I really wanted to say to her was, "Oh, Mum, Drew's perfect. He's amazing. He's gorgeous and I think I'm in love with him" but I knew not to give too much away. Yes, we're girlfriend and boyfriend and yes, we love each other but that's all she needed to know. For the time being. The real challenge would be how to break the news that my boyfriend is different. And by different, I mean dead. I don't think there would ever be a right time to broach the subject.

"Well, the weekend isn't over yet but, Henri, that's lovely," Mum interrupted my thoughts, "I'd love to meet him. Remember, he can come here any time."

I wasn't going to tell her that he's already been in my room. Overnight too, for that matter.

"I know, Mum," I smiled, "I think he just likes the company under his own roof. I think he enjoys playing house while his folks are away. He knows he can come here, but…"

"That's all you can do, Henri. Don't force the issue. He'll come if he wants to."

"I know. Do you mind if I just go up to my room and listen to my music for a bit?"

"Of course not, go for it."

I skipped up the stairs, into my room and threw my bag to the floor. Sitting on my bed, I played out all that had happened in such a short space of time. New house. New school. New boyfriend, however real or not he may be. A new friend. A new life.

I looked over at my diary on my study table. It called out to me, urging me to fill it with details of all these new experiences. I knew I had to comply. I needed to get all this down on paper, as if committing it to the pages would cement it in my history. It had to be real then, didn't it?

"Am I going to see you at any point today?" Mum shouted up the stairs.

"Sorry, Mum. Coming," I shouted back down.

I shut my diary and put it in my desk drawer. I couldn't believe how long I had been writing in it, lost in my own little paradise of words and music.

"About time," my Mum said, a playful tone to her voice, "come on, sit down and let's have dinner."

I sat across from her, taking in the plate of food in front of me. It looked delicious and I couldn't stop the rumbling noise my stomach made. Without hesitation, I picked up my cutlery and tucked in. "That was lovely, Mum," I said after I forced the last morsel into my mouth.

"Glad you've enjoyed it."

I nodded, feeling stuffed to the brim.

Silence settled between us but if my Mum thought she could get away without telling me all about her new romance, she could think again.

"So, you've got a lot to tell me."

"What about?"

"Um, John? Your date?"

"I've already told you, sweetheart. It was great. I had a lovely time. Nothing more to tell."

"Right, I see," I smiled knowingly at her.

"Don't look at me like that," she said, blushing red, "honestly, that's it."

"Come off it, Mum, he stayed over."

"Well, okay then…"

Mum polished off a whole bottle of wine as we chatted away. I can't remember the last time she had talked so candidly and happily. Of course, she omitted certain details, but it didn't take a genius to know that she had slept with John. Probably the reason why she drank all that she did; a little Dutch courage never hurt anyone. She seemed different, in a great way. She was glowing, radiating confidence. It was good to see her this way, like she used to be.

"Mum, I really need to go to bed now otherwise I'll be shuffling round like one of the walking dead at school tomorrow."

"Oh blimey," she said, snapping out of her happy daze, "yes, you carry on up, sweetheart."

I smiled sleepily.

"Come and give me a big hug," she continued.

I leaned in to her and she wrapped her arms around me. There really is nothing better than a Mum hug. It doesn't matter how old you are because in one, simple, loving gesture, you are a child again.

"Night, Mum."

"Goodnight, darling."

DAY 16

"Oh, thank you so much for joining us finally," the supply teacher huffed.

"I'm sorry," I said, scurrying quickly to my desk, head down, eyes to the ground, "I slept past my alarm."

It was true. Well, kind of. I never set my alarm. And this morning, well, let's just say my Mum had decided she was having a lie in too.

"Well, at least you didn't come up with some laughable excuse," she sighed, "I won't recap so you'll just have to find someone who will."

Seriously? I shrugged my shoulders and my gaze fell on Stacey sitting on the table to my left. She looked like a shadow of her former self. She glanced at me and I quickly looked away and to the front of the class.

After an hour of discussing the metaphorical themes in Orwell's 'Animal Farm', the bell rang. Now, that usually meant me shooting up from my seat and getting the hell out of class as quick as my legs would take me. Not today though.

Stacey hadn't moved an inch from her table. It was like looking at a statue. She was frozen to the spot. I walked up to her and pulled up a chair. Sat down across from her.

"Stacey. You okay?"

Silence.

I kicked my chair back and got up. If you're going to be like that, forget it, I thought. I turned around and headed for the door.

"Wait. Henri."

I spun back around. Sat opposite her again.

"You okay?" I asked her a second time.

"I don't think I am. I don't think I ever will be."

"It's understandable."

She nodded.

"I can't do this, Henri."

"You can. You will."

"I've hardly slept since it happened. I'm going mad, Henri. Seriously."

What could I say? Nothing that would help anyway.

"I really appreciate this," she went on, "I don't deserve your sympathy. I'm a horrible person, Henri. Maybe what happened to me was karma. Maybe I deserved it."

Well, yes, you did.

"Stacey, I wouldn't wish that on anyone, not even you."

"I've been having bad thoughts. Bad, bad thoughts."

"What kind of bad thoughts?"

"I don't want to be here. I can't."

"You're just exhausted. That's what it is. You just said you've hardly slept."

"It's not that."

"Oh, I think it is."

"It's not!" she spat the words at me, "That thing, that whatever-it-was that attacked me? He's speaking to me."

"He?"

"Yes, he."

"Well, that's good."

"Excuse me?"

"Sorry Stacey, that came out completely wrong. What I meant is it's good that you're remembering."

"Right. Okay. I guess. This is why I'm not coping, Henri. I don't want to remember. I want to forget. Everything. He speaks to me. Keeps getting in my head. He says I should do it. He's even given me some tips," she laughed sadly.

"I just want you to know that I am truly sorry. For everything. I hope you can forgive me," she said as she got up and walked out of class.

Art was next on the timetable. Along with English, it was the only lesson that could ever bring a smile to my face, but I doubt that would happen today. Not after what Stacey had told me. I couldn't stop thinking about it and I had the strongest feeling that nobody would be seeing her at school again. I just hoped our conversation might have changed her feelings. I don't think I could deal with knowing that I was the last person she spoke to.

Today's task was to draw a portrait from memory using only pencil and charcoal. I sat at my easel in the corner, the spot I had assigned myself last week. I decided on my Mum as the subject and began to work.

"Oh Henri, this is just wonderful," the teacher said, drawing my attention to my work. I wonder if anyone else noticed my mouth drop open in shock? I wasn't looking at a drawing of my Mum, not at all. Drew stared right back at me from the page. Without sounding too egotistical, I could see why the teacher thought it was so good. It was so real. It was too real. It looked more like a photo than a drawing.

"Thank you," I said sheepishly, quickly gathering up my drawing equipment.

"It's so realistic," she mirrored my thoughts, "he reminds me of someone. I'm assuming he's a he?"

"He is, yes."

She nodded slowly, thoughtfully.

"It's Drew, isn't it? Drew Hardy?" she asked.

"It is."

"Well, it's beautiful, Henri. It really is."

"Thank you," I said, smiling awkwardly.

The bell sounded, and I headed off to put all my things away. I didn't put my picture away though. I folded it up and slipped it in my trouser pocket.

The fresh, cool air took my breath away as I ploughed through the doors and out onto the playing field. I looked instinctively to our remote, out of the way tree and saw Drew. I couldn't stop myself from breaking into a sprint. Thankfully, there was only a handful of students milling around and thankfully, they didn't even notice me. I threw myself at Drew and he caught me with ease.

"You will not believe how happy I am to see you!" I said, into his scruffy, green jumper.

He lifted my chin up to his face and kissed me deeply.

"Likewise," he said, pulling away, leaving me

standing there with my eyes closed.

"What's the matter?"

"Oh nothing," I lied.

"Nothing? Oh really?" he said, leaning his forehead to mine, "come on, Henri. I know when something's not right with you. What's up?"

I let his question sound out in my head. Yes, of course I was preoccupied. It was bad enough knowing that, at some point, I'd have to tell him exactly what he was. Now, I'd got the added pressure of wondering whether Stacey would go through with ending her own life.

"Now's not the time. Just leave it, huh?"

"I knew it. It's me, isn't it? What have I done?"

I cupped Drew's face in my hands and kissed him gently.

"You haven't done anything."

He had though, hadn't he? Okay, he'd done nothing to hurt me, but it must have been him that assaulted Stacey. Maybe he was still getting to her. I really, truly hoped he wasn't but at the same time, a tiny little part of me was glad that Stacey had been warned off me.

"Hey, can I stay over on Friday?"

"Course you can. It's not like I have to clear it with anyone, is it? I could have a hundred-strong orgy in that house and my folks wouldn't give a shit!"

"I'll check with my Mum first though. Sorry. I wish I didn't have to."

"No, you don't, believe me."

"I know. You're right. I'm sorry. Anyway, I'll check and let you know as soon as, okay?"

"Cool. And will you be burdening me with your problems?"

"Oh, a burden now, am I?" I smiled.

"Did I say that?"

We both laughed.

"Come here, you," he said, pulling me into him. I put up no resistance. If only we could stay like this forever.

I slung my bag, and then my coat, over the hooks at the bottom of the stairs.

"Hi Mum."

No answer. Weird. I walked through to the kitchen, drawn by the smell of something wonderful. The slow-cooker was on the worktop, its contents bubbling away on low. I opened the lid and breathed in the aroma of another family favourite – lamb stew.

I opened the fridge, pulled out the water-filter jug and poured myself a tall glass. Taking a large gulp, I felt the ice-cold water refresh me. I turned around and saw a folded piece of paper, my name on the front, propped up between the salt and pepper pots. I opened it and started to read.

Hi sweetheart

Hope you've had a good day. I'm so sorry but I've been called into work. One of the girls phoned in sick for her shift and apparently, I'm the only one who can cover. I'm not too happy about it but we could use the money.

Anyway, like I say, I hope you don't mind. There's stew in the slow-cooker and there's also a bottle of wine in the rack too. If you do have some, make sure you leave a glass for me!

Love you,

xx Mom xx

I smiled, and I took the lid off the slow cooker and using the ladle she had left next to it, I spooned more than I could probably stomach into a bowl. I took a spoon from the cutlery drawer and a wine glass from the cupboard, spotted the bottle of wine in the rack. I poured a healthy amount of the rich, claret into my glass.

Once I'd put my food and drink on the dining table, I headed over to the record player, selected Pet Sounds and put it on to play.

The stew was delicious, it really hit the spot. I went through to the living room, put my wine on the coffee table and turned the record over. I settled down onto the settee, sipped at my wine and let the music envelope me.

"I think we need to talk," he says, sitting down, facing me.

"About?"

"You know what."

"Enlighten me," I say, knowing full well what he's getting at.

"There's something going on with me, isn't there? You know something, don't you?"

I gulp and accept that this is it. I have to tell him.

"Please, Henri?"

"Henri, it's me."

I blinked open my eyes and for a second, felt completely disorientated.

"What? Oh hi, Drew."

"Hey."

"How did you get in?" I slurred, my head still

spinning from sleep.

"Front door. You really need to make sure you lock it when you're on your own."

"Oh right. Of course," I smiled awkwardly. Now that he mentioned it, I didn't remember turning the key.

"Is it just me," he said, "but do I detect a note of disappointment in your voice?"

"What would I be disappointed about?"

"About me being here."

"No. No, not at all. I just wasn't expecting to see you until school tomorrow."

"Oh, okay," he said, disappointment still evident on his face.

"Sorry, Drew. It's just because I've woke up suddenly and I don't think I'm fully awake yet."

He nodded.

"Henri, I know we agreed we'd see each other on Friday but I really needed to see you tonight."

"Well, I'm not complaining," I said as I sat up and kissed him on his gorgeous mouth. He kissed back deeply and then I felt wetness on my face, but it wasn't from me. He was crying. I could feel him trembling.

"Hey, what's the matter?" I asked.

"I need to talk to you," he said, pulling away slowly and shaking his head.

"Go ahead, I'm all ears."

"I went for a walk today," he sniffed, barely holding back sobs, "A really long walk. I needed to think," he paused, eyes avoiding mine.

"Okay?"

"And my walk took me to the church and through the cemetery."

Shit, he knows!

194

"And I don't know how to say this, Henri. I don't know how to explain…"

"What?" I asked, feigning innocence.

"I saw a headstone, Henri. I saw our grave. All our names were on it, mine and my folks. Oh man, I just… I'm going crazy, aren't I? I'm hallucinating. I mean, that's the only explanation for it, right?"

I couldn't answer him. Couldn't utter a single word. Couldn't bring myself to look at him.

"What? What is it, Henri? You're saying I'm dead? Is that what this is?" he laughed, nervously.

"Just let me explain, Drew. It's not as simple as you think!"

"Oh really?" he laughed again but it really wasn't funny. In fact, it scared me, "so are you telling me you're dating a ghost?"

I nodded. How could I explain any of this to him without it sounding like the worst nightmare or the biggest joke ever told. He got up and started pulling at his beautiful, dirty-blonde mess of hair. If there was anything to physically depict what crazy was, it was Drew, right now.

"This is just one huge fucking joke, right?"

I didn't want to shake my head. I really didn't.

"So, if I'm a ghost, how come I can do this?" he asked as he pulled me sharply to him, "and this?" he said, smothering my mouth with his.

"I know," I said breathlessly as I broke the kiss short, "I thought exactly the same, but it does make some kind of crazy sense. It explains your invisibility."

"Oh, for Christ's sake, Henri, I was just kidding about that. It was just a figure of speech."

"I know that but it's truer than you realise. It's why Stacey and her pals think I'm crazy. When they came after me on the field and stood right in front of us? They couldn't see you. And then the other night in the club? Nancy said I was having a conversation with nothing."

"I just can't get my head round all this, Henri."

"I wouldn't expect you too. I'm still struggling so God knows how you must be feeling."

"So, what the hell are you still doing with me?" he asked, voice cracking, "Why haven't you run a mile?"

"Because I can't, Drew. Because I won't. Because I don't want to. That and the fact I just can't shake you off," I laughed, hoping to inject a little, light hearted humour into a situation that was far from funny.

I wasn't expecting the small smile that broke on to his face even though his eyes brimmed with tears.

"So, how did I... What happened?"

"Are you sure about this?" I asked, caution flooding my tone.

"With all due respect, Henri, I've just found out I'm a fucking spirit so why not go the whole hog and tell me how I came to be... this."

Was Drew still here, stuck, because he didn't know how he'd died? Was that what was stopping him from moving on? I hoped it was, and wasn't, all at the same time. Would he vanish in a puff of smoke and leave me forever if I told him? No. That couldn't happen. I didn't want it to, but it was selfish of me to even think about lying to him, especially if that lie would keep him from finally being at peace. I breathed deeply and mentally crossed my fingers.

"Come with me," I said, taking his very real feeling hand, leading him to the stairs, "I need to show you something."

Drew stared blankly at the laptop screen. Once again, tears began to fill his eyes.

"So, it's real then? It's really real?"

"I wish I could tell you differently, but it would be one, big, fat lie and that's the last thing you need from me right now."

"What the fuck?!" Drew shouted, "No. No way. My Dad? He killed us?"

He was still right in front of me. He hadn't vanished in a puff of smoke. Maybe it was too early for that. Maybe that would come later.

"I'm so, so sorry."

"Shit. I knew I wasn't his biggest fan or anything but Jesus Christ, that's just…"

He stumbled over to my bed like he was drunk and sat down on it. He held his head in his hands.

"I know nothing I say could ever make this better," I said as I sat next to him and put my arm around his shoulders, "I have no idea what you're going through, and I don't want to say I understand because I don't. I just want you to know that it doesn't change how I feel about you."

His eyes bored into mine, still wet with tears.

"How can this not change how you feel about me?" he asked, prodding a finger at his chest, "how can you be with someone who isn't actually here, who isn't real?"

"I don't know," I replied, shaking my head, "I can't explain it, but I don't want to be with anyone else. I only want to be with you. You are real to me. I don't know why you are and to be honest, I really don't care."

"It's sick is what it is!"

"We're not hurting anyone by being together, so

why?"

"I know that, Henri but come on, this is all so messed up."

"But it's a mess I want to be part of, Drew. Believe me, I had all the same thoughts that you're having now. If anything, it's made me more determined to stick this out with you. I'm right here with you. I'm not going anywhere. I love you, Drew. I've never felt like this before."

"What did you say?"

"I love you."

"Say it again."

"I. Love. You."

He pulled my face to his and kissed me deeply. It was electric, explosive. It felt like it meant everything to him. There was so much need in him. He broke away breathlessly.

"You mean that?"

"With all I am," I answered sincerely.

"I love you too, Henri. So much."

All the excitement, if that's what you could call it, took it out on both of us. For a while, we just sat on my bed, glazed expressions fixed on our faces.

"So, it's definitely only you that can see me?" Drew asked.

"As far as I can tell."

"That ain't a bad thing, I suppose."

"How do you mean?"

"It means I can stay here with you any time. If your Mum can't see me, she'll never know. Think of the fun we can have!"

Yeah, loads of fun until she catches me talking to thin air.

DAY 17

"Henri," I heard right outside my door, "you up?"

I grunted. Of course I was up. If I wasn't before, I certainly was now. I mean, how many hours sleep can a person get by on, seriously? If the answer was two, then you'd be correct.

"Yes," I called out to my Mum and rolled over to find Drew lying next to me, half naked and staring into my eyes.

"Don't go," he said, "stay here with me. Just tell your Mum you're ill."

Now that sounded like heaven and, it could be argued that I was ill. Two hours of fitful sleep is enough to make anyone feel poorly. Drew's words filled my head and temptation was beginning to get the better of me.

"She'll know though," I whispered, "she knows me well enough to know when I'm lying."

"Well, mean it. You've got to totally mean what

you're saying," he smiled.

I know, I know.

"Okay, Mum," I moaned, hoping she'd hear my attempt at feeling sorry for myself. There was a knock on the door.

"You okay, sweetheart?" she asked, "Can I come in?"

BINGO!

"Yeah," I coughed and spluttered. The door opened, and she came straight at me, hand held aloft, ready to check my temperature.

"Aren't you feeling well?" she asked, placing the palm of her hand on my forehead, looking up to the ceiling as if it would miraculously give her a diagnosis.

"I don't think so," I moaned again, really laying it on thick, "I think it's just because I haven't slept well, and it's made my head hurt."

"Open your mouth. Let's have a little look."

I opened wide. Why she wanted to look down my throat was beyond me. I hadn't said my throat was sore. I suppose it's just a Mum thing. Even though there was absolutely nothing wrong with me, I still said "ah" with more feeling than was necessary.

"It doesn't look swollen," she said, her head practically wedged in my mouth, "but you do feel hot and you definitely don't sound right. Why don't you take the day off school?"

"Oh, I don't know," I replied melodramatically, "I think it's too early to start having time off school. What kind of impression will that set?"

"Don't be ridiculous, Henri! You're clearly not very well. What good would you be if you were there?"

I shrugged.

"Nothing, that's what," she continued, "now, I'll phone the school to explain and if they want to get funny about it, they can get funny with me."

I smiled at her and she tucked me up under my duvet.

"Now just try to get some rest okay, sweetheart?"

I nodded. She kissed my forehead and left the room. I felt Drew's hands slip around my waist from behind and felt more than glad that I had pulled this particular sickie.

"Hey, what are you doing?" Drew mumbled.

"Getting up. I've had my sleep out."

"And?"

"Well, I want to get washed and changed. I hate lazing about."

"But you're not lazing about," he smirked, "you're ill, remember?"

"Duh, I know," I smiled at him. I've never been able to stay in bed when I'm not tired enough to. Can't see the point in it.

"It's not like you can go anywhere is it?" he continued, "I mean, if you're well enough to go out, you're well enough to go to school. That's what my Mum used to tell me when she actually gave a shit."

"I know that, Drew," I said, employing my best, resting bitch face.

"Sorry," he said, meekly.

"It's okay," I sighed, "Can I just get ready now, though?" I turned my back to him and pulled my Nirvana t-shirt over my head, "Here's what I'm definitely doing this morning; going down to get some breakfast."

"Should I just wait here then?"

"I think that's for the best."

Drew smiled awkwardly, obviously sensing he was annoying me.

"I won't be long," I assured him as you would do a small child.

Whether it was psychological, I don't know, but as I began to walk down the stairs, I started to feel ill, as if I could pass out at any minute.

Mum was standing at the kitchen counter, magazine open in front of her and a piece of toast in hand. Whatever she was reading, she was engrossed and when I let out a feeble, little cough, she very nearly choked on her food.

"Oh hi," she said, finally catching her breath, "I never heard you come down."

"Sorry, Mum. I didn't mean to startle you."

"Don't be silly. I was just reading this article and…," she trailed off, "are you hungry? Do you think you could manage a bit of breakfast?"

"I think so," I coughed for effect.

"Good girl," she said, rushing around the kitchen, "what do you fancy?"

"Whatever's the least trouble," I said but really, all that was going around in my head was an image of a huge plate, laden with eggs, bacon, grilled tomato, sausage, baked beans and a hash brown.

"How about a full English?"

She's a mind reader, I thought. I hoped she couldn't read too deep. She really didn't want to know what was going on in my head right now. I nodded anyway and grinned widely.

"That's settled then," she went on, "sit down and I'll get you a nice glass of orange juice. What you need is a good dose of vitamin c." She squeezed my shoulders affectionately.

I sat, watching her potter around, humming along happily to a tune I had never heard. I don't think I'm alone in taking the life I have for granted. It suddenly dawned on me that I did, even though I didn't mean to. It got me thinking about Drew and I wondered if he had ever woken to the sound of his Mum busying herself in the heart of the home. It's a comfort to me. Has he ever known that comfort?

"Here you go," Mum said, placing a steaming plate of food in front of me. I put my face right over it and inhaled deeply. It's not often that I fancy a big breakfast. I usually go for toast or cereal, maybe even fruit, but my mouth watered at the feast laid out before me.

"Thanks, Mum. I love you."

"Love you, too," she replied, ruffling my hair.

She skipped off merrily, and started cleaning the pots and pans and utensils, washing and stacking them in the drainer to dry.

I don't think I've ever seen my Mum truly stop and relax. Yes, a cup of coffee first thing in the morning but she usually stands up for that, and of course, dinner is always at the table, with a glass of wine, but as soon as she's settled, she's up and at it again. I guess I can see where I get it from, my constant desire to be doing something. Filling my time rather than letting it go to waste.

She plonked herself back down, sitting opposite me with a fresh cup of coffee in hand.

"How are you feeling now?"

"Better," I replied, immediately feeling guilty.

"Good, good. I suppose I shouldn't say this but

I'm glad you're at home. Oh, listen to me getting all sentimental."

Sentimental?

"Everything okay, Mum?"

"Yes, everything's fine. I'm just being silly."

"Come off it, Mum," I said, knowing full well that something was bothering her, "there's something the matter. You can't hide it from me."

"Just something I was reading earlier."

"When I came down?"

"Yes, sweetheart."

"What was it about?"

"Kids without parents. Kids just being left to their own devices; being left home alone," she said, shaking her head, "It makes me feel guilty when I think about you here, all alone, at night, whilst I'm at work."

"Well, you don't need to feel that way. I'm old enough to look after myself."

"I know. I know that. And I would never, ever have taken a bar job if I thought you couldn't. At least I can be here when you get home from school. I know it's only for a few hours, but…"

"Look, Mum," I said, pushing my plate to one side and taking a gulp of orange juice to wash down the remnants of breakfast left in my mouth, "I'm a big girl now. You really haven't got to worry about a thing."

"I don't doubt that for a second, sweetheart but until you've had a child of your own, you'll never understand. Once you become a Mum, you will always be a Mum. You don't retire from it."

"I know, Mum. I know."

I had heard the Mum speech more than a few times over the last couple of years. It was just her way of saying that no matter how old I am, I will always be her little girl. I am proud to be her little girl. I couldn't be any prouder of her, not just for being my Mum but also for who she is.

"Do you enjoy your job?" I went on.

"Well, it's not been long but yes, I think I do. I'm not a stranger to bar work and I know what I'm doing. It feels good."

"Well then, there you go. You're not hurting either of us by working nights at the bar. Do what makes you happy, Mum. I mean that."

She smiled wide, brightly.

"We're doing okay, aren't we?"

"More than okay, Mum."

"Hey, you," I whispered to Drew as I walked into my room. He was sat on the edge of the bed, head hanging down, "What's up?"

He looked up at me and it wasn't hard to notice that he'd been crying.

"Ah, nothing," he answered solemnly, "just having one of my emo moments."

I sank down next to him and put my arm round his shoulders and he quickly rested his head against my cheek.

"I'm sorry I was a bit sharp with you earlier. I didn't mean to upset you."

"You didn't upset me," he mumbled, "really, you didn't."

"What is it then? Talk to me."

"Henri," he sighed, "I'm so happy."

"Doesn't sound like it!"

"I am. I really am. I mean, you're the girl of my dreams. I know it's corny, but you are. You blow me away. Finally, things seem to be clicking into place. But," he took a deep breath, "I'm dead! I've had to wait until I'm dead just to get everything I've ever dreamed of and that kind of bothers me, you know? It just isn't fair!"

"I don't know what to say," I said, squeezing him just that little bit harder, "All I know is that I'm so happy you're my boyfriend, ghost or not."

He lifted his head from my shoulder, turned my face to his and kissed me.

Silence filled my room. It was so loud it hurt.

"Henri?" I heard my Mum shout as she ascended the stairs. I gestured for Drew to keep quiet and make himself scarce, and then promptly reminded myself that he wouldn't be seen or heard.

"Yes, Mum?"

"Can I come in?"

"Course you can."

My door opened slowly, and she poked her head round it.

"How you are doing?"

"I feel much better actually, Mum."

"Look, I've had a text from work," she said looking guilty and hopeful at the same time, "and I've been asked if I can go in earlier. Again. I've said you're sick and that I'd have to see how you feel."

"When do they need you?" I asked, hoping she would be out the door within the hour.

"Well, as soon as possible, really."

Fine by me.

"Just go, Mum. Honestly, I feel much better than I did earlier. If I need you, I'll phone. Okay?"

"Promise?"

"Promise."

She gave me a big hug and kissed me gently on the cheek.

"Okay then," she said, "well I'll just go and get ready then I'll be off."

I nodded my approval. She smiled at me and shut the door.

I waited until I heard the front door open, shut and then lock.

"Woohoo!" Drew shouted, "When's she due back?"

"I imagine it'll be the usual – about midnight. She might finish early if she's gone in early."

"Cool. So, what do you fancy doing, skipper?"

"Cinema?"

"Excellent idea. What do you want to watch?"

"Don't know. Shall we just turn up and see what's on?" I asked.

"Hell yeah! That's exactly what I used to do," he beamed, "Don't get me wrong, I watched some absolute shit but mostly I would hit on a gem or two."

It felt weird getting off the bus with someone that no one else could see. I had already warned Drew not to talk to me, speak, or do anything that might make me laugh. Imagine the daggers I would have got if I hadn't? Thankfully it was only one bus into town.

We got off the bus at the main depot in town and made the short walk to the cinema. Popcorn was purchased, along with along with a large drink and then I, we, looked at screening times. The next film due to start was a horror.

Brilliant. Just brilliant.

We sat down. It was just us, and two men, sitting

right at the very back of the theatre. Of course, to them, there was just the three of us, a fact that did not make me feel any happier about the situation.

"You okay?" Drew asked, putting his hand on my trembling knee.

"Yeah. Fine," I lied.

"Cool."

The room dropped darker and the trailers began. I'm not a particularly religious person but I prayed to God that I could get through the film without looking like a total idiot.

The end credits rolled up the screen and they could not have come quick enough. If the lights would have been on, Drew and the two men at the back, would probably have noticed my pale, pallid face in all its glory. I stood up swiftly and quickly made my way towards the exit. I didn't even check to see if Drew was behind me. I just wanted out.

One of the men shot up in front of me, preventing me from opening the door.

"Hi there," he said, "did you enjoy the film?"

As a child, my Mum had drummed the you-must-never-talk-to-stranger's speech into me but of course, as you get older, you have to talk to strangers. How else would you make new friends? How the hell would you ever get on in life. But there are strangers and then there are strangers. These men were the latter. Suddenly, Mums words came back to me fast, loud and clear. I ignored the man and attempted to move past. My attempt was quickly thwarted.

"Hey, I'm talking to you," he said, this time nowhere near as friendly.

"Excuse me," I replied, hoping he couldn't sense that I was royally shitting myself, "I'd like to get past please."

He shook his head and stayed stock still.

I looked around for the other man but saw no one. I could sense Drew behind me.

"I'm here," he said, "I'm right here."

Great, I thought, I appreciate it and all that, it's just a shame you're not actually real enough to knock this dickhead out!

I tried to get past the man again, this time not even asking. He put his arm out, across the door.

"I'll ask again. What did you think of the film?"

"Don't say anything," Drew said beside me, "don't let him get to you. We've got this. I promise."

"Look, I just want to be friends, that's all," the man went on.

"I bet you do, you fucking pervert!" Drew bellowed a shout the man would never hear.

"Please, I just want to leave," I said, my voice trembling.

"Nope."

"Look, my boyfriend's in the Men's. He'll be wondering where I am."

"So," he smirked, "Let him wonder."

"Let me out now or I'll phone the police."

"What for?" his smirk turned to a full-on grin, "I'm not doing anything wrong."

Drew, do something, please!

The guy took his arm down from across the doorway.

"Go on then. Off you go," he said.

I ran, leaving Drew standing.

The hustle and bustle in the foyer made me feel more at ease.

"Hey," Drew said, approaching me. I would have done anything to just throw my arms around him but again, I'd get some pretty weird looks from members of the public. I looked into his eyes and hoped he would pick up on my silent plea to get out of there. He got it straight away and we headed to the doors.

We didn't get too far before I did exactly what I had wanted to do in the cinema. There was no need to worry this time. There wasn't a single other soul in sight. I kissed Drew deeply.

"It's okay. You're okay," he sighed.

I didn't answer him as I nuzzled my face into the crook of his neck. He rubbed my back, comforting me with every stroke of his hand.

"What did you do to him?"

"What makes you think I did anything, Henri?"

"Right. Yeah. Come on, spit it out."

"Oh okay, if you insist," he smiled, "Let's just say I gave him a little scare. That's all you need to know."

It's all I wanted to know.

"Hey, maybe that's why I'm here," he went on, "I'm obviously your guardian angel."

Maybe he was. It was a comforting thought.

"What do you want to do now?" he went on.

"Can we just go home?"

"Which one?"

"Mine, please."

He nodded, and we walked in silence but for the first time since we'd been together, it was a silence we both wanted.

We had barely been in the house for half an hour when there was a knock at the door. Drew froze, a far-away look on his face.

"What's the matter?"

"Nothing. It's nothing," he said, looking totally unconvincing.

"No, I don't buy that."

"It's just weird. I don't know what I'm feeling. I just know that something doesn't seem right."

I looked at him, completely baffled and walked towards it.

"Don't!" he said, taking my hand.

"What the hell, Drew?"

"Don't answer it."

"What do you mean, don't answer it?"

"Your Mum would want you to stay safe."

"I know. Christ though, Drew. What do you think I do if the postman comes and I'm the only one here?"

"Look, Henri, I've got a bad feeling about this. Please don't answer the door. Come on, we'll go and hide."

I yanked my arm from his grasp and tutted at him. I pulled the door open and, standing in front of me, were two police officers.

"Henrietta Turner?" the female officer asked.

"Yes?" I nodded.

"Could we come in for a moment?"

I opened the door wide and silently gestured for them to come in. Drew was right. I never should have opened the door because, for some reason, I knew what they were going to tell me.

"Henri, please take a seat. We need to talk about your Mum."

"How bad is she?" I sobbed. Did I want to know the

answer?

"She's in Intensive Care," the female officer said.

"So, that's bad then, right?"

"Well, she's in a critical condition but she's stable at the moment," she answered, an audible wobble to her voice.

"Can I see her?"

"That's why we're here. We'll escort you to the hospital."

I shook my head, tears tumbling down my face. I grabbed my coat and bag from their hook and followed the police officers out of the house.

I didn't want to set foot in the ICU, but I had no choice. The female officer held my arm, guiding me inside as gently as she could.

"Are you okay, Henrietta?" she asked quietly. I nodded and took a deep, quivering breath.

"Now, we have to warn you," the male officer said firmly, "she's hooked up to machines and without meaning to upset you any further, she's been beaten very badly. I'm afraid it's not pleasant."

Yes. Beaten. Badly beaten. That's what the police had told me in the car. Why didn't whoever did this just take the money and run? It's not as if my Mum had been closing up and some drunken idiot had kicked up a stink at throwing out time. This had happened in broad daylight.

Some sorry excuse for a human being beat her to a pulp for the pittance that was in the till. They had beat her and left her for dead for seventy pounds worth of float. I would never wish death on anyone but whoever did this to her deserved a long, slow, painful one.

"Mom," I cried as I took in the extent of her injuries. The policeman wasn't wrong, "Oh Mom. I'm here now. Right here."

No answer came from her bloodied, swollen mouth but then I didn't expect one to.

"We'll leave you to it, sweetheart," the police woman whispered before tapping her partner on the arm. He nodded, eyes struggling to find mine.

"Thank you."

I wanted to stroke my Mum's face. I wanted to gather her up in my arms and hold her there forever, but I couldn't. I couldn't because there was no way round all the tubes trailing out of her. There was only an IV drip in her right hand though, so I picked it up and kissed it, letting my tears fall onto her bruised skin.

I totally forgot about Drew. I looked around and as if on cue, he appeared at the end of my Mum's bed.

"Oh, Henri. I am so sorry," he said, opening his arms out wide, ready for me to dive headfirst into them. I shuffled round the bed and did exactly that.

"I'm so glad you're here," I whispered, "I couldn't see you. I thought you'd left me."

"Been here all along, honey. You probably couldn't see me because of all the madness and worry."

"I know. I'm sorry I doubted you."

"Don't apologise, for anything. You have absolutely nothing to be sorry for."

His arms squeezed a little tighter around me and I felt safe. It would have been the easiest thing to stay wrapped up in him but the machines around my Mum started going crazy. I couldn't tell which bleep was coming from where. The curtain flew open and half a dozen, scrubbed up men and women rushed through Drew and surrounded her, totally blocking my view.

"What's happening?" I shouted.

"Can we please get Miss. Turner out of here," one of the men said, "someone take her away."

"No! Don't touch me. I'm not leaving her."

I felt a hand gently caress my shoulder.

"Henri, come on. Just let them do what they need to do. You can come back in as soon as they're done," Drew whispered.

A female nurse took me gently by the arm and said, pretty much word for word, exactly what Drew had. I let her lead me away from my Mum and out of the ward. She found a chair and gently pushed me down onto the seat.

"We'll let you back in soon, I promise," she said, "the doctor just needs to try and stabilise your Mum, okay?"

I nodded to show my understanding, but it was also a nod to myself. Both of us knew she was lying. I allowed my head to drop into my open palms and even though I knew it would draw attention, I broke down in floods of tears. I needed Drew by my side. I needed to feel him. Needed to know he was there.

I felt a hand on my shoulder and through my tears, I realised it was the female police officer. I thought she left with her colleague, so it was both a comfort and a surprise to find she was still there.

"Why don't you come for a walk with me? Get out of here for a little while. You'll be the first to know when you're able to go back in and see your Mum."

"Thanks, but no thanks," I said as politely as possible, "I'm not setting foot from here."

"What about a hot drink then? Coffee? Tea?"

"I'm fine, thank you."

"Okay, well just let me know if you need anything at all."

I nodded.

I liked her.

"Henri," I heard. Felt a hand shaking me gently, "Henri, wake up, sweetheart."

I opened my eyes, felt a smile forming on my lips. The smile disappeared when I saw that the face in front of mine was not my Mum's but the female officer.

The doctor who had ordered me to leave stood to the side of her. His body language told me all I needed to know. I gulped and felt my eyes brim with more tears.

"Is she?"

"We did everything we could, Miss Turner. I'm very sorry."

I jumped up and ran around the corner, into her room. The doctor, nurse and police officer quickly followed. They stood back quietly, respectfully, allowing me this moment with my Mum.

"Can you leave us alone, please?" I asked as calmly as I could.

"Of course," the doctor answered. The three of them left just as quietly as they came in.

Drew rose from the hospital chair, next to the bed which held her still, lifeless body. He looked drained, exhausted.

"Henri, I am so, so sorry," he said, his eyes almost

as full of tears as mine.

I picked up her hand. It felt like it had always felt. Was she supposed to feel dead? I wasn't expecting the scream that erupted from my mouth.

I felt Drew behind me. Felt his hand on my shoulder.

"Henri. Henri, look," he said.

I slowly raised my head from the tear-soaked bed sheet.

"Look," he said again, this time pointing towards the very end of the bed.

My Mum stood there, looking at her body on the bed and then looking at her fingers, her arms, everything she could see. She ran her hands up and down her body. Not upset but shocked. My eyes flitted between the two versions of my Mum and although I knew exactly what this meant and even though I could barely see for tears, a sense of calm and relief flooded through me.

"Hi, sweetheart," she said.

"Hi, Mum," I cried.

"You're here!"

"Of course I am. Where else would I be?"

"I'm sorry, sweetie," she said, taking my hands in hers, "I didn't mean for this to happen. I don't want to leave you, but I have to. Please forgive me?"

She started to cry, and it was the saddest sound I've ever heard.

"Oh, Mum. Don't. Don't say that," I said, just about stifling my sobs.

"I didn't mean to give up, Henri. I fought as hard as I could."

"I know. You always have."

"I tried, sweetheart."

I walked up to her, put my arms round her. I could feel her, just like I feel Drew. I hoped she could feel me too.

"I love you, Henri," she sighed, "more than anything in this whole world. Please know that I will always be with you. You must trust me on that, okay?"

I nodded, just about holding back yet more heaving sobs.

She turned to Drew. Looked him up and down.

"You're the boy in the news! I'm so sorry about what happened to you."

Drew looked down at his feet and then back at her.

"You're here for me, aren't you?"

"Yeah, I think so."

"Are you two?" my Mum stuttered, "do you know each other?"

"We're close, yes," I gulped hard, knowing exactly what I was going to say next, "Mum, this is Drew."

"What? You're Drew? I mean, you're a ghost. How does that work?"

Drew looked at me, silently urging me to answer something I wasn't all that clear on myself.

"I don't know, Mom," I said finally, "it just does. Anyway, we don't need to get into that."

"So, you're actually together then?" she pried further.

"Yes," Drew answered simply.

"It's not like I can do anything about it now though, eh?" She smiled and looked at Drew, "I hope you're taking care of her?"

"He is," I answered for him.

A glimmering, white, almost iridescent oval appeared in thin air.

"Wow, look at that," my Mum gasped, "it's beautiful! Is that our cue to leave, Drew?"

Oh my God. It was happening.

"It is," he answered, reaching for her hand, "It's time to go."

"What? No! You can't. I can't lose you both!"

He gently pulled her right up to it.

"Please don't go!" I shouted this time, as if the increase in volume would change everything.

"I'm sorry, Henri but we really have to go," Drew said, "I love you so much."

"I love you too."

"Goodbye, sweetheart. Love you to the moon and back," my Mum smiled, clearly holding back tears.

I didn't stop the tears from falling.

"I love you too, Mom. So much," I said then looked at Drew, "Drew, please come back to me."

I heard his breath catch in the back of his throat as they walked together into the light.

"Can you take me home please?" I asked the female police officer.

"Of course, Henri. Oh, by the way, I'm Alice and this is Frank" she said, pointing at her colleague, "it's about time you knew our names."

"Thank you, Alice. Thanks, Frank."

Frank nodded.

"We'll take you home as soon as you've spoken to Penelope here. She's from Social Services," he said, gesturing to a woman in a sharp, navy blue, two-piece suit and a crisp, white shirt, who looked, quite frankly, as if she had been sucking on a lemon.

I shook my head.

"Seriously? Right now?"

"I'm sorry, Henri. There's nothing we can do," Alice said, "just speak to her and get it out of the way. She's got to do this."

"Right. Okay. Whatever."

Penelope approached me with caution, as if I was going to bite her if she came too close.

"Hi, Henri," she began, "my name's…"

"Penelope. I know," I finished.

She looked down at the floor then back up at me.

"I am very sorry for your loss, Henri and I know this is probably the furthest thing from your mind right now, but we need to go over a few things. Legalities and whatnot."

"Whatnot? Ooh, now that sounds interesting," I said sarcastically, "Shall we just talk about that?"

Silence.

"Look, I get it. You're just doing your job but seriously, can't it wait. Just for another day, at least?"

"I'm afraid not," Penelope found her voice again.

"Come on then, let's get this done."

"Let's find somewhere a little more comfortable," she said, "we've got quite a bit to go through."

Great. Just great.

We walked the corridor in silence until Penelope slowed.

"Ah, here we are," she said, pushing open a door. It was one of those family rooms. One of those rooms where you get told the worst. It just seemed like any old room to me.

I walked in, ducking under her arm. She closed the door behind us.

Penelope sat down, straightened her skirt and shoved her hand into her bag as if she was rooting for an emergency bar of chocolate. She pulled out a pen, put it in her mouth and dived straight back in. This time her loot was a notepad. She clicked her pen and looked at me.

"Once again, I would just like to offer my sincere condolences, Henri," she said, sounding like she really meant it.

"Thank you."

"Now, Henri the law states that at your age you can live on your own. You can rent your own place. You are an adult."

"Great. Thanks."

"But I'm not just here to spout stats at you about what you can and can't do. I mean, I am here to let you know your rights," she corrected herself, "but my primary concern is your welfare."

"I can look after myself, Penelope."

"I don't doubt that for a second, Henri but you've just…"

"Lost my Mum? Yeah, I'm aware of that."

"And it's awful, particularly because it was just the two of you."

I felt my eyes begin to well up. It was. Not is. Not anymore.

"So," Penelope went on, placing her hand on my knee, "I just want to make sure that you're going to be okay. No, that's wrong, what a thing to say. I'm sorry, Henri."

"It's okay," I sniffed.

"I need to be sure you can live independently. I need to make sure you can cope. Let's just tackle the practicalities first and then we'll discuss any support you might be entitled to."

"I don't need any money. I'm not a charity."

"I know that, but you will be entitled to some help, financial and personal. Let's just get the ball rolling, okay?"

I nodded.

"Okay."

"So, that's me done," Penelope said.

"Really?"

"Well, yes, until our next meeting. In the meantime, is there anyone else we can contact? A family member, perhaps?"

Um, yeah, there's my long-lost father, I thought. It was more than tempting to brush under the carpet the fact that my father was off somewhere, living another life with other people but it would be just my luck, wouldn't it? She would, no doubt, find out I was lying and to be honest, I couldn't deal with any more aggro. I'd got more than enough on my plate already.

"There's my Dad," I came clean, the words stinging as they tumbled from my mouth.

Penelope took down what little details I had for him, scribbling on her note pad like a woman possessed.

"Okay, Henri. That's good. So, I'll get in touch with him."

"If you must," I said, rolling my eyes. I knew this would happen, "but he's not bothered about me, about us, since he left. He didn't care, he doesn't care, and I doubt he's going to start."

"Henri, whatever's gone on between you and your Dad, he needs to know the situation and that he has a legal responsibility to you. I understand why you might not want him involved but I'm afraid that's the law."

I nodded. Penelope was right. Deep down, I knew that.

"Is that it, then?"

"That's all for now, Henri but I'll be in touch again soon."

If you must.

The house was so silent. So empty. It felt huge, like one person was nowhere near enough to fill it. I threw my bag down to the floor and could have easily done the same to myself and stayed there forever. In one, devastating blow, I lost my Mum and the love of my life. My heart hurt. Really hurt. I always thought being heartbroken was just a turn of phrase. A way to put into words exactly how upset you are. But it's real. My heart felt like it could explode with this all-consuming pain.

I glanced blankly around the kitchen and living room. Everything looked the same but totally different.

I could feel fresh tears forming, another wave ready to crash and fall down my face. I let it happen. No point in trying to keep it all in. I cried, I sobbed and when my eyes closed, I didn't fight.

There's a noise on the landing. No, not a noise. A feeling.

"You can come in," I call out to him, "It's okay, Drew."

I sit upright, and my door opens slowly. He's standing

there, and he's been crying. His face is dripping wet. His eyes are red raw. He comes to me and lays his head on my lap, wraps his arms around my waist. His shoulders are shaking and a new wave of heart wrenching sobbing spills from his mouth.

"Don't cry," I tell him, "I hate to see you so sad."

"I'm just so sorry," he murmurs, "just so, so sorry."

I hold him tighter even though I know he's not going to be sticking around.

LUCY ONIONS

DAY 18

I knew I had to phone in school. My Mum couldn't cover for me this time. I picked up the house phone and dialed. Principal Stokes wasn't available to speak to. In a meeting or something. When I explained the reason for my absence to the school receptionist, there was a very awkward, heavy silence and many apologies. She offered help and told me to take as much time as I needed. A small sense of relief washed over me. I was told to expect a phone call from the Principal at some point.

I may have slept all night, but I didn't feel any better for it. I felt groggy, my head thick with lethargy. Would I be awake to answer a follow up phone call from school? Hard to tell. What was I going to do now? What was the protocol in this situation? There were so many practicalities to consider but my brain was having none of it.

I rubbed my eyes and realised in an instant that I'd been asleep, again. I don't remember dozing off.

The red light on the answer machine was flashing and I knew who would have left the message. I should have played the message straight away. Instead, I listened to the greeting my Mum had recorded the day we moved in.

"Hi. We can't get to the phone right now because we're busy having fun. If you need us, leave a message after the tone. We'll try and get back to you, honest!"

I slumped to the floor and cried. Cried like I would never stop. How could anyone do that to a woman who was on her own and vulnerable? Why would anyone want to do that? To my Mum? Didn't they know that's what she was? My Mum. And then, Drew.

As if it wasn't bad enough to lose her, this unseen power thought it was okay to take the only boy I have ever loved away from me, too. What the hell was the point in me being here anymore? I had my Dad, wherever the hell he was, and I had Nancy, my best friend, the sister I never had, but to be honest, it didn't seem like enough. If I did it, if I ended it right now, would Drew and my Mum be there to take me wherever it is we go?

I made my way up to the bathroom. The mirrored cabinet above the sink looked amazing. I knew what was in there. My sure-fire way of getting out of here. Mum had a bottle of super-strong painkillers and sleeping pills. She hid them right up the top, behind her lotions and potions but with me being the nosey-parker I am, it didn't take long to find them and find out what they were. I knew she used the sleeping pills far more than she let on. When Dad left, she went months without proper sleep. I took out the bottles and opened them, pouring pills from both into my hands. I threw the pills into my mouth and they almost entirely filled the cavity. I knew it would taste horrendous but there was no way I could swallow them all, even with water. I pinched my nose and began to chomp. I gagged as soon as the taste hit the back of my throat. I tipped our toothbrushes out of the tumbler then swilled and filled it up with water. I took a gulp to help wash down the clag of crushed pills. It took a good few gulps to completely clear my mouth.

I perched myself on the edge of the bath and wondered how long it would take for me to slip away. I plugged the hole in the bath and turned both taps on full. If the pills took their time, if they didn't work at all, at least I could count on a watery end. I hoped that the pills did their job because I couldn't really imagine what it must feel like to drown. If I panicked too much, would I be brave enough to fight it? To let the water fill my lungs and consume me?

As the water continued to gush out, I had an epiphany. I couldn't go! What would my Mum say if she saw me? It would break her heart. I couldn't do that to her, no matter how much I wanted to be with her again.

I shoved my fingers to the back of my throat and pushed them, slowly, further back. I felt my tongue and the muscles in my throat contract around them. It was a familiar, comforting feeling. I'd had enough experience of making myself sick in the not so distant past. It was such a good stress relief. It was the one thing I could control at a time when there really wasn't much else I could. It didn't take too much effort for the first wave of nausea to hit.

I retched and heaved until my body could not give up any more to the toilet bowl. I hoped I had got rid of every single, last fragment of every pill. I hoped it was enough.

There was a knock on the door and then even more, fast and fervent. I rinsed my mouth with mouthwash to get rid of the rancid taste and swore under my breath.

"Hang on!" I shouted as I slowly and carefully made my way downstairs. It may have been the pills that had made me feel so groggy or it may have been because I'd spewed my guts up. I hoped it was the latter. I hoped I'd got rid of the pills just in time.

"Henri," Nancy bawled, running at me, her arms open, "Oh my God. Are you okay?"

I hugged her back. I wasn't expecting to be happy to see anyone, but Nancy was an oasis in a world full of shit.

"I'm so glad you're here," I sighed.

She squeezed me even harder.

"Please, come in."

She headed straight for the kitchen, opening and shutting cupboards.

"Can I make you a drink?" She asked, "Get you anything?"

"Thanks, Nancy but I'm fine," I lied.

"I'm sorry, Henri. It's just me trying to be helpful."

"I know. Thank you."

She smiled awkwardly.

"Anyway, I just wanted to come around to check on you," she went on, "I just wanted you to know you're not alone."

I hugged her again, hard.

I told her all about what happened with Mum and even though my head screamed no, don't do it, I went ahead and told her what Drew had done. That he led her into the light. Into the next world.

"Oh my God, Henri," she sighed, shaking her head, "I don't know what to say. I..."

"It's okay," I stopped her, "to be honest, if the roles were reversed, I wouldn't know what to say to you either."

"Wait a minute," she said as she headed to the front door and stepped out onto the porch. She came back with a rucksack slung over her shoulder and in her hand, a plastic bag full of clinking bottles.

"Now, you can say no if you want to," she said, "but you need someone with you. You shouldn't be alone at the moment, rattling around in here like a lost soul. Are you okay with me staying?"

"I couldn't think of anything better."

"Good, me neither."

I felt my eyes well up. I had no one now. I didn't think I'd ever have to need anyone other than my Mum, but I needed her. I needed Nancy and if this was how life was going to be from now on, I could think of a lot worse.

DAY 19

"Hey," Nancy said as she met me at the bottom of the stairs, a slice of limp toast dangling from her hand, "I need to pop out and get some smells."

"Smells?" I giggled quietly, weakly, "Have you got a fetish or something? Do you go around sniffing random objects and people?"

I imagined Nancy running around sniffing the air. I giggled again.

She giggled too.

"Seriously though, if I don't get some new deodorant soon, you won't want me living with you."

"Now you mention it, I have noticed a funny smell…"

Nancy lifted her arms above her head and sniffed at her armpits deeply.

"I'm joking, silly."

"You little…" she laughed, "I might even splash out on some new perfume."

"Covering all corners, eh?"

She nodded.

"Why don't you come with me, Henri? We can grab a coffee and something sweet, sticky and indulgent."

I wasn't in the mood. I knew she was just trying to take my mind off things, just for a little while, but I didn't want to take my mind off things. Not yet.

"I'm not really in the mood, Nancy. Do you mind if I don't come?"

"Oh, Henri, of course not," she said, stroking my arm, "I won't be long then. I'll just get what I need and come straight back."

"Take your time, honestly. I'm not going anywhere." Those last words held so much weight. If it wasn't for her, I couldn't have promised such a thing.

She pulled me into a hug.

"If you change your mind, just phone me," she said.

"Yes, Miss!"

The house fell silent once again. Nancy had bought a happy chaos when I thought I would never know happiness again. It followed her as she left. Half of me hated it. The other half was thankful for the quiet, grateful to have some time to itself.

I headed to the kitchen and I stared out the window, onto the back garden.

"Henri?" I spun round hoping to see Drew.

"Hello?"

Nothing.

Just my imagination.

"Henri?" I heard again, "can you hear me?"

"Yes! Yes, I can. Drew?"

"Yes, it's me."

"Oh my God! You've come back?"

"Well, no. Not exactly. Can you see me?"

"No!"

"That's the thing, right. I don't think I'll be coming back."

"What? Why?"

"I don't know, Henri. I'm so sorry."

I swallowed the lump in my throat but up it came again, and I started to cry.

"I wish I could hold you. I can't stand being away from you, Henri. I just wanted you to know that your Mum is fine. I want you to know that I am too. "

My tears came heavy and blurred the room around me. I totally gave in to my grief, to the darkness I could feel swallowing me whole and then the home phone rang out it's shrill, tinny alarm. With energy I didn't think I possessed, I practically dived on top of the phone and snatched up the receiver.

"Hello?" I mumbled.

"Hi, Henri. Its Principal Stokes."

Great, just great.

"Hi, Mr. Stokes. How are you?"

"I'm fine, Henri," he answered, tone full of pity, "Are you? I mean, oh dear, what a ridiculous question to ask."

"It's okay, Sir. Don't worry. What else is there to say?"

"Yes, you're right. Still, it's …"

"It's fine, honestly," I interrupted, "anyway, if you're wondering when I'll be back at school…"

"That is not the reason for my phone call. Far from it. I won't be expecting you back until you feel able to do so. You can't put a time limit on this kind of thing, on grief. If you are worried about school-work though, not that it would be high on your list of priorities right now, I can email you with homework and such."

"That would be good, Sir. Thank you."

I gave him my email address.

"Henri, is there anything else you need? Anything at all?"

"No, Sir. It's fine but thank you for asking."

"Just take your time. Take as long as you need. Goodbye, Henri."

The phone went dead, and I put it back down. I couldn't miss school. I didn't want to be away from it for too long, but I also knew it was too early to go back. I knew my heart and mind wouldn't be in it. It's so wrong for me to feel like this. But losing the two most important people in your life tends to make you feel a little out of sorts. I had to remember that. Maybe it was exactly what I needed? To focus on something other than my Mum and Drew.

Can't I just have one moments peace? I thought as I answered the knocking at the door. I was getting sick and tired of the sound.

"Hi, Henri."

"Hi, Penelope."

"Can I come in?"

With a little reluctance, I gestured for her to enter. She sat down awkwardly on a chair at the dining table. I sat opposite.

"So, you know why I'm here, Henri. I'm just going to ask some questions and all I want you to do is answer them as honestly as possible. Then I'll just need to have a little walk through the house. Is that okay?"

"Of course. Don't worry about it," I lied.

Penelope went through a list of closed questions. I answered them all honestly apart from the question relating to alcohol consumption. Of course, I lied about that. Luckily, there wasn't a bottle of anything alcoholic in view and that wasn't because I'd hidden it.

"Well, everything looks in order, Henri," Penelope said as she walked back into the living room after her little snoop around, "I can see why you wouldn't want to be anywhere else. It's a lovely home."

"It is. Thanks. My Mum made it so," I said, just about managing to hide the tremor in my voice.

Penelope nodded sympathetically.

"I've contacted your father, Henri, as we discussed. He's now aware of the situation and I can tell you he's very upset about it all. As a result, he's said you are more than welcome to go and live with him."

"Seriously? Is he joking?"

"No. This is not a joking matter, Henri. He is your father and although neither he, nor we, can make you do something you don't want to, he still has a responsibility to make sure you're okay."

"Whatever."

Penelope smiled awkwardly.

"So, where do we go from here?" I asked, nervous to hear her reply.

"Well, regarding staying here, in your family home, that's fine but I need to make sure you have the financial means to. Do you have any money coming in?"

"As in, do I have a job?"

Penelope nodded.

"No, but I can get one easily enough."

"Okay, and do you have access to your Mum's accounts? Any paperwork?"

"I know where she kept all that kind of stuff."

"Do you know if your Mum left a Will?"

"I can't tell you that for definite but I'm sure she would have made one. My Mum was like that, you see. Had everything in order."

"I'm sure she did," Penelope went on, "it's a Mother's prerogative. Believe me. When my daughter turned five, my husband and I drew up our will. If I hadn't have taken the bull by horns, we'd still be without one. So, Henri, at your earliest convenience, I would like you to check through your Mum's legal paperwork and we'll take it from there, okay?"

"I can do that."

"Here's my card," she said, handing one to me, "it's got my direct line on. When you have found everything I've asked for, get in touch."

I nodded.

"If you need anything at all in the meantime, please call me."

She pulled me into a hug that I really was not expecting.

"See you soon, Henri."

I smiled at her as she walked out the door and headed over to the record player. I pulled Revolver by The Beatles from the shelf and set it to play.

That's exactly what I needed now. I needed music to break through the piercing silence. Maybe it was all I needed. As long as I had music, nothing else mattered.

"Honey, I'm home!" Nancy called happily.

"Hi. You okay?"

"I am now. How're you doing?"

"Same as when you walked out and left me," I teased.

"I shouldn't have gone. I could have just used some of your stuff."

"Nancy, I'm winding you up."

"Well stop it" she laughed back, "anyway, what're you up to there?"

Nancy rested her chin on my shoulder.

"Ooh, job-hunting, huh?"

"Something like that."

Penelope had planted a seed. I needed to get a job. If I needed to pay bills and buy groceries, it was a must.

"Well, why don't I see if I can get you in at the pub?"

"That's a great idea. I've never worked in a pub before though?"

"Look, if I can do it, anyone can," Nancy laughed.

"Cool."

"I'll have a word with my manager on my next shift."

"Great stuff. Thanks, Nancy."

There was always the shop too. I could always ask John about a job.

I'd been thinking about what Penelope had said all day. I knew Mum had a solicitor because she had taken on Mum and Dad's divorce case. They clicked on their very first meeting, became quite friendly with each other. Both had had the same kind of life experiences.

I knew Nancy was here to keep me company, but I was intent on finding all the information Penelope had asked for. I might as well get it out the way. The quicker this ball started rolling, the better.

"What you up to now?" Nancy asked as I darted towards the cupboard under the stairs.

"I've got to sort out some legal paperwork for social services. I'm sorry, Nancy but I need to get this done."

"Hey, don't apologise," she said, "I'll just amuse myself until you're ready to do it for me."

"I amuse you then, do I?"

"Of course you do. Why do you think I'm friends with you?"

We both laughed.

I opened the door to the cupboard under the stairs and flicked the light switch. Mum was obsessive when it came to organising and keeping things neat and tidy. The cupboard was no exception.

I pulled open the top drawer of the filing cabinet and flicked through multi-coloured dividers until I got to the one marked, Solicitor Stuff. It was mostly full of paperwork from the divorce but at the very back of it was a sub-folder, simply named, 'For when I'm gone'.

My hands started to shake as I took the folder out. I don't know why. Maybe I just didn't want to face up to the fact that this was it, she really was gone. I took a document out of the file and let my eyes skirt over it, not wanting to read into too much detail. It was a copy of Mum's last will and testament and, to cut a long story short, she had left me everything.

Then I started reading it, properly. The house was

paid off. I guessed it must have been the money from the divorce that had sorted that out. She'd got savings and ISA's. That's no surprise. I knew she was good with money.

There was a telephone number at the very bottom of the page. I know that Penelope had said to pass on any information like this to her but even so, I picked up the landline and punched the number. I was trembling. Nervous to be talking legalities and embarrassed to be doing it so early. I had absolutely nothing to fear.

The female solicitor was nothing but sympathetic and explained everything clearly, omitting the jargon I expected a solicitor to spout. She booked me in for an appointment for the following Monday, after school. I explained I had no means of getting to her offices other than maybe finding a bus that would at least get me close. I needn't have worried. She told me it was no problem at all. That she would come to me, under one condition. I had to supply the coffee. Now that, I can do!

She didn't speak down to me. Didn't patronise. Once she had confirmed all the details for good measure, we said our goodbyes and she put the phone down. I phoned Penelope immediately after and explained everything. I apologised for taking matters into my own hands, thought she would be angry at me. She praised me for my initiative and courage and told me she would be attending the meeting. I could see now that she wasn't the ogre I thought she was. I felt light. Felt like a weight had been lifted. I could just grieve now without worrying whether I would have a roof over my head in the coming weeks, months, years. Okay, it would never take the pain away. Nothing could ever do that. I had lost far too much. But it was one less thing to worry about, that's for sure.

DAY 20

"I don't have to go in, you know," Nancy said, "I told Stokes that I would be staying with you."

"I know, and I really do appreciate it, but I don't want your absence to reflect badly in your report."

"Henri, I couldn't give a crap about that. It's just paper."

"I'm sure your Mum thinks the same."

"She understands. It's not like I'm just skipping school for the sake of it. And anyway, it's not like she can ground me anymore. I'm not a child."

"I know that too but look, Nancy, I'm okay. If you don't need to have time off, don't."

She sighed and picked her bag up.

"Are you absolutely sure about this?"

I nodded.

"Hey, I'm going to phone school anyway, but can you tell Stokes I'll be back on Monday?" I asked.

"Yup," Nancy said as she walked out of the house.

I had prepared dinner. Without any help. All on my own. I set out two plates, two sets of cutleries, two wine glasses and dished up. I sat in my usual place and looked across to where my Mum would have been and smiled at my best friend. My first ever attempt at a roast dinner (who cares that it wasn't Sunday!) and she wasn't around to share it with me. I swallowed hard, trying to get rid of the lump in my throat. I poured two glasses of Cabernet Sauvignon and handed one to Nancy. We raised our glasses in unison.

"To you, Mum!" was all I could manage before taking a gulp of my drink. After a few more sips, I loosened up.

"Thank you, Mum. Thank you so much," I went on, eyes closed, "You haven't got to worry about anything. I'm going to be just fine. I wish I would have just taken the time, whilst you were here, to say thank you more. To tell you I love you, lots, lots more. I do, Mum. I love you so much. I miss you so much, but I promise you, I'll be fine."

Nancy sniffed, wiped her cheek.

I drained my glass empty and poured another large helping.

The beef didn't taste the same. Neither did the roast potatoes. Nothing tasted the same, for that matter even though I cooked everything exactly as I'd watched my Mum do it.

I used to sit in the kitchen as a child, mesmerised by the sights, smells and sounds that were a result of her cooking. Then as I grew older, I used to prepare the vegetables for her and pay attention to every, minute detail and timing. She always made it look so easy. It was second nature. It just goes to show, no matter how hard you try, your dinner's will never taste like your

Mum's.

I only realised we'd polished off two bottles of wine as I poured the last of it into our glasses. We were both a little tipsy and tired, so I placed Ten by Pearl Jam on to the record player and we slouched down on the sofa. I closed my eyes and almost immediately felt myself start to drift away with the music.

He is standing in front of me, as plain as the nose on my face.

"Is this real? Am I asleep or awake?"

"You're asleep, honey."

"So, is this the only way I'm going to be able to see you from now on?"

"I think so, yes."

"Well, in that case, I want to always be asleep."

"Ha! I think Stokes would have something to say about that! When are you back at school?"

"Monday, but maybe I could have a little more time off. I could sleep at the drop of a hat at the moment. He's told me to only come back when I feel I can, so there's no rush."

"Henri, I would love nothing more than to see you every day again even if you do have to be asleep for me to do it, but I think you need to get back to your normal routine."

"You're saying that like I've been out of touch with reality for ages!"

"Well, that's not how I mean it to sound but I do think it's going to help. You know your Mum would want you to carry on as usual, right?"

"Of course I know that!" I shout at him.

"I'm sorry, Henri. I'm not here to patronise you. If it helps any, I want to be here with you. I've never wanted anything so badly."

I woke with a start, thinking about the conversation I'd just had with Drew. He was right, I needed to get back into my old routine. It would be so easy to hide myself away but at some point, I'd need to venture out, show my face. School would help. The structure would bring some stability back into my life. It wouldn't cure what I was feeling, it wouldn't take the heartache away, but it would allow me to focus.

I thought of my Mum and knew exactly what she would say if she was still here. She wouldn't let me sit and mope at home, she'd be the one to push me out that door. She's not here though so I can either carry on the way I am or show her some respect and try and live like I know she would want me to. It would take time, of course it would. Luckily, I've got time, plenty of it.

DAY 21

The house wasn't a mess, not by a long shot, but I had let things slip a little. Understandable, under the circumstances, but even so. I had a feeling that the act of cleaning up and tidying away would take my mind off things, if only for a little while.

The sun had found its way through a gap in the closed curtains and was casting its light over Nancy, sleeping soundly on the sofa. We both ended up sleeping where we sat and already, I was paying for it, for not going to bed. My neck was aching and by the looks of it, Nancy's would be too.

I opened the kitchen windows and inhaled deeply as a cool breeze wafted past, refreshing me as it did. I went upstairs and opened more, in my room and the bathroom. This house needed air.

I left my best friend to sleep and headed up to my room. I wrestled with my duvet and after much huffing and puffing, managed to separate it from its cover. I pulled my pillow covers and under sheet off far more easily.

I stood for a while outside my Mum's room. Couldn't quite pluck up the courage, although why I needed courage, I can't quite say. Why was I so nervous? It was her room. I had nothing to fear. I slowly pushed the door open and just as I should've expected, her room was immaculate. Not a single thing out of place. It felt weird. Like she'd never been there. No sign of disorganisation whatsoever.

I slumped onto her bed and ran my hands over her duvet. I turned and lay face down, burying my nose into the soft bed sheets then shuffled upwards and lay my head on her pillow. It smelled like her shampoo. The shampoo she'd used since I was a kid. I can't remember her hair smelling any different. I decided that there was no way I was washing her bed sheets. I needed to keep that smell, her smell, as long as I could.

I took my bed sheets and dirty laundry downstairs and loaded them into the washing machine. Just like the washing powder, the fabric conditioner was for sensitive skin. Mum had used the same stuff since I was a kid too. She always said it reminded her that once, I was a baby. I poured a cup of powder in its compartment and did the same with the conditioner.

Mum kept all the cleaning products under the sink, all neat and tidy in an old washing bowl. I pulled the bowl out and grabbed a pair of gloves for cleaning. I looked around the kitchen and living room and the only thought in my head was, let's do this!

We fell onto the sofa and looked around us.

"Good job, well done, eh?" Nancy said, wiping her

forehead.

"I'm sorry I woke you up."

"Don't be silly. I'm glad you did."

I was too.

"Thanks for helping, Nancy."

"No problem. Feels good, doesn't it?"

It certainly did.

We had spun round the house like human tornadoes and just as I had thought, busying myself with household chores had given me just that little bit of respite.

There was a knock on the door. I got up, smoothed my hair down and checked myself over in the mirror. The house work had made me sweat and I could still feel it prickling my skin. I wiped my forehead quickly. I looked through the spy hole. It was John. He looked grey. The only colour came from the flowers he had in his hands. I lifted the latch, unlocked the door and opened it.

"Hi, John."

"Hi, Henri."

"Hi, John," Nancy called from the kitchen.

"Hi," he called back.

"Where are my manners? Sorry, John, come in."

He stepped through and I closed the door behind him.

Silence.

Awkward silence.

One of us would have to break it.

"How are you?" I asked him.

He shook his head.

"How am I?" he said, clearly angry at himself for not asking me the same question, "How are you? I mean, oh, I'm sorry, Henri. It's a stupid question."

"No, it's not, John. It's the first thing you would ask. It's natural. Anyway, come in. Let's not talk at the door."

He limply handed me the flowers and followed me into the kitchen, his head hung low.

"Sorry, this is Nancy, my best friend."

"Hi, Nancy."

"Hello again, John," Nancy smiled, looked at me, "I'll just be upstairs, okay," she went on, leaving the two of us alone.

"These are lovely, John, thank you," I said, snipping the ends of the stems, "would you like a drink? Tea? Coffee? Something stronger?"

"A glass of water will be fine," he answered.

I took a tall glass from the cupboard and filled it with fresh, filtered water from the jug.

"Here you go," I said, handing the glass to him.

"Thank you," he said, taking it from me.

"It's a pleasure."

Silence.

Awkward silence.

He was nervous, that much was clear.

"John, it's okay, you know?"

"I know. I just don't know what to say."

"I understand. I'd be the same."

"Actually, I do know what to say. I'm sorry I haven't contacted you until now. I'm sorry I wasn't with your Mum. I'm sorry I couldn't do anything."

He broke down, sobbing. Heavy, painful sobs.

"John, there was nothing either of us could have done. You don't need to be sorry."

He nodded sadly.

"I just needed you to know that. I really liked her, Henri."

"I know. She liked you too."

He nodded again. Downed the rest of his water.

"I really am so, so sorry."

"Seriously, John, stop. Please."

"I'm s…"

"No! Enough."

Silence.

Awkward silence.

"Henri, if you need anything, anything at all, you just let me know. Have you got anyone looking after you?"

"I've got social services on side and they've notified my Dad of the situation, although what good that will do is yet to be seen."

"So, you're staying here on your own? What about your boyfriend? Will he be staying?"

Now I fell silent. I felt tears well in my eyes and a lump form in my throat. I was just about coping with talk of my Mum. Just. Add Drew to the chat and that was it. I blinked, hoping the tears would retreat to where they had come from. Instead, they rolled down my cheeks.

"Oh, Henri. I'm sorry, I…"

I scowled at him.

"No more apologies," I reiterated, "no, he won't be staying here."

"Oh, I see," he said, "you guys okay?"

"Let's just say I won't be seeing him as much from now on."

"Oh," he said, leaving it at that.

"Luckily, my best friend, Nancy will be staying from time to time, so you haven't got to worry."

He smiled.

"Well, that's good. Anyway, I'm going to go now, leave you in peace. Remember, just let me know if you need anything."

"I will," I smiled, "erm, actually, I don't suppose you need an extra set of hands at the shop, do you? I could do with a little, part time job."

"Well, I'm not advertising, but I suppose it would help to have you. Company for me, some extra money for you."

"Brilliant, thank you," I said, grinning, "when do you want me to start?"

"Henri, there's no rush. Whenever you're ready, okay?"

"Okay."

"Well, take care," he said, turning away from me. He spun back around, "Oh, actually, would you please let me know when the funeral is? I'd like to be there."

"Of course I will."

"No! I scream at him, that's not fair."

"I'm sorry," he says, "I'm so sorry."

"You have to come back!"

He shakes his head. Tears tumble down his cheeks. He chokes on the sobs coming from his mouth.

"You know this is the last thing on earth I want."

"Well I need to be with you. I can't stand this."

"No. Don't you even dare. Don't you dare do what I think you're thinking about."

"It's the only way, Drew."

"Can't we just carry on like this? We can still be with each other, like this."

"I know. I know that but it's just not enough."

"It's going to have to be, Henri. It will have to be."

DAY 22

I sit up suddenly, my hair soaking wet, my pillow damp. I know I can't do it. I know I mustn't. I want to though, I really do. But then there's Nancy. I can't do it to her. And no matter what I think of my Dad, I can't do it to him either.

I kick my legs out of bed and make my way to the bathroom. It's early but I need to shower. I need to wash the sweat off me. I need to wash away the dream.

I stand under the stream and let the hot water flow over me. I'd held on to the hope that Drew would come back for long enough. I had to be realistic now. He wasn't coming back. That's what he'd said. He was never here in the first place. Just a soul, not a person.

Whether it was the after effects of the shower, I don't know but I felt this sense of clarity. Like I had a purpose again, like the loss of the two people who meant the most to me in the whole world didn't define me.

The talk with John and my dream with Drew had clearly had some impact on me and I knew that the only place I could go now was forward.

I'd never eight am on a Sunday before. The sun was up, the birds were singing and the only thing that threatened to shatter this idyll was my rumbling stomach. I felt hungry, physically and mentally. Hungry not just for food but for a new start.

I put the percolator on and delighted in the sound of my brewing coffee. Whilst I was waiting for the first hot drink of the day, I grabbed a book from the bookcase and dropped it on the kitchen table. I made a simple breakfast of toast and jam then sat and ate far too quickly with my head stuck in someone else's story.

"Hi, Henri," Nancy's voice filled the room.

"Hey, you," I said, slightly annoyed that I'd been disturbed but happy to hear her.

"You okay?"

"You know what, Nancy, I am. I feel alright today."

"That's great. It really is."

"I know. Are you okay?"

"I'm good."

"That's good."

"And what are your plans for today?"

"You ask that as if I have a life."

"Oh, Henri."

"Oh, Nancy."

"Seriously, what are you up to?"

"What does it look like I'm doing?" I said, holding the book up to her.

"I broke the silence, right? I'm sorry."

"I'm happy to have the silence broken if it's you that's breaking it."

"You're too kind, Henri."

We both laughed.

"I'm only going to ask once more," Nancy said, getting her breath back, "what are you doing today? If the answer is nothing, do you fancy coming home with me for dinner? Mum's cooking lamb shank and all the trimmings. There's plenty to go around."

"You know what, that sounds great."

Nancy's smile seemed too big for her face and it was infectious.

I knew I needed to get out. I wasn't exactly climbing the walls yet, but it wouldn't be long before I was if I didn't drag myself out. I wasn't really ready to see Nancy and her Mum in the same room, together, doing mother and daughter things but I had to. I had to support her as much as she was supporting me.

I decided to make a little effort, dressing in black leggings and a burnt red tunic. I put on a minimal amount of make-up. I know we weren't going anywhere special, but I wanted to look okay.

"Ooh, look at you!" Nancy squealed in excitement, "you look gorgeous."

I rolled my eyes.

"Seriously, you do. I always say that putting a bit of makeup on makes you feel just that little bit better."

"It's just makeup, Nancy. It's going to take a lot more than this to make me feel better."

"Oh my God, I'm sorry. I can be such an insensitive bitch sometimes. I didn't mean…"

"Hey," I pulled her into a hug, "I know you didn't. You're not an insensitive bitch."

I gently pushed her away.

"You do look lovely, though," she said.

"Hi, Mum," Nancy said, storming past me.

"Hi, sweetheart," her Mum said, hugging her.

Mrs. Walker's eyes found mine and she let go of Nancy.

"Hi, Henri. I'm glad you came. It's good to see you."

"Thanks, Mrs. Walker. It's good to see you too."

She walked up to me and pulled me into a hug.

Silence.

Awkward silence.

"I'm so looking forward to this, Henri. Are you?" Nancy asked, clearly trying to break it.

"I am," I smiled, wishing I could feel as excited as she clearly was.

"Mm, something smells awesome, Mum" she said, heading straight to the kitchen.

Nancy was right, something did smell awesome. Lamb and garlic and rosemary. My mouth started to water.

"Well, I hope you've both got an appetite."

My stomach rumbled as if on cue.

I pulled out a bottle of red wine from my bag and held it out to Mrs. Walker.

"Oh, Henri, you didn't need to bring anything," she said, "just having you here is enough."

"Thank you but please, take it."

She took the bottle from me.

"Thank you, Henri. It's lovely of you."

I smiled at her.

She smiled back.

"Do you want to stay here tonight?" Nancy asked before taking another gulp of red wine, "I know Mum would love it if you did."

Nancy's Mum had left us to it, said she had work to do in her office. We were sitting on the sofa, full up and tired from the meal, and the wine was going down nicely. Maybe it wouldn't hurt to stay out of the house for a little while longer.

"Yeah, I will. It'll be nice."

Nancy smiled from ear to ear.

"Hang on though, I haven't bought my stuff for school tomorrow. Sorry, Nancy. Another time, yeah?"

"Aww, come on, Henri!" she pleaded, "I've got uniform you can borrow. We're about the same size, aren't we?"

"Well, yeah, but…"

"Please?" she whined.

"Okay then. I'll stay."

"Yay," she squealed.

I laughed at her.

"I know I can get a bit over excited sometimes. I can't help it. It's just the way I am."

"And the way you are is just fine."

She looked down into her wine.

"Think you could squeeze in dessert?" she asked.

"Depends what it is."

"Just ice cream, I'm afraid."

"Oh, I can always make room for ice cream."

"So, are you all ready for tomorrow?" Nancy slurred slightly.

"I think so. Is it wrong for me to say that I'm actually looking forward to it?"

"Hell no. It'll do you good."

"That's exactly what I'm thinking."

"Just take your time, take every day as it comes. That's all you can do."

"I know."

"More wine?"

"Not for me, thanks. I don't want to feel rough for tomorrow."

"I suppose you're right."

"Hey, I forgot to say, I spoke to John."

"And?"

"I've got myself a job."

Nancy pulled me into a hug.

"Oh, Henri, that's great. I haven't had chance to ask at work, so you've beat me to it."

"Is that okay?"

"Is what okay?"

"That I've managed to sort myself out."

"Of course it is, silly. I'm over the moon for you."

"Thanks, Nancy," I said, pulling out of her grip, "right, time for bed."

"It's only ten o clock!"

"That it is but I'm exhausted. You stay up if you want."

"No, it's okay. I suppose I better hit the sack too," she yawned, "come on then."

I followed behind her up the stairs and giggled as she stubbed her toe against the bannister. She was in obvious pain, jumping on one leg with her foot in her hand but I couldn't help but laugh.

"Oh yeah, very funny."

I couldn't take her seriously.

"Anyway, goodnight, Henri," Nancy yawned.

"Night, Nancy," I yawned back.

"I'm so proud of you, Henri."

"Why?"

"What you're doing, going back to school, getting a job, it's brilliant."

"It's not exactly original, Drew. I'm not the first to lose a loved one."

"I know that but you're doing it. You're getting your life back and it makes me so happy. I know your Mum would be so proud of you, too."

"I miss her, Drew, so much."

"I know."

"I miss you too, so, so much."

"I miss you too. I can't begin to tell you how much."

He walks up to the side of the bed. Lies down next to me. His face isn't even an inch from mine. My skin prickles. His breath trembles.

I wake up.

LUCY ONIONS

DAY 23

I didn't need my alarm to wake me up, but it went off anyway. I let it ring out, not because I enjoyed it's sound so much, but I figured it would eventually wake Nancy up.

I looked over at the uniform that had been left out for me. Nancy's Mum must have put it there at some point.

I dressed slowly, feeling my stomach churn with hunger and maybe even nerves. I washed as quickly as I had dressed and went downstairs. I knew I had to eat something, but I knew I couldn't handle breakfast.

"Good morning, Henri," Mrs. Walker smiled, "did you sleep well?"

"Not too bad," I said as my stomach groaned loudly.

"Someone sounds hungry!" She laughed, "What would you like?"

Yes, I was hungry, really hungry, but I was scared

of what eating too much would do to me.

"I'll just take this banana," I replied, grabbing one from the fruit bowl on the kitchen table, "do you mind?"

"Absolutely not, you've got to eat something. You take whatever you want."

"Thank you."

"Don't mention it. Has my daughter surfaced yet?"

I shook my head.

"Nancy," Mrs. Walker shouted up the stairs, "are you up?"

"Coming," she called back.

I watched her walk down the stairs and right up to me.

"How are you feeling?"

"Fine, thanks."

She looked fine, too. She looked as if yesterday hadn't even happened. Like we hadn't touched even a drop of wine.

"How are you feeling?" she asked.

"Good."

That's as much as I could say. Could I really do this? Could I really face school?

"So, what you got first?" she asked hopefully.

"Physics," I sighed. I wasn't exactly excited by the prospect.

"Oh, pants!"

"I've got to go and see Stokes though first. Just check in, you know?"

"Okey dokey. Well let's catch up at lunch then, okay? We can talk about what films we'll be watching at yours later."

"You know the solicitor's coming around after school, right?"

Actually, had I told her about the solicitor?

"I do now."

Clearly not.

"Oh my God, I thought I'd told you. I'm sorry."

"Henri, chill. It's fine. I'm not your M..." her face dropped instantly.

"Hey, don't worry," I assured her, but it didn't do much to help ease the horrified look on her face, "Nancy, it's fine. Honestly."

"Well, I have enough stuff in my overnight bag to last me a few days at yours," she said, her face breaking into a grin, "but if you would prefer me to go home tonight, I completely understand."

"No, no. I still want you to come around."

"As long as you're sure?"

"I am."

"Well look, I'll make myself scarce. I'll just stay in your room until you've finished."

We hugged each other instinctively.

"I have to go now. Get all this stuff out the way. I'll see you later."

I walked away, past Nancy, towards the main entrance, feeling the butterflies in my stomach start to flutter their wings.

I just made it to Physics as the last student in line filed into class. Thankfully, I saw a desk right at the back and I smiled, happy to know no one would be able to stare at me, well at least not without looking blatantly obvious.

I got out my pencil case, textbook and exercise book and shoved my bag down by my feet. Poised, pen in hand, ready to start taking notes, I felt myself zoning out. I turned my head to the left, finding the windows. I stared long and hard, hoping and wishing that Drew would appear but my eyes were rewarded with no such a view. I snapped my gaze back to the front of class. My eyes may have been locked on, but my mind wasn't.

The hairs on the back of my neck prickled and a rush of cold air raised goose bumps on my skin. I turned, facing the direction of the icy blast. Nothing. I turned back round, my teeth gritted.

"Help me!"

I span round again, hoping my imagination was playing tricks on me. Something told me that wasn't the case.

"Henri, help me," the voice called again, clearer this time. So clear that I knew exactly who it belonged to.

"Stacey?" I asked, my voice barely a whisper.

"Henri, help me!"

"How'd it go?" Nancy said, squeezing me tight.

"As well as could be expected. Glad it's over now though."

"I'm sure it'll get better once you're back into it. It was always going to be hard but you're doing the right thing. You know that, don't you?"

I nodded because I didn't want her to notice that I was on the verge of tears. Of course she was right. I knew today would be hard. I really didn't expect it not to be but man, it blew whatever expectation I had out of the water. Could I handle another day of the same?

A yellow, Volkswagen Beetle was parked at the end of the drive. It was an original and in immaculate condition.

"That must be the solicitor then?" Nancy said, breaking the silence.

"Could be. Then again, it could be Penelope."

"Penelope?"

"Social services. Everything's got to go through them now."

We headed to the car and waited at the driver's side door. The woman behind the wheel had absolutely no idea we were there as she tapped away irately on her phone. I giggled, amused at her obliviousness. Her head jerked up and she looked straight at us. She shoved her phone into her bag and opened the door.

"Oh sorry, I didn't realise you were... You haven't been standing there long, have you?"

"No, we just got here," I said, "sorry to have kept you waiting."

"You haven't. I just got here early. You would be amazed at how much work you can get done in a car. It's more of an office than my actual office. You must be Henri? And your friend?"

"Nancy," I said.

"Nice to meet you too, Nancy."

"And you," Nancy replied.

The woman nodded and zoned out for a moment. I let out a pretend cough in the hope it would bring her round. It did.

"Oh, sorry," she laughed awkwardly, "please excuse me. My brain is feeling a little overworked at the moment. I'm Jessica. Jessica Stern."

We shook hands through her rolled down, car

window.

"Don't worry about it. Do you want to come inside then, or will we be doing business out here on the drive?"

"Oh dear," she answered, shaking her head, "You must think me very unprofessional."

"Nope," I assured her.

"Thank you for your understanding. Right, let's go inside then."

Nancy headed straight for the stairs.

"Hey," I said, gently tugging at her arm, "you can stay down here, you know? I don't mind."

"I know but I think you need to have this time to yourself. If you need me though, just shout."

I smiled and pulled her into a hug.

"Oh, by the way, my name's Jessica. Jessica Stern."

"I know."

"You do?"

"Yes, you told me outside. It also says so on your card and letter-headed paper."

She shook her head and let out an exasperated sigh.

"Of course," she said, "as you can tell, I'm just having one of those days."

I smiled. I felt sorry for her. She seemed so stressed.

There was a knock on the door. I opened it.

"Hi, Penelope."

"Hi, Henri," she said, sounding just as flustered as Jessica Stern, "I'm sorry I'm late. What a day."

I didn't realise she was late until I remembered that I'd phoned her to tell her about the home visit from the solicitor. I gestured for her to enter. Jessica stood up, smoothing down her crumpled skirt.

Penelope held her hand out to her and they shook hands.

"Hello, I'm Penelope. I'm with social services. I'm dealing with Henri's case."

"Pleasure to meet you," Jessica replied, "I'm Jessica Stern, Henri's acting solicitor."

"Would you like a coffee or tea or something?" I asked them both.

"Coffee would be wonderful," Penelope replied, "One sugar and literally a splash of milk."

I looked at Jessica.

"Same here. Thank you, Henri."

"Coming right up," I said on my way to the kitchen.

"I suppose I should really cut down," I heard Jessica tell Penelope, "I drink far too much but to be honest, it's the only way I can operate at the moment. I mean, I know four cups a day isn't great but it's less than some people I know."

"Oh, tell me about it," Penelope said, "It's a wonder I ever sleep."

They stopped talking at the very same second they saw me standing in front of the pair of them, two steaming hot mugs in my hand.

"Here you go," I said, holding their drinks out to them. They both took their mugs of coffee from me with both hands. Both holding them under their noses.

"Hmm, just the job," Penelope sighed, taking a quick slurp. She put her drink on the coffee table, "right, let's crack on, shall we?"

"So?" Nancy asked, coming up behind me as I waved the two, caffeine fuelled women off.

I turned around and pulled her into my arms. I had no words. There just weren't enough to explain exactly how I was feeling. She rubbed my back.

"It's okay. You don't have to tell me anything."

I unwrapped my arms from around her. I couldn't stay like it forever even though the thought of it was certainly tempting. She smiled warmly. I smiled back.

"Do you want a coffee?" she asked.

"Nah, it's okay. I've had two already. I think that'll do for now."

"Well, alright but just let me know if you need anything," she said, and I could sense she was disappointed.

I nodded at her but felt guilt wash over me. This girl had been fantastic since I lost my Mum. Since Drew disappeared. The least I could do was tell her what's what with the Solicitor. Tell her what life had in store for me now. She was the only person I had left, the only person I could truly trust now that my Mum and Drew were gone.

"So basically, I've got everything Mum worked so bloody hard for," I spurted, feeling instantly relieved at the outpouring of words, "I haven't got to worry about a thing. Nothing at all."

"Well, I suppose that's something?"

"I guess."

"But?"

"But I would rather have everything to worry about if it means having her here."

"Oh, Henri," she said, stroking my arm, "I know. I know."

"She left a note too."

"Oh."

"It hurts, Nancy. It really hurts."

Nancy shook her head and sighed.

I headed to the kitchen, pulled two tumblers out of the cupboard, dropped some ice cubes into each and cracked open the whiskey. I took the drinks back into the living room.

"Here," I said, holding a glass out to her. She took it without a word. We both sipped at our drinks in silence.

"Do you want to see it? The note?" I said, feeling the liquid burn my throat a little.

She carefully unfolded the piece of paper, handling it like it was some antique artefact, and started to read.

"My beautiful girl," she began. I felt my throat tighten immediately, "this is going to sound so clichéd but if you are reading this letter, it means I am no longer here. I feel silly even writing it, but the fact of the matter is, it's true."

She looked over at me, tears falling down her cheeks.

"I don't know the reason why I'm no longer with you and to be honest, that's of no interest to me. I don't want to be anywhere other than with you, my darling, but as my parents always used to tell me, 'the only sure thing in life is death'.

I just want you to know that I love you so much, my beautiful little girl. I don't know if there's such a thing as an afterlife but, no matter what happens, I will always be by your side even if you don't know it."

My throat tightened even more, and I could just about hold back the sob that was threatening to fly out of me. Just get through this, I thought, just listen.

"Everything is in order anyway, Henri," Nancy read on, quietly, "I think I've managed to cover everything but if there any loose ends to tie up, the solicitor will deal with all that.

You are such a bright, caring, loving girl and I know how upset you'll be when you read this. Bloody hell, it's heart-breaking for me to even write it. It's going to be difficult at first and even though you'll never forget, you will move on and make a life for yourself. A simply wonderful life."

She looked at me, her eyes full to the brim with tears. She let out a trembling, wobbly sigh and carried on.

"All I ask is that you just try your hardest in everything you do. I know that won't be hard because you give everything your all anyway. But as much as I want you to work, please don't forget to have as much fun as possible and live everyday as though it's your last. Have no regrets. Live. Be happy.

Anyway, I'm going now before my tears wash the ink away. I love you, Henri. More than life.

Yours forever. Mum xxx."

Nancy let the note slip from her fingers.

"Oh my God, Henri," she said simply, sadly.

We sat in silence. You could have heard the tiniest of pins drop. I felt like I'd been holding my breath all the time my best friend was reading to me.

She looked up at me, her eyes searching.

"You okay?" she whispered.

I nodded but I wasn't. Not at all.

"I'm going to pop out and get some shopping," Nancy said, "we're running a bit low."

"Okay," I mumbled.

"Do you want to come with me? Get out of here for a little while?"

I shook my head. That was the last thing I wanted

to do.

"Well, I'll try not to be too long," she said.

Be as long as you want. I don't mind.

Nancy walked out and as the door closed behind her, I let out a sigh of relief. I just wanted to be alone, just for a little while.

I sat in silence, letting it surround me. I wasn't in the mood for music of any sort, which for me is weird. I just wanted quiet. I didn't fight with my eyelids as they slowly shut.

"I'll get it," Nancy shouted up to me. The phone stopped ringing a second later.

I couldn't hear what she was saying as I lay like a starfish on my bed.

"Henri," she shouted this time, "it's for you. It's the hospital."

Without hesitation, I raced down the stairs. I lost my balance on the bottom two but somehow managed to stop myself from falling flat out. Nancy held out the phone to me, her other hand covering the mouth piece.

"They're ready to release your Mum," she whispered.

I gulped as I took the phone from her.

"Hello?" I said, struggling to keep my voice from breaking.

"Hello, Henri. It is Henri, isn't it?"

I nodded slowly and immediately realised she couldn't hear me nod.

"It is," my voice caught in my throat.

"I'm Pru. I work at the mortuary. I'm phoning to let you know that we're ready to release your Mum. She'll be taken to the Chapel of Rest tomorrow morning, so you'll be able to see her and make arrangements for the funeral with the Funeral

Directors on the high street."

My eyes welled up with fresh tears. I gulped down the lump in my throat.

"I'm sorry, Henri," she said, obviously realising I was upset, "I'm afraid there's never a nice way to put this."

"I know but thank you anyway."

"Oh, don't thank me, sweetheart. No one should be thanked for imparting this kind of information. The death certificate will go straight to the Funeral Directors rather than you having to collect it first. I just want to offer my sincere condolences, Henri. You take care now."

"You too."

DAY 24

I phoned school and spoke to Principal Stokes. I told him I needed to take the day off to sort the funeral out and that I wouldn't be back at school until after it. I apologised for the bad timing, having only been at school for one day before taking even more time off. He was very understanding. I really didn't have anything to worry about.

Nancy was in the kitchen, busying herself with preparing breakfast. She was humming to herself and whisking up eggs for scrambling.

"Hey," I said, pulling out a chair from under the dining table.

"Shit," she span round, "you scared me!"

"Sorry. Didn't mean to."

"I know. I know," she giggled and then immediately stopped, "are you okay?"

"I suppose so."

"You know you don't have to see her if you if you

don't want to?"

"I know," I said, taking the mug of coffee she held out to me, "I need to though. I need to say goodbye one last time. Is it wrong for me to feel curious, too? Oh my God, that sounds so creepy."

"Doesn't sound creepy at all," Nancy said, taking a sip of her own coffee, "I would feel exactly the same."

She put her drink down, turned off the hobs she was using to cook our eggs and bacon on, and threw her arms around my shoulders. She didn't have to say anything. Didn't need to. Just feeling her surround me was enough.

"Could you come with me?" I whispered.

"If you want me to, I will."

"Really? I mean, do you think your Mum would mind? What about school?"

"First off, my Mum will be totally okay with it and I'll just tell the school the truth. Tell them that I'm supporting my very best friend on a very hard, emotional day."

"Thank you so much, Nancy."

"I would like to say it's a pleasure," she said, a gentle, understanding smile on her lips, "I mean, it is to be by your side, but I just wish circumstances were different."

"Hi. I have an appointment at eleven. It's Henri Turner."

The lady behind the reception desk looked to be in her late fifties or early sixties. She was incredibly stylish in her silk, ivory blouse and her tortoise-shell style, rimmed glasses. She looked down at her paperwork and ticked something, me, off her list.

"Ah, yes. Hello Miss. Turner," she said sympathetically, "take a seat, dear. Someone will be you as soon as possible. Would you both like a drink while you're waiting to go in?"

"No thank you," I answered for the both of us, not even thinking that Nancy might want some kind of liquid refreshment. I knew that if anything was to hit my stomach, food or drink, it would no doubt come straight back up, with force. I was having a hard job keeping my breakfast down.

"Okay. Well if you need anything, just give me a shout," she smiled.

We both nodded.

"Hey," Nancy whispered, elbowing me gently in the ribs, "you sure you don't want a drink?"

She lifted her bag off her lap, opened it so that only we could see the silver hip flask peeking out.

I shook my head.

She shrugged, put the flask quickly to her lips, took a sip and winced.

"Okay, go on then," I whispered. I guessed a little bit of Dutch courage wouldn't do any harm. I took a deep sip, gulping down the whisky and winced, just like Nancy had, as the liquid burned its way down my throat. The temptation to snatch the flask from Nancy and guzzle down the rest of its contents was strong, but what would my Mum think of me if I went in drunk?

Nancy grabbed my hand and held on for dear life as we entered the viewing room. I walked in with my eyes closed. I don't know why. Maybe I thought it was more respectful. Maybe I was just plain scared.

"I'll just be out here if you need me," the Funeral

Director said before closing the door.

Nancy gasped. I opened my eyes.

Mum lay there, looking just as if she was asleep. She looked beautiful. She looked real. The more I stared, the more I expected her to sit up and give me a hug.

Nancy was crying. I was strangely calm. I didn't feel upset. I didn't feel happy. I didn't know how to feel. It was all so surreal.

I lay her favourite photo of us on her chest. The one from the Fleetwood Mac gig on her fortieth birthday. I stroked her cold, hard hands and kissed her forehead.

"I'll love you forever, Mum."

After dealing with all the funeral and cremation arrangements, we finally left the building. We'd only been there just over an hour, but I felt like a whole day. It was hard leaving my Mum there, knowing I would never see her again.

"Let's go to the pub," Nancy spat out, totally out of the blue, "you need a drink. We both do."

DAY 25

My mouth felt like I'd swallowed the Sahara and I had a raging thirst. I slowly forced my eyelids open and instantly shut them again as the room span around me. I gulped and felt saliva fill my mouth, the sure sign of sickness. I shifted my legs off the sofa and sat up, my head throbbing in pain from the effort. I sucked in a deep breath and forced myself to stand, wincing with even more discomfort.

To my left, Nancy lay sprawled out on the other sofa and didn't look like she'd be coming around any time soon. I quietly blamed her for getting us in to this state although it hadn't taken too much persuasion for me to knock back the beers.

I sighed, headed to the kitchen, poured a pint glass of water and drank it in three mouthfuls. I burped and covered my mouth, nausea washing over me. The feeling got worse as I ran upstairs and flung open the bathroom door. I just about made it in time.

I washed, brushed my teeth twice and made my way to my room. If I'd have slept in my room, I would have been woken by my alarm, but I hadn't, and I groaned as I looked at my clock. Ten thirty am, no point in going to school now.

"Henri," Nancy called croakily from downstairs, "you okay?"

I headed back into the living room and we looked each other up and down.

"I take it that's a no then," she said.

I shook my head.

"Oh my God, I feel like shit," she went on.

"Same here."

"We must have been really going for it."

"It would seem so," I smiled, starting to remember Nancy getting up on the karaoke and singing, or should I say, murdering, 'Hey Jude' by The Beatles. Whatever she was doing, she got the whole pub up and singing along with her.

"I'm assuming we're not going into school?" she asked sheepishly.

"Well I'm not. No way. Don't think I can face it."

"Okay, that's it then, pajama day starts here. I'll phone in."

My stomached rumbled, hungry after emptying itself so I left Nancy on the phone and headed back into the kitchen to throw some breakfast together.

"I really didn't think I was going to manage that but thanks, Henri, it's exactly what I needed," Nancy said, wiping her mouth with the back of her hand.

"It's a pleasure. What did the school say?"

"They were fine. Obviously, I didn't tell them real

reason we weren't going in," she winked.

I smiled halfheartedly.

"So, what shall we do then, apart from slob out?"

"Whatever we do, we won't be involving alcohol of any sort."

"Spoilsport."

"Seriously, Nancy."

"I know, I know. Do you think I'm stupid? Just the thought of…"

I felt my stomach churn.

"The only beverage I'd be drinking, other than water, is tea, copious amounts of it.

It was a day of total relaxation. We played records, read our books and didn't even bother with the tv because, come on, the crap they show in the daytime just isn't worth the effort.

Nancy was desperate for Chinese food, so we ordered a meal for one which was plenty enough for both of us to enjoy without feeling like we'd made pigs of ourselves.

I washed, dried and put our plates and cutlery away and slumped on to the sofa next to my best friend. Nancy looked at me, smiling in contentment and for just the briefest of moments, I felt like I hadn't a care in the world.

DAY 26

We made it to school with plenty of time to spare. The only people milling around were a bunch of the usual early birds, the ones that the "in" crowd would call nerds, a handful of kitchen staff and a few teachers.

"This is wrong," Nancy said, "what have we become?"

I laughed.

"Seriously," she went on, "this will be the first and the last time I'm ever getting here this early. It's ridiculous."

"I don't know what the big deal is, Nancy. It's only half an hour."

"And that's more than enough, thank you very much."

I laughed again and turned around as I heard a car pull into a parking space behind us. Principal Stokes smiled eagerly at me.

"Henri," he said as he got out of the driver's seat,

"it's good to see you."

"Thanks. Good to see you, too."

He locked the car, bleep bleep.

"I wasn't expecting you to be honest, what with tomorrow. How are you feeling?"

"Okay, I suppose," I shrugged. I'd almost forgotten, allowed myself to push it to the back of my mind and suddenly, I felt terrible. I felt tears prick my eyes and it took everything I had to hold them back.

Nancy seemed to sense the change in atmosphere and I could feel her looking at me. She rubbed my back.

"Well, you know where I am if you need anything, Henri," he went on.

"Thanks, Sir."

"You've got to eat, Henri!" Nancy scolded.

What's wrong with an apple and a coffee? I thought.

"I'm really not that hungry."

"I don't care. I'm not opposed to force feeding if the need arises. Don't think I'm joking."

I reluctantly picked up a ham and pickle sandwich. Anything to shut her up.

"Happy now?"

"Well, it's an improvement."

The weather was perfect, not too hot, not cold. There was a refreshing breeze cutting through the hazy heat. It was obvious the groundsman had been in at some point, the smell of freshly cut grass was gorgeous. There was no way I was eating my lunch inside. Nancy clearly had the same idea.

"Come on, let's go outside," she said.

We headed out and as soon as our feet hit the asphalt, I looked over to the back of the playing field and felt a sudden pang of sadness. I don't think I'd ever be able to look at our tree in the same way again. It was just a tree, now. I swallowed back the lump in my throat.

"You okay?" Nancy asked.

I nodded. I don't think she believed me.

"Come on, let's go and sit over there," she said, picking up my hand and practically dragging me to the nearest picnic table.

I look at my sandwich and it turns my stomach, but I won't hear the last of it if I don't eat so I pick one up and take a bite. We eat in silence until I spot Stacey's friends heading out of the cafeteria doors. They look upset, pale.

"Hey," I whisper over to Nancy. She doesn't hear me.

"Nancy," I whisper a little louder.

"Hm?"

"Look, quick," I nod over to the girls.

"God, they look like death warmed up. Let's hope they're not coming down with some terrible illness because that would be a real shame."

"Nancy!"

"Oh what? Don't tell me you don't feel the same."

I shrug.

"Here we go again. Henri, don't waste your time on those bitches. They don't deserve it."

"Maybe so, but…"

"You know your problem," Nancy said, putting her sandwich down and looking straight at me, "you care too much."

"I wouldn't call that a problem. I'd rather care

than not."

"I'm sorry. Take no notice of me. I just don't think they deserve your care. What have they ever done for you?"

"I know, I know. At least I'm the better person."

I get up and walk over to them. They turn their backs, clearly not wanting to get into conversation.

"Hey."

Nothing.

"Are you alright?"

Still nothing.

"Whatever," I say and walk away.

"Henri, stop," I hear and turn back.

"Yes?"

"Can we talk?" one of them says.

I nod and sit down across from them.

Silence.

"Well?" I ask.

"It's Stacey," the acting ring leader speaks up again.

No shit.

"Yes?"

"We haven't seen her."

No, neither have I. So, what?

"Okay, and?"

The group takes a collective sigh. There's a strange look on each of their faces. Fear? Are they scared?

"I don't know how to put this," the same girl says, "but we've heard her. Every one of us."

They all nod.

"It's like she's a ghost or something."

Shit.

"Oh, okay."

Silence.

"I've heard her too."

"What?"

"Stacey. She spoke to me too."

"No. No way. Why would she speak to you, Henri? It's not like you were the best of pals."

"I know, believe me, I know. But I think you might be right."

"That she's a fucking ghost?"

I shake my head. I don't know what else to say to Stacey's second in command.

"You're a fucking weirdo, Henri. I've always said so," she said, standing up and gesturing to her friends, "come on, let's get away from her."

I start to realise Nancy was right. Maybe I need to toughen up.

"So?"

"I should have listened to you, Nancy."

"That's hindsight for you," she says, "you're a better person than me though. Don't ever change. I mean that."

I smile at her.

"So, spill. What's their deal?"

I explained that conversation in full. Nancy was all ears. We headed back inside and made our way to the common room. Unsurprisingly, Stacey's friends were huddled in a corner. They looked even more freaked out than they did outside.

There's a knock at the glass, see through door. It's not like we can't see Principal Stokes standing right behind it but manners maketh the man. He opens the door and looks around the room, stopping when his eyes land on Stacey's friends. He starts talking to them but we're not close enough to hear what's being said but, looking at their shocked expressions, we make a calculated guess that it's got everything to do with their best friend.

We approach the group, and, against my better judgment, I ask if everything's okay. I can tell Nancy is really not happy about our intervention but at the same time, she's more than eager to find out what's going on.

Stacey's Mum phoned the school to let them know that her daughter is in hospital, her condition is stable. She had asked for the message to be passed on to her friends so that they could visit her

The girls get up to leave.

"Are you going to see her?"

"Of course we are, Henri. Stokes said we can finish early. We're going straight to the hospital now."

"Well, we hope she's okay."

Nancy clearly doesn't agree with me.

"I'm going to see her."

"What? Come again?"

"I'm going to go and visit. Later."

"Why?"

"I don't know. I feel like I need to."

"Is it such a good idea though, really? It's going to be a long day tomorrow. Why don't you just chill out tonight?"

"No, I've made my mind up. I hear what you're saying Nancy, I do, but I've got to see her."

"Well, I think you're being silly but that's why I love you, I suppose. If you're that set on it, I'll come with you."

"Um, actually, I wanted to go alone. Do you mind?"

"No, I don't. To be honest, I was only going to be nosy. You know what I'm like."

"I'll fill you in on all the details, I promise."

"You better."

I walk in through the automatic, hospital doors and I start to wonder whether coming back was such a good idea. I close my eyes, take a deep breath as I walk up to the reception desk. I cough, hoping to interrupt the lady sitting behind it.

"One moment, please," she says, finishing typing, "Hello, how can I help?"

"I've come to see Stacey. Stacey Kemp."

"Are you a relation?"

"No," I shake my head, "I'm a friend from school. Stacey's Mum phoned school to tell us she was in hospital and that we could visit her."

"She did leave me a note explaining something like that, but her friends came earlier today."

"I know they did. I couldn't come with them as I had a test," I lied.

She looked quizzically at me, trying to work me out.

"Please. I really want to see her. I haven't stopped thinking about her since our Principal told us the news at lunchtime."

"Well…"

"Please," I pleaded, turning on the puppy dog eyes.

"Okay, that's fine but visiting is over in an hour. When you hear the bell, that's your signal to leave."

"Thank you. What ward is she in?"

"She's in her own room. Go down this corridor," she said, pointing her finger in the direction I was to follow, "third room on the right."

"Thank you, again."

I walked calmly past the first two rooms, glancing sideways through their open doors. In the first, a boy, I'm guessing around the same age as me, lay in bed. His bruised eyes were closed. A family were sitting around their daughter's bed in the second. The daughter, if that's what she was to them, was sitting up, giggling at her little brother who was doing a pretty good impression of a monkey. The Dad was sitting on the foot of the bed, smiling at his daughter whilst the Mum was sitting in a chair by the side of her.

And then I got to Stacey's room. The door was closed, and I took a deep breath before opening. I don't know why but I felt nervous.

"Stacey?" I whisper as I open the door.

She looks at me like she's about to cry.

"Henri."

I walk up to the side of her bed and pulled a chair over to sit on.

"I hope you don't mind me coming to see you?"

"No, I don't," she smiled, "I wasn't expecting you. I'm not exactly your favourite person."

"Look, don't worry about that. I wouldn't be here if I didn't want to."

I look down at her wrists. They're bandaged up. It's not hard to guess why she's here.

"Oh, Stacey. What happened?"

"I think that's pretty obvious," she said, lifting her arm up to show me what I had already seen.

"Why?"

"I haven't felt great since the attack. It really got to me. It freaked me out, but I started to believe that I deserved it. I did deserve it."

"No one deserves that, Stacey. I can't imagine how terrifying it must have been."

"It's karma, Henri. I've dished out so much crap to other people. I've made other people's lives a misery, including yours."

"I don't disagree, but I wouldn't have wished this on you."

"And that's why you're so much better than me. Henri, I'm so sorry for what I put you through. I'll never be able to apologise enough. That's why I tried to end it. I'm not even any good at that."

All I could think of was Drew. I hoped he hadn't been bullying her into doing this. I know he was only trying to protect me. Hadn't he scared her enough by attacking her?

"Can I talk to you?"

"Of course you can."

"I haven't been able to talk to anyone, not properly anyway, for such a long time."

"What about your friends? Can't you talk to them?"

"They're not my friends. They're just girls who decided to cling on to me. I don't have any real friends."

"Oh, okay."

"I'm not a confident person, Henri."

"But you seem so…"

"It's all an act. I'm a coward, a weakling. And I'm the way I am, a bully, because I'm a victim too. I know that's no excuse, but I don't know any different."

"I'm sorry to hear that. So, who was bullying you? I've never seen anyone at school causing you any grief."

"Oh, it's got nothing to do with school. I'm talking about my abusive, alcoholic of a mother."

"Oh no, Stacey."

"Oh yeah. She can do some damage when she's got a bottle of vodka in her. I'm only living at home because I can't afford to get my own place. She hates me, Henri, and I hate her."

"You need to speak to the police."

"I can't. I'm too scared of what she'll do. If I just keep my head down and try not to do anything to upset her, and believe me, it doesn't take much, things are okay, but I just can't live like it anymore, Henri."

"No one could, Stacey. It's not your fault though."

"I know it isn't but being a bully is. I didn't have to terrorise you, or the other kids I've picked on in the past, I had a choice. I picked the wrong option, and this seemed like the only way I could right my wrongs," she lifted her hands up to me again, "but something, someone, changed my mind, told me I could make things better, that I could be better. He told me this wasn't the way and with all the strength I had left, I dialled 999 and then I passed out."

"He? Who stopped you going any further, Stacey?"

I knew what she was going to tell me.

"You won't believe me."

"Try me."

"It was Drew. Drew Hardy. He was at our school. He was such a nice guy. I didn't really know much about him. No one did. He kept himself to himself."

I felt a lump in my throat and did everything I

could not to cry.

"And then he was gone. Just disappeared," Stacey went on, "and that's when the news broke. His Dad shot him and his Mum. I mean, that's just fucking horrendous, isn't it? It's heart breaking. Henri, you would have liked him, I'm sure. There's not many like that boy."

Tears filled my eyes and I thought, no, there's no one like him. No one at all.

My head was spinning from the news and when the bell rang, marking the end of visiting time, I said goodbye to Stacey and left the room. I couldn't get out of the hospital quick enough and as soon as I got outside, I sucked in air, my chest heaving, and I started to cry, really cry. I looked up to the sky and smiled.

"No way," Nancy said, putting her wine down, eyes and mouth wide open.

"I know, right?"

"If there's one person I would least expect to kill themselves, it's Stacey. She's so confident, way too cocky for my liking. The attack must have really done a job on her."

"It would seem so. But there were other factors, Nancy. The attack was just the tip of the iceberg."

"Oh?"

"Issues at home. Her Mum isn't exactly a model parent. She's not had the best upbringing, shall we say. I actually feel really sorry for her, Nancy."

"It doesn't excuse her actions though, Henri. She's not been an angel, has she?"

"I know. I totally agree. She apologised to me."

"So, she should."

"And there's something else."

"Go on," she said, picking her wine glass back up and taking a sip.

"She was stopped."

"Oh my God! Her Mum?"

"No. Drew. He came to her, stopped her before it was too late."

"He saved her?"

I nodded.

"What if she didn't want to be saved?"

I shook my head, didn't know how to respond to that. Drew did the right thing though, I know he did. Maybe it's exactly what needed to happen. It's not her fault she is like she is. Maybe Stacey would turn things around now she's got this second chance. Everyone deserves a second chance, don't they?

We finished our simple dinner of jacket potatoes and baked beans and finished the bottle of wine I'd opened as soon as I got in from the hospital. I was exhausted and even though the thought of staying up late, talking the night away, over wine, with my best friend was tempting, I knew I needed to sleep, to wake up refreshed in the morning, ready to take on the day ahead.

DAY 27

"I just want to wish you all the very best for today, Henri," said Principal Stokes.

"Thank you, Sir. That means a lot."

"It's a pleasure and remember, take whatever time you need."

"Thank you again, Sir. Goodbye."

"Goodbye, Henri. Take care of yourself," he said and hung up.

I wanted to cry. Again. But I didn't. I would be doing enough of it at the funeral.

I wasn't expecting a big turn-out. Not by a long shot. After all, we hadn't been in town that long. Our life was really only just starting again when she got taken away. But the church was full. I spotted so many old friends of hers. Some looked on, as blank and lifeless as corpses themselves. Most were crying. Not just the odd-tear-rolling-down-the-cheek kind of cry. No, they were sobbing hysterically. It made me a little angry. How could they cry like that when my eyes were barely watering?

And then it began. Mum came into the room to her favourite song of all time, God Only Knows by The Beach Boys. I felt a wide grin breaking on my face. I was not going to cry. I would not shed a tear. And then, as if the other half of me, the emotional half, was sick of being negated, I broke down. Fell apart at the seams. I didn't want to be sensible anymore.

Nancy's clammy hand was clasped firmly around mine. She was looking down. Too afraid to look at me or ahead of her.

The song played out and the service started.

As much as I could have beat the living daylights out of my Mum's boss, I didn't put up a fight when he offered to pay for her wake. Guilty conscience? I think so. I was glad to have all the responsibility taken away from me. I don't think I could have handled all the mourners being in the house. I would have had to mingle then. The Red Lion was neutral ground for everyone and people got into their little cliques pretty much straight away. I was happy. Well, not happy, obviously, but glad to just sit with Nancy in a cozy little nook. Away from people who would no doubt want to tell me how sorry they were.

"You okay?" my best friend asked.

I nodded.

"Want another?" she asked again, holding up her empty glass.

"Please," I answered, downing what little was left

of my whiskey.

She got up gingerly and headed to the bar. She'd only had two drinks herself, but it seemed to be affecting her much more than me.

I kept my gaze low, hoping to avoid eye contact with anyone. I kept my gaze low, hoping to avoid eye contact with anyone. Unfortunately, my efforts to distance myself were thwarted but then, amongst all the people offering their deepest condolences, something made me look up. Something made me take notice. It was a feeling more than anything else.

I saw Nancy waiting, rather impatiently, at the bar and then my eyes pulled to the left, towards the bar hatch. I gasped, feeling my mouth drop open.

"Dad?" I mouthed as I walked towards the man I thought I would never see again.

"Henri," he said simply.

"What the hell?"

"I know. I know."

"No. You really don't!"

"Can we go outside? I really need to talk to you."

I nodded, simply because I didn't want to cause a scene. I led the way to the beer garden.

"I know I'm the last person you want to see right now, but no matter what's happened between us, you're still my daughter and your Mum was once my wife. I know you think I don't give a damn, Henri but you would not believe how much I do!"

"Save it for someone who actually cares, Dad," I growled.

"Look, I'm not asking for anything, Henri, but I needed to be here today. She was the love of my life. I know you won't believe that, but she was."

"So, you just show up to the wake to drown your sorrows? You were obviously far too upset to come to the funeral!"

"Henri, I was at the church and the crematorium," he said sharply.

"Whatever! You're only here because social services told you to be!" I spat.

"Of course they contacted me, Henri. I'm your father. But believe what you want. Just because you didn't see me doesn't mean I wasn't there."

I broke down for what felt like the millionth time. He gently and gingerly put his arm around my shoulders and as much as I wanted to pull away from him, I didn't. I turned into him and put my head against his chest. He eased up and I could feel the tension between us fall away. He wrapped his arms around me and held me tight. I couldn't remember the last time my Dad had hugged me, but I remembered, straight away, how good it felt. Up until he left, I was always his little girl. He used to say that no matter what, I would always be. I cried and cried into his chest, leaving a large wet patch on his shirt.

"Sorry," I sniffed, pointing at the mark.

"Don't be. Never be," he said quietly, "Would you like a drink?"

"No thanks. Nancy's already at the bar," I answered, pointing towards her.

He nodded.

"Best friend?" he asked.

"Yup."

"So, how are you doing?"

I shook my head. Seriously? I thought.

"Sorry, totally wrong question, right?"

I nodded.

"Truth be told, Henri, I just don't know what else to say."

"Well, that's one thing we definitely have in common, right now."

"I can only apologise for being a shit father."

"I can't argue with you on that but thank you for the apology."

"I know it's early days, sweetheart, but I will do everything in my power to make up for not being around. I promise you that I won't ever leave you again."

"Oh, okay. So, you've been dropped by your girlfriend then?"

"Ouch," he said, and I realised how sharp I was being. He didn't deserve my sympathy, that's for sure but I didn't need to kick him any further down than he already was.

"Sorry. That was wrong of me."

"No, it's okay. I'm sure I would feel the same way."

"So, are you here for good, then?"

"If you want me to be?"

Did I want him to be?

"I think the question is, do you want to be? Do you want to be here for me?"

"Of course I do. Why do you think I'm here?"

"If you want to be here for me so badly, why has it only taken you until now to find me."

He shook his head.

"I can't answer that, Henri. There is no answer. There's no excuse at all."

I looked at him quizzically.

The door to the beer garden opened and John stepped out.

"Everything okay, Henri?" he asked, looking at me, then my Dad.

"It's fine, John."

"I saw you come out and you've been a little while. I was concerned."

My Dad looked down at the floor.

"Thanks, but honestly, I'm fine. John, meet my Dad. Dad, meet John."

"Oh, um, hello," John said, holding out his hand, "nice to meet you."

"You too," Dad replied.

"I'll leave you to it, Henri," John said, placing a hand on my shoulder, "I'm only inside if you want me."

"Thanks, John."

"May I ask?" Dad said, looking at the closed door.

"It's John," I said and winced as I realised my Dad would have obviously picked up on that.

"I gathered that, Henri. How do you know each other?"

"He's Mum's boyfriend. Well, he was."

That shut him up. Cat's got your tongue now, hasn't it?

"Oh, right, well I'm glad she found someone to make her happy. I know I didn't do the best job of that."

"No shit!" I laughed, "Yes, she was very happy with John, even though they weren't together that long before she…"

We both fell quiet. The sentence didn't need to be finished.

"Anyway, I'm here now, whenever you need me, I promise."

He handed me a sticky note with his address and number scribbled on it and we headed back inside.

"Oh, what's this?" Nancy asked, carefully carrying our drinks back from the bar, "accepting numbers from older men are we now, Henri?"

My Dad's cheeks turned a deep red and mine certainly felt as though they had done the same.

"Nancy, this is my Dad. Dad, this is Nancy."

He didn't speak. It looked like he couldn't.

"Shit," she said, drawing the word out, "Oh my God. I'm so sorry. I …"

"It's fine," I assured her, "You weren't to know."

"No, I know. But…" she said, looking my Dad up and down disapprovingly.

"Hello, Nancy. Nice to meet you," my Dad said, holding his hand out to shake hers. She didn't reciprocate. He shrugged.

"I'd like to say the same," she said.

I looked straight at her, half mad, half in agreement.

"Look, I'm sorry," she said, "I'm just looking out for my best friend. I'm a little protective."

I smiled at her.

My Dad smiled at us.

"I totally understand, Nancy. I do," he said, "Like I say, it's nice to meet you and I'm glad Henri has such a great friend. I'm going to go now, Henri. I just wanted to let you know that I'm here. I wish circumstances were better and I am truly sorry for what I put you and your Mum through."

"Whatever," I nodded and watched him walk out of the pub. He was going to have to try much harder to weasel his way back into my good books.

"Well, what a day," Nancy said as the last few mourners stumbled out of the pub, "that was a right turn up for the books with your Dad, wasn't it?"

"Wasn't it just," I replied, downing the last of my drink, watching Nancy wince as she finished hers.

"Shall we head home?" she asked, and I felt a sense of comfort wash over me. It made me happy to know she thought of my home as hers too.

"Sounds great."

"You know what? I think I'm going to go straight to bed. Do you mind?" I asked Nancy through yawns.

"Of course not," she yawned back, "I don't think it'll be much longer before I call it a night either. Would you like a nightcap or a hot chocolate or something?"

"Nah, I'm cool thanks. I'll just grab a glass of water."

"Okey dokey. If you don't mind, I'm just going to stay up a while longer and watch a film or something."

"That's fine," I replied, filling a glass from the kitchen tap, "you carry on. I'm just so tired and I'm not the best company when I'm exhausted. 'Night, Nancy."

"Ni-night, honey."

I stood in the bathroom, looking at my reflection in the mirror of the bathroom cabinet. My eye makeup had run, and I looked done in. I opened the cabinet and pulled a wipe from its packet. I closed the door and gasped in shock. Drew stood behind me and I span round, ready to pull him into my arms but there was nothing but air in front of me. I turned back to the mirror to find he wasn't there either. I honestly didn't think I had any more tears left in me, but I began to cry. I thought I was done crying, if only for a little while.

"God. I wish you were here, Drew," I said loudly, hoping he'd hear me, wherever he was. No answer came. Just sad, lonely, empty silence.

I wiped away the mess of makeup, brushed my teeth and put my pajamas on. I took a gulp of water and slumped to my bed, not even bothering to pull the duvet up over me.

"Henri. I'm here."

"Drew?" I cry.

"Hey. How are you?"

"As well as I can be, I suppose. I can't explain it. It was the worst day, but it wasn't as bad as I was expecting, either. It's so messed up."

"Not messed up at all. I get that."

"Did I just see you in the bathroom? Were you really there?"

"Yes. I'm sorry if I scared you."

"You took me by surprise, that's for sure. So, it looks like we've stepped up a gear. Dreams and now, reflections? I'm going to be the vainest narcoleptic I know!"

"You know a few, then?"

"Oh yes, loads. So, what's next? What's the next step?"

Silence.

Sad silence.

"Drew?" I ask again, "Speak to me!"

He looks into my eyes, his are filling up with tears. I know what he's going to tell me. I don't want to hear it.

"This is it, Henri. I've come to say goodbye."

Silence.

Sad, sad silence.

I think we both knew this was coming.

"No. No, no, no! I didn't. I had hope. I still have hope."

"I wish this wasn't the end. I don't want it to be, but it is. I'll always be yours though, Henri. I'll always be with you."

With Thanks

I know, I know. There's always a page where the author thanks a load of people. I for one *always* read the "thank you" page because I'm plain nosy and even though I don't expect you'll have read on this far, I'm going to do one anyway.

Thank you to my husband, Simon. I've said it before and I'll say it again – I wouldn't be where I am today without you. I couldn't do all this if I didn't have you. We've had many ups and downs (thankfully, more ups) and I know life will continue to test us but as long as we're together, we'll step off this rollercoaster with smiles on our faces.

Molly, you blazed your way into our world in 2010 and hit us like a ton of bricks. You've filled our hearts with so much joy, love and happiness. I know we don't always see eye to eye but you're my biggest achievement ever and our pride and joy. You're a one off, Molly. Never change.

To my Mum and Dad – thanks for always telling it like it is and for all your love, support and encouragement. Where would I be without you both? Thanks for being the best grandparents ever, too.

To my little Sister, Ella. You are one in a million, one of a kind. I don't know what I'd do without you. Thanks for being my best friend in the entire universe. You're the coolest Aunty ever and the fact that you've made me an Aunty to my two gorgeous nephews, well – I can't tell you how much that means to me. Max, Harry – I love you millions.

To my brother in law, and fellow soul singer, Paul –

you're alright too, I suppose! No, seriously, you are.

Thanks to my crazy, rockin', next door neighbour and best mate, BB. You truly are amazing and just as mental as me, and thanks to Leigh and Kearon too because they have to put up with the craziness that is *us*.

Huge thanks to all my fellow authors and book club buddies (you know who you all are!). I love the fact that we go off on tangents and that, most importantly, we just *get* each other regardless of whatever we're jabbering on about.

Special thanks to the awesome, James Josiah who knows exactly how to pick me up when I'm in a rut with my writing, when I doubt myself and wonder if I should go ahead and publish the stuff I pour out on to paper. Thanks for editing. Thanks for listening. Thanks for your advice. Thanks for being bloody brilliant. My sincere thanks also to Natalie Rix of Monnath Books for her proof reading services, her friendship and her words of encouragement.

Thank you to the incredible, Nick J Townsend who has worked his magic and turned the characters in this book, and the last (Shout the Call) into real beings. I mean, they've always been real in my head but the moment I see them, on paper, in full colour – well, it's just the best feeling.

Last, but by no means least, I have to say thanks for the music and bands that have provided the perfect writing soundtrack for If You Should Ever Leave Me. Thanks to The Beatles, Bowie, Carole King, Fleetwood Mac, Haim, Hozier James, Jack Savoretti, James Bay, Lana Del Rey, My Chemical Romance, Nirvana, Pearl Jam, Prince, Soundgarden, The Used, The Wildhearts and Terrorvision. The list could go on. And on. And on. The band that deserve the most thanks though – The Beach Boys. Without *Pet Sounds*, there wouldn't be God Only Knows and without *God Only Knows*, this book wouldn't be here.

ABOUT THE AUTHOR

Lucy Onions hails from sunny Walsall in the West Midlands. She resides in a 2-bed, semi-detached with her husband, Simon, her daughter, Molly and a Staffordshire Bull Terrier called Pringle.

When she's not writing, Lucy is a photographer (**www.lucyonionsphotography.com**), a lead singer (**www.souldoutuk.com**) and she runs a lovely little book-club called Walsall Book Social, which all means she's always stupidly busy but that's the way she rock 'n' rolls.

She hopes you've enjoyed reading the book as much as she did writing it. She'd love it even more if you left her a little review of it. Somewhere.

If you would like to find out any more about her writing and what's coming up next, you can find out more here: **www.facebook.com/LucyOnionsAuthor**